To Bill

Thank y—
Support so —.
Here's another Musical
odyssey for you....

A MUSE

[signature]

Kieran Saint Leonard

HYPERIDEAN PRESS

Copyright © 2025 by Kieran Saint Leonard

All rights reserved. No part of this publication may be reproduced, distributed or transmitted in any form or by any means without prior written permission.

This a work of fiction, any resemblance to existing persons and institutions result from the author's imagination and are used fictiously.

Hyperidean Press
www.hyperideanpress.com

A Muse / Kieran Saint Leonard – First Edition May 2025

Edited by Dr. Udith Dematagoda

Cover Images by Emma Elizabeth Tillman ©2025

ISBN 978-1-9163767-9-3

For Fern, and my friend Joe

What is the price of Experience? Do men buy it for a song?
Or wisdom for a dance in the street? No, it is bought with the price
Of all that man hath, his house, his wife, his children.
Wisdom is sold in the desolate market where none come to buy

William Blake, *The Four Zoas*

Where do we exist? In ourselves, looking out from the solipsistic prison of belief? Or are we just integral in the minds of others, mere constructs in the minds of those who experience us?

Are we subject or object?

What exactly is a Muse?

THE CHURCH OF THE HORSES

I

Bell, book and candle. The skeleton key click of kitten's claws on cold church flagstones. The inky depths of the Yorkshire Moors cloying around the bible-black walls of my new home. The Church of the Horses.

Curious now in hindsight to think that the first sacred invocations of the Goddess were echoing there amongst those barbarous isolations. Within the walls of the church the fated alchemical compound of desire and nameless fear that our great move north had already begun transubstantiating. The sulphur and mercury mixture curdling in my blood, nourishing and unfurling its fine shapely wings ready to commence its shadowy work. Unlike *The Odyssey*, things had not begun well.

It started snowing with prophetic determination from the night we moved in just two days before Christmas. That same day our first holy and beloved cat Harold had died cruelly and portentously as we packed our possessions into a van to head north out of London to the remote moors of Yorkshire.

My fiancée sat beside me in the van, inconsolable at the unjust and foul twist of terrible fate that had carried off our cat. The day we had planned and dreamt of for months; the fresh start, the clean slate, the romance of moving away from the capital city, where we had met and always lived, a move to a dramatic new chapter of self-imposed exile, to the remote fate-tempting adventure of an abandoned church in the middle of nowhere.

We had got off to the worst possible start. I had been running through songs with my band at a nearby venue in North London, preparing for our celebratory send-off gig and farewell party, when my fiancée tending to the last of the packing alone in the flat had turned around to see Harold laying stricken and mewling horribly on the kitchen floor.

As I was meandering through the sinuous melodic curlicues of the second verse of *Like a Rolling Stone* less than a mile away she had gathered up the cat's body, already the life leaving it, and in blind panic ran down the high street towards a vet – a vet who was already redundant. The cat was gone.

A magisterial pain had entwined a rigour-like grip upon us as we drove up the rain-torn motorway with his little cat body already stiffening in the back of the van. With every passing mile the gravity pull of grief intensified and the tugging strands of remembrance and nostalgia for our old life in London multiplied silently and insidiously into a choking filament net of perfect concert-pitch regret. Inconsolable agony. 'His heart just gave out.' The relentless grey rain and road and occasional stifled sob communicated all there was to say. The first act of our new life was to lay our beloved cat to rest in the black clay of North Yorkshire. A tree was selected, and the ground beneath it was cleared by the shovel blade I wielded inexpertly and gracelessly into the sodden soil. Rain ran down my neck and into the rivulets of grief, and before too long I was on my hands and knees sobbing and clawing at the soil with both my hands. Then he was laid down in his favourite blanket, words were said, my fiancée and I hanging onto each other like desperate survivors of some unspeakable tragedy. It occurred to me later that tragedy was in fact our lives. Or so at that time it seemed.

II

Sacrifice and ritual. Somehow we ignored the occult undertones of moving to this deconsecrated temple. Ancient, foreboding and haunted. Nonetheless we settled into homemaking amidst the graves of centuries-dead villagers; we nested in our neo-gothic church.

Discordantly oversized, too big a construction for such a tiny village, so remote and unremarkable as to only be known by its proximity to the bleak geometry of the emptiness it bordered upon: *O The Low Moor*. The black church perched upon the Low Moor. Like a tick on the back of some amorphous beast.

O Goddess! Yes. It is a song of sorts. One that is impossible to sing along with or to dance to. I heard its first stirring amongst the settling timbers of that profane church. A deadening blanket of snow settling on the oblique classical angles of a centuries old edifice of worship that had somehow become my new home. God help me. I heard its murmurings stirring there in those vaulted negative spaces, carried on the drafts and currents spiralling and circling amongst those arches whose once pious purpose and occluded masonic meaning had now been unconsciously subverted in my mind into a sort of invisible spiritual prison.

You see, I simply cannot drive a car. This was a relatively insignificant detail in my previous life in London but here, up here on the moors, driving was the difference between society and civilisation. My kingdom for a cab ride.

I did in fact hear *the song* the very first night I was alone in the church. It was a deadening month after Christmas. January had felt like a particularly drawn-out comedown to a dreary and misguided party.

But, I was in fact not truly alone;.You see, the day after we had moved in, the day after we had buried Harold the Cat, we had taken the only course of remedial action open to the totally heartbroken and grief-stricken: the desperate act of replacement. Two miles down the snaking road that crested the village we had spied with the keen eyes of grief a sign saying 'Cats for Sale'.

With no boxes unpacked and very little said, we found ourselves the following morning climbing into our recently-acquired little grey Peugeot car (itself symbolic of adulthood and independence) to acquire yet another symbol of love and solidarity, a new bloody cat. Two bloody cats. Keith and Nancy, named after our only two friends in Yorkshire. A month later, on that night when I first heard the stirrings of the song that would lead me across Christendom on the trail of its arcane harmonic resonances, its enchanting intervals and ephemeral midnight cadences...leading me to the edge of the abyss.

It had been a snowbound and intensely claustrophobic month of self-examination and the occasional back-biting argument counterpointed by fleeting hedonistic visits from intrigued and much pined-for London friends. We were begging our friends to visit. Enticing them with tales of hide and seek in the skeleton-populated crypt, drunken candlelit graveyard marauding, Alexandrine volumes of booze and all the drugs they could wantonly insufflate.

Dionysus, O sweet Dionysus, we are alive and well and living in Low Moor.

A month of lamp, rug, shelf, box, unpacking, purchasing, glassware unwrapping, kettle, picture hanging; ardent mindless homemaking. A month of day drinking. The hour that alcohol would begin to unfurl its microclimate around our existence became incrementally earlier each day. It always went unremarked upon, like some sinister tide creeping in around our ankles.

In hindsight I see that pinprick of time somewhat more clearly and yet it all feels less explicable now.

The bleak realities of living day to day in a fifteenth-century church, surrounded by a sprawling unkempt graveyard, adrift on a desolate moor in Yorkshire, are not to be understated. I had sold myself (and my concerned friends) on the 'big move' as if it were a well-considered, deliberate decision to escape the merciless murmurings of

London, to flee the music scene to which I had become so willingly, yet unhappily, entwined.

To my fiancée however it was a return to the Kingdom of her childhood. Surrounding ourselves in the unbridled wilds of the countryside was an attempt to insulate ourselves from the fraying emotional attrition of this atomising age. Foolish wayfarers we, how many earnest wanderers before us had made similar pyrrhic journeys, and met with the same ignominious fate: Chronic boredom. We were bored out of our minds. It was amazing how rapidly the gothic novelty had worn off.

Each amaranthine day felt like aching tedium might actually carry us off; real sheer slow torturous death at the hands of a clock. I began to catch myself fantasising that some demon of pure madness was lurking waiting to pounce from behind a gravestone, or from one of the long shadows of the pews we'd dragged in to lounge around at the kitchen table.

The kitchen table was the original consecrated altar we had found preserved in the front of the church. We dusted it off and sacrilegiously hacked its legs off to make it a more comfortable height for a dining table, this again, in hindsight, was perhaps not the wisest of moves. One night I would even read my friend's tarot cards from this altar. *Mea Culpa*.

My fiancée had got her heart's desire in accordance with an unspoken pact we had made two years earlier when I was in the throes of recording my first album, now a testament to the halcyon days of our relationship. In exchange for supporting me then, she got her wish now - leaving London to return to the North. The realities of this wish now manifested daily in the cold crucible of the church; and it soon became clear that we had accidentally fallen into the mortal abyss that lay between the wish and its actuality.

My first evening alone. Memories of the church always lead me off at a tangent. Stark digressions. I was all alone aside from the cats.

I put down my guitar and slid off my chair onto the recently purchased rug, scooped up a kitten, topped up my wine and rolled a cigarette. I had gradually accustomed myself to a steady decline in contact from my friends, the gradual onset of self-imposed social hypothermia, the slow ossifying chill of isolation. Time had lost all meaning within days of moving in. The nearest human being was at least a solid mile away, tucked up in that godforsaken village. If there was anyone any closer then that I didn't want to know about it. I had occasionally seen odd skittering shadows shifting about amongst the treeline at the edge of the graveyard. I chose not to give these shadows much thought.

My fiancée was working late at her new job, some twenty miles over the moor towards Leeds. I wasn't really sure what her new job was. I'd been deep in my day drinking cups when she had excitedly told me about it.

Glancing down at my phone I noticed that Mr Sands had messaged me. He was rehearsing for a concert at the Royal Albert Hall...*The Royal Albert Hall*...it felt as far away as the rings of Saturn. He suggested we rendezvous when he finished as he wanted to see the Church. He said it sounded 'Groovy.'

I paused, my eyes narrowed, weighing up his suggestion. Mr Sands always seemed to have difficulty grasping the geography of the UK, either wildly over- or underestimating distances. After a moment's consideration I replied with self-knowing aridity that the church was five hours' drive north of London so unless he was intending on dispatching a helicopter I doubted very much I would be seeing him this evening.

Exhaling, I dropped the phone back on to the rug and gazed up at the vaulted ceiling, my thoughts reaching to the cobwebbed oak trusses and leafing lazily through the film of recent memories I had formed in this place. I felt like I was in three or four places at once. This had been happening a lot. Temporal displacement, a sense of internal alienation from myself. Egoic estrangement. I didn't find the sensation particularly unpleasant.

Earlier that day I had been reading about 'thin places'. The ancient pagan Celts and later Christians used the term to describe mesmerising places like the wind-swept isle of Iona in Scotland or the rocky peaks of Croagh Patrick in Ireland. Heaven and earth, the Celtic saying goes, are only three feet apart, but in thin places that distance is even shorter.

I was becoming increasingly certain that the Church of the Horses was one of these 'thin places'.

The first arresting historical event I had uncovered was that in the midst of The Great War one of the largest munitions factories in England had been located in our new home, the village of Low Moor. The only reason that I could think of for that was that the village's remoteness and minuscule population reduced the risks involved in the manufacturing of massive bombs – that is to say, things designed for killing. It must be an extremely sensitive and tricky business manufacturing massive bombs, I thought, relighting the tip of my cigarette.

On the sunny morning of 21st August 1916 a fire broke out in one of the factory buildings, followed a few minutes later by a devastating blast when the fire reached the phosphorus store. This vast explosion had eviscerated the entire complex and immediately killed 40 people including all the on-site workers, a railwayman, the six firemen who had attended the initial blaze, not to mention a solitary dog. Phosphorus burns at 5000 degrees Fahrenheit. The blast could be heard in London.

This dog had been sniffing around in the factory yard at the unfortunate moment the explosion occurred and had (according to reliable witnesses) been blown all the way to Manchester, where his scorched collar and smouldering remains were discovered that morning by a fairly unlucky boot-shine boy.

I find myself reclining and thinking fondly of that dog. So swiftly and unwillingly propelled with such catastrophic force high up into the stratosphere, up through the grey blanketing clouds in a vast arcing parabola, a hair's breadth from leaving Earth's embrace. Hurtling over the rolling moorlands of the West Riding of Yorkshire, such incredible speed and infeasible altitude for a dog, and then the terminal velocity descent down into the cobbled street below. A sacrifice to aviation.

It was subsequently declared something of a miracle that the church had withstood the blast. Every other building in the surrounding radius had been flattened. The implications of this dark miracle made me feel uneasy, for reasons I found difficult to define.

I lay there on the rug, in the centuries-come-what-may-still-standing church, listening to the silent snow settle on the graves outside, experiencing an emotion not unakin to jealousy for that heaven-bound hound. *At least he found a way out of here.*

I wondered if the explosion or indeed the tremendous upward velocity of the dog had somehow ripped a hole in the fabric of space-time in this locale and created one of these 'thin places'. Or perhaps was it the thin place that had caused the catastrophe. It all felt vaguely hallucinatory. That flaming dog. I gulped my wine. I wonder what the poor bastard's name was.

Sometime later that same night: I hadn't moved from my position on the floor. It occurred to me that once, not so long ago, this exact spot had been a place of vigorous weekly Christian congregation. How many villagers had shuffled over these stones on which I now lay? How many had knelt and prayed for grace and redemption, stood and sang the hymnal, wept, renounced Satan and buried passionate lusts deep into the bosom of a God who now seemed so intensely and aggressively absent – at least from my current horizontal rug-bound perspective. This train of thought led me to ruminate on all the new sins that I had recently committed in my new home. I lay there smoking and considering these very mortal sins, my mortal sins in my church. I rolled over to the record player, flipped through the unpacked records and selected one.

Patti Smith's Horses thundered into the room from the woolly well-engineered West German hi-fi speakers positioned equidistant at either end of the knave. I gazed down into Keith the Cat's sanguine blue eyes.

I looked up into the vaulted oak-trussed ceiling. Was it possible that a vaulted ceiling could actually oppress? With each passing moment, the knowledge of the relentless accrual of snowflakes gathering flatly, silently drifting, Mandelbrot set upon Mandelbrot set, began to weigh heavy upon my heart. I too was being buried alive. *My living room is becoming my living tomb.* I shuddered.

Patti's enraptured incantations were carrying me off into that netherworld, a psychological hinterland I seemed to have been inhabiting more and more frequently, not always when I was alone. Even in the company of visiting friends I would catch myself slipping into this rosy reverie, the twilight interior world. Slipping wilfully into a palace of subtly shaded silks and opulent ermines, spiced wine, tobacco and hashish thighing on the air, Araby-oiled sweet-scented skin, delicately-bejewelled henna-inked feet dancing and twisting in the red and black earth, swaying shimmering dances, sadnesses glistening perfectly vermillion across a Saharan landscape, as midnight blue zephyrs blew long low straining notes that broke perfect silences over the infinitely tessellated night-time skyline. All of this locked within my howling borderline state of mind, the desolate valleys, canyons and carparks of incomprehensible neural networks mapping a near-infinite web of coin-toss experiences as yet to kingdom come. A city of angels awaits, and so far beyond the tepidly terrestrial boundaries of those snowbound, church-bound, mind-numbing out-there going nowhere grey roads and dismal moorlands, the present dark shapes and outlines that reigned me in so. God damn you low farm buildings and constipated cottages crouching murky-framed behind middle class mediaeval mullioned stained-glass warping windows of the most ancient forgotten worship rites. Country fair be gone! O yes! Therein, deep, warm and womblike, in an absolute reverie on my dusty Persian rug I lay. Hearing the quivering song she or some other Goddess sang.

My phone buzzed. At the same moment Patti concluded narrating the fated destiny of the boy Johnny, and I was no longer daydreaming leaning on the parking metre. I extended my hand to reach for the phone, assuming it to be my fiancée, as Patti rhapsodised, dancing somewhere out there on distant Redondo beach.

It was an email, unexpected at this hour, unexpected at any hour these days.

Had I listened more closely in this moment I would have undoubtedly heard the levers and wheels of the great god Los celestial musical machine, subtly shift his cadence, alter his key and commence a new surreptitious whirr of fateful euphonic motion. I didn't, however. Instead, I paused to take a drag of my cigarette before scrolling down to open the message. *O Deus Ex Machina miserere animae tuae sit tibi Deus.* And so did the Goddess begin.

III

Ten minutes later I stepped out of the heavy oaken doors into the blank hoary night of northern England gripped in high winter. Yorkshire's cold embrace slipped its willowy fingers under my shirt, testing my tenuous resolve and trying my taut nerves. I walked down the white ribbon path of snow into the graveyard. Absolute silence surrounded me. The church looked more imposing than usual, silhouetted brilliant black against the snow. I walked to a particular grave that had caught my attention on the day we had first moved in.

The year on the headstone was 1823 and the name was Fred – an unfortunate child, the first born of one of the local milliner families died age 5 years, followed in the same grave by his brother, also Fred, died age 3 years, followed by the third brother Fred, died 18 months. Three Freds laying there together abed. Hard to find anything meaningful to say about that kind of luck. I was fascinated by the dead Freds' grave. A perversely affecting *memento mori*.

I stood gazing at the grave, bathed in the eerie half-starlight. My pulse was a gentle timpani in my ears, the chill settling in my bones. I heard a soft crackling noise and, looking back the way I had come past the pool of light by the church doors, I shuddered, transfixed. There was a large dog on fire, entirely engulfed in a ball of flickering blue-green flames. The flaming hound just stood there, head cocked, looking askance at me.

I blinked my eyes but still the awful visage persisted. No sound save the awful crackling accompanied by the faint scent of singed fur on the icy air.

In a sudden wretched motion it struggled to draw itself erect. It teetered horribly on its hind legs in a profane and mocking imitation of a man and in this fashion took its first trembling steps towards me.

IV

My friend Higgs answered the phone disconcertingly quickly. It always throws me off my conversational stride when there aren't at least three rings for me to gather my thoughts and collect myself. I stood in the great hall of the church, leaning on an upturned pew, trying not to think about the vision I'd just seen outside, thinking instead of the email I'd just received.

-Everything ok?

-Do you know it's almost rude how quickly you answer the phone?

-Right.

-Anything I can do for you, Leonard? Or were you just ringing to tell me that I answer my phone too quickly.

-Something's come up.

-I see. Let me just get my coat.

-I haven't told you what it is yet.

-No need, I will see you in...I hear him pause to check something, Three hours.

There was a click and the line went dead.

I couldn't really grasp how it was possible that Higgs would be arriving so soon, nor why he would set out with virtually no explanation in the dead of winter, in the middle of the night, in the midst of a howling snowstorm, but his methods and means have consistently evaded scrutiny.

Suddenly excited for his arrival, I first went to the kitchen counter and poured myself the first of several large Irish whiskeys. Downing this, I retraced my steps and firmly bolted the great doors, a shiver running up my spine as I drove the bolt home. I then retired to my chair by the murmuring fire. I stoked it and dispatched a couple of bone-dense logs into its glowing maw. I settled in the armchair to consider my next move.

The storm racked the church. I began to feel ill at ease, unnerved. The message, and then that weird walking dog, all ablaze... The night had taken a terrible turn. The fire spat and crackled. I found it mirrored my mood. Its infernal red glowing jaws now like the very mouth of the troubling matter. Yes, it was restless and wanted to sink its hungry teeth into something, gnaw at the timbers of the church that shouldered and shuddered under the storm outside, and yes outside the wind blew to the crack of doom, and the snow drifted yet higher and higher still around those silent stone crossed graves, bookmarks of time and life, abnegating pages of oblivion, being no use at all, of course, to their true owners, the long dead.

The email. *O thy Hermetic messenger*. I read it all over once again very carefully.

I sat in silence.

It then occurred to me that I still hadn't heard from my fiancée. Was this perhaps another cause for concern? At that moment it was hard to say. Feeling suddenly fatigued, I succumbed to the fire and the whiskey as they did their nepenthetic work.

I awoke to a horrendous banging. I leapt up, smiling like a deranged yogi, my whiskey glass skidding across the floor, my phone almost flying directly into the roaring fire. The screen shattered on the hearth. The church itself seemed to be suffering some kind of fit or seizure. Something was definitely trying to force its way in through the front door. There was a great blustering of air overhead. It sounded like the storm was raging both inside and outside of the structure. There was a great and terrible thrumming of the aether. I stumbled into the dimly lit knave as the relentless hammering at the doors continued. What in God's name was it that was trying to gain ingress to my holy fortress?

A horribly deformed face leered at the portico window, I screamed, the storm heaved out its blustering heart as if in a chorusing, whistling reply to my own bloodcurdling wail. Neither of the cats stirred an insouciant whisker. The thing's face loomed in again, rattling at the casement and emitting a guttural pre-linguistic moan.

There was a moment that I thought I had actually started to die of fright, yes I felt myself slipping away. The shadowy church swam, a crimson vignette crept about the periphery of my vision but after a deep breath all remained belligerently material and solid before my watering eyes. Steeling my soul I summoned the courage to peer more closely at the dreadful looming countenance at the window, distorted as it was through the centuries old glass. My heart beat hard to behold such horror, but I also felt unexpectedly very much alive, and all of a sudden I was laughing. I was laughing before I had really understood what was funny.

I stepped towards the portico as my sense of humour and my vision aligned:

It was Higgs.

I could now hear the muffled snowbound words he was yelling.

-Let me in.

As I heaved the great door open, it caught the wind and almost pulled me headlong onto the frozen flagstones. Higgs' fleet reactions stepped in and he caught both me and the door mid-flight. The blizzard had worsened in the hours I had dozed and was now a raging maelstrom.

Higgs' face was blanched white, his eyebrows dusted with a glaze of frost. His cropped brown hair powdered white with snow, creating a faintly humorous confectionery finish to his demeanour. Steadying myself I was just about to speak when I noticed that the ominous blustering sound was even louder out here. Somehow it was so loud as to be almost over-powering the howling gale itself. It was then that I glanced skyward and noticed that the thick snow falling appeared to have turned black. As black as the mantle that shrouds the blind.

-It's all black! I screamed

-No, it's all bats.

What I had thought of as snowflakes were in fact hundreds, possibly thousands of bats pouring out the aperture on the uppermost left side of the defunct belfry.

I gasped gazing in wonder at this chiropteratic onslaught. Terrifying and enthralling, it felt precisely like the awful geometry of a mesmerising dream. Some dreadful artery to the infernal had been cut loose, allowing this haemorrhage to flood over Low Moor.

-Christ.

-Let's get inside

The wind hawked Higgs' words away. We turned tumbling out of the stygian night and into the church, slamming the door behind us.

-Lovely place you have here, Leonard,

he said, shrugging off his sheepskin coat and stamping the snow from his shoes. The storm of bats and snow howled outside.

His gaze met mine for a moment.

-I can only assume the storm must have disturbed their seasonal roosting. The old priest- from the parish, who made the arrangements for us moving into the place, had mentioned them. He said they weren't to be disturbed, some unusual breed or other, fiercely protected by royal order. I had forgotten all about them until just now, I hadn't realised how many of the bastards there were up there.

-It's a nice touch. A very affecting welcome.

-How did you get here so quickly?

-The last train out from King's Cross and then a taxi as far as the village and then I walked the rest. Can't say I thought much of the village, by the way.

-It's very good of you to come.

Embracing his shoulder warmly I switched the main lights on, flooding the church in light, and set about fixing two tumblers of distilled hospitality.

-Good Lord, I had forgotten the size of this place. From the photos you sent me it's hard to get a true sense of the scale. What on Earth do you do here all day?

-That's a good question...There's something we need to discuss.

V

Higgs read the entire contents of the message. His gaze settled for a moment on the cracked screen, meditatively swilling the last of the dram in his hand.

-So I am to understand that this 'Tiberius Red' has cordially invited you to join him on a magnificent musical tour of Europe, completely unexpectedly? Apropos of nothing? Have you had any dealings with him previously? Is he a friend of yours?

-None at all, and I don't know him from Adam. I was aware of him purely through his association with my friend Raphael. You know, my old pal the poet, beautiful gadabout. Well, he and Tiberius spent some decadent times together in London and New York a few years back.

I paused, theatrically catching Higg's eye and slowly sipped my whisky. I was clearly enjoying having company. Higgs' face remained neutral, undrawn. I took another hefty sip and continued.

-Tiberius Red. The name, is steeped in sibylline mystery, intrigue, even a degree of infamy. Rumours abound, very few of them reliable. He emerged from the subterranean New York art scene a decade ago. His dark star rising as an avant-garde composer, lyricist, filmmaker, abstract painter and, it is rumoured, amongst those in society, (to whom, when they whisper, it is wise to listen), an accomplished practitioner of the more esoteric arts.

A candle guttered. I suspected I may have laid it on a tad thick. Higgs placed his whiskey to one side.

-So this Tiberius is some sort of magician? What kind of magician? Is he not just a musician who's invited you on tour?

The words hung in the air, disturbed only by the fire settling in the grate. A solitary glowing ember fell onto the hearth, its rubicund colour fading rapidly as it cooled.

-Well, I imagine he would prefer the term 'magus.' Raphael told me that Tiberius had studied both painting and the dark arts in some far flung places.

I hastily refreshed our glasses from the now one-third empty bottle of Jameson.

Higgs was gazing out through the mullioned windows, his eyes gently misted.

- It's bleak out there. What you been doing here all this time?

-Thinking mainly. Standing stock still, like a long-legged fly, gazing at my problems.

I paused

-Now, I have asked you how you got here so quickly in the middle of the night, but there is something else that troubles me.

Higgs eyes returned to mine. Something of the defensive aspect of a challenged chess player settled there for a moment.

- Why did you come here in the middle of the night?

With that, the open palm of the gale slapped hard into the west-facing side of the church, causing a shudder to run through its fabric. The centuries-old stained glass braced inwards and somewhere something audibly smashed to pieces. Neither of us flinched, we silently sipped our whiskeys and after a moment Higgs spoke

-I was waiting for something I think. Waiting, and perhaps expecting something.

-And then you called. Alright, that's enough of that. Now then – what do you want to do, Leonard?

Reaching into a satchel by his feet, he retrieved a battered laptop. Opening it, he looked up. His eyes met mine; a wince of caution flared.

-I should probably look into some flights. Tiberius's message says that the first night of the tour begins in Hamburg tomorrow evening.

-I can't possibly.

But I knew it was all too possible. My presence in Hamburg tomorrow night was as possible as my very current presence before the fireplace. A gaudy streetcar flashed across my mind. I was neither subject nor object at that moment. Higgs was on the phone to a travel agent, negotiating already. I lit a cigarette and gazed into the fire, ablaze both within and without.

***

Some time later, I was standing at the top of the spiral staircase at the very centre of the church, looking down at Higgs below.

-I will wake you up at 5, he said softly.

I nodded. He looked tired.

-We have to get to Manchester airport somehow, but leave it to me. In the meantime, pack and try and get some sleep. I will need to discuss the itinerary for this tour with you at some point, as it's *unusual*...Well, anyway. Not now. Go and get some sleep.

I nodded, and stepped into my room. It occurred to me I hadn't mentioned seeing the flaming apparition to Higgs. I was sure there would be a moment in the future to do so.

Switching on a low table lamp, I threw my usual touring attire into my capacious leather travel bag:

Two black shirts

Two white Shirts

black suit jacket

black suit trousers

Six pairs of black socks

One white t-shirt

Phone charger

Notebook

Turning to my bedroom desk, I rifled through the detritus to find two sacred and holy relics that I never travel without: a battered paperback of 'The Complete Poems of William Blake', and my Rider-Waite Tarot deck in its soft black Napa leather pouch. I gazed down at my bag of black clothes and effects.

*-Though I am black, I am not the devil. So the old wives'
tale goes.* I said this out loud, stuffing the book and the tarot
cards into the brimming- bag.

Black the colour of death; the colour of all things dark and
shadowy, phantom or spectral, unknown or often deadly:
black is the colour of evil personified. But there are some
beneficent things associated with my favourite colour: It is
the colour of fecund, fertile earth, which the most ancient
human civilizations blindly worshipped. It is the colour of
dignity, elegance and sophistication, the preferred colour
of Madame Dior and her little black dress. The Egyptians
believed that black cats had dark and divine powers, and of
course we all know better than to dare to deny that they
don't. Indeed, the Pharaohs themselves thought cats were
insouciant gods who walked amongst us, one black paw in
and one black paw out of our narrow avenue of reality. To
the Japanese black is the colour of the soul as it leaves the
body. Both the early Christians and the Cherokee Indians
believed it represented the shroud of death when it was
incarnate on Earth, the begowned Grim Reaper. For the
Hindus it is the delicate colour of beautiful and terrifying
Shiva, the Destroyer and Creator of worlds. Early African
legend tells of how people became black themselves by
eating the liver of the first ox that was ever sacrificed to the
earliest of Demiurges.

-Sometimes we all have to make sacrifices, I said, gazing
at my yellowing copy of Do Androids Dream of Electric
Sheep? You just won't fit, dear Philip K. Dick. I tossed
the paperback lightly onto the bed. My packing for the
unknown was complete. My black list of packing ticked.

Considering a final cigarette, my weary mind wandered, imagining the very first black list. Fitting imagery for a man currently standing in the exact centre of a radiating pattern of the rose stained-glass window, encased in the great arching nave where our stone-cold bedroom was located. 'A man's own mandala should never be in his bedroom,' I vaguely remembered reading somewhere.

Without undressing, I fell backwards onto the bed. I lay there and let the light of my mind play upon the strange events of the evening. Fragments of thoughts, the living inertia of my life, the nothingness colliding with the suddenness, unexpected visitation, welcomed visitations, the unexpected: unexpected. All brought forth by a mysterious message. How one moment a few hours earlier I had been supine on the rug without a single earthly commitment to occupy my time. Now, I was in bed about to depart first thing.

The gibbous moonlight shone through the stained glass, casting coloured patterns on the oak-planked floor by the bedstead. *How long until I'll be back in this bed?* was one question. *Where in God's name is my fiancé?* was another.

I sat bolt upright. She must have been caught in the storm.

I grabbed my phone and dialled her number. It went straight to answerphone. She must have had to stay at her workplace. She hadn't called – again, because of the storm – it must be – I rationalised, willing my racing thoughts to surcease.

Best leave her a note.

My Love, sit down here with me, nestle into the gentle fractures of my red blanket. Keep quiet in the crooked bent of spired and ancient architecture hard hewn from soft, tar-black stone all carefully cut and considered for vaulted wild worship. Clustered pagans pliant amidst settled silent stone. All hard corners, marble and arches elbowing out the old myths. Here in this place of no pity a strong and solitary thought can be caught and held like a mad black moth in a moonbeam, or a fox dancing and screaming with a mouthful of bright crimson innards of lamb's throat and lungs dangling from its gaudy maw, like an obscene necklace glistening. Here in my isolated temple, ringed radial with the death markers of those who once walked youthful and bright-eyed now deep and warm in weed-wedded soils with bones white as night.

This is the old mind at work. An inner ink-blot running across the page with pale watery progress. And so on and so on it goes, across cold and heathen moor, where the light plays tricks and nothing wilful stays.

All my Love,
Leonard.

With this I turned off the lamp and returned to bed.

In the last quivering moments before the red velvet curtain of consciousness fell, I heard strained notes of profane music playing savagely on the blizzard wind. Out there on the moor– God knew where, somewhere in the ordnance survey oblivion beyond the graveyard – came the fragments of a very strange song. It came again playing on the gale like a terrible overture.

I awoke sometime later in the night by yet another awful
sound

It came again.

Again and again,

It was the tortured wailing of a dog.

A soaring, heaven- or hellbound hound, white-hot and
howling, howling, aloft and eternally aflame.

MYSTERY TOUR

I

-Welcome aboard British Airways 8.56 flight to Hamburg International. Our flight...

The neutral white lighting of the aircraft cabin irradiated my last monochrome memories of the church on the moor. I was wearing my green French greatcoat, and a pair of Spanish leather riding boots that I had acquired the previous year on an excursion to Cadiz. I considered these two items of apparel a sort of psychic suit of armour.

As the aircraft began to gather speed for flight, I had the feeling of transition, of actually moving in time, not just in space. It is at moments like this that I do not truly know myself. I realised I had not said goodbye to either of my cats at the church, and simply left the note for my fiancée. I would be seeing them all soon enough. The engine noise drowned out the laughter of the gods.

II

I dozed fitfully on the flight, surfacing with snatches of strange images that remained superimposed on my mind as I came to, lingering like an untraceable aftertaste as I gazed at the undulating duvet of cloud outside the cabin window. Cannibal cats, a billion bats, profane love letters, smouldering dog collars, incendiary violins, pages of books written in an unknown language, silver chalices of crimson wine flexing and arcing endlessly through the azure air. Were these the psychological sacraments of inscrutable events yet to come?

Germany appeared to be in the grip of some kind of once-in-a-century continental blizzard. As the plane dipped beneath the cloud level, Hamburg emerged, a vast grim and grey industrial complex. It occurred to me that all I had seen was endless white snow and black buildings for the last month.

I felt neurologically glacial. I didn't like the sound of that thought. It occurred to me that I was walking the twilight tightrope of the tropics of gothic. I finished my third Bloody Mary and prepared for landing.

While Higgs waited for our luggage and my battered guitar case to emerge from the carousel, I strolled to the kiosk for cigarettes. The disproportionate fiscal triumph of purchasing two packets of Gauloises for five euros immediately lifted my post-flight drink-dazed malaise.

We smoked silently in the -4° afternoon sunlight, emitting meditative glowing exhalations of smoke that hung solidly in the air for a moment, each breath glistening like an abstract statue before dissipating on the freezing breeze. We waited for a taxi amidst this aeronautical ballet of planes, a delicate moment of cumulus-nimbus calm.

-Higgs, has the next ice age recently commenced without my noticing?

-I am thinking that we should go straight to the theatre. We can introduce ourselves, you can prepare, and then we can deal with the hotel before the show.

-I need to warm up.

-You will.

-I haven't even thought of what songs to play.

III

The Reeperbahn. I have always loved the sound and shape of the word in my mouth. In German it is also known as *die sündigste Meile*, a statement of teutonic linguistic precision: the most sinful mile.

Turning onto the pervert-populated, neon-lit, mile-long fuckfest, I cracked a smile, remembering how fond I was of this industrialised thoroughfare of iniquity. An avenue of anything. A human safari park. Somehow despite the street's uncompromising dedication to all ideologies of the explicit, erotic and illicit, it couldn't help but be beautiful, disarming and charming. It was a refined optical narcotic. Every available square inch was an instant tonic. From the backseat window of the cab, I took in all that street had to offer through my greedy keyhole eyes. I felt a rising richness and a welcome ache of hedonistic remembrance returning to my blood.

The cab pulled to an abrupt halt, and we stepped into the bracing ColdWar weather. Getting into the spirit of things, I dramatically popped the collar of my greatcoat and gazed up at one of the most nauseating buildings I had ever seen. Nazi megalomania incarnate in concrete.

I was about to have my first encounter with two of the most graceful examples of humanity I had ever been so fortunate as to meet.

IV

Tiberius Red wore a black and white fur coat of an unspecified species (it couldn't possibly really be a panda – could it?) and a crimson wide-brimmed hat; he was smoking what appeared to be a long ivory pipe and watching a mildly pornographic video on his laptop.

He was not expecting me as I entered his candle-lit and perfume-incensed dressing room-cum-mobile kasbah. His brilliant blue eyes connected with mine above his black, jungly beard, which concealed the continent of his face. A sharp sense of intrusion was instantly apparent and I feared an unwitting and unforgivable transgression had passed with me over the threshold.

-Mr Leonard, how wonderful you could make it at such short notice.

His voice was warm, with a New York accent that seemed to speak to me straight from some absurd Blaxploitation movie. He stood delicately for a man of his saturnine presence, moving directly towards me at the door and extending a cold, disquietingly clawlike hand.

- Sorry for intruding. I didn't realise this was your private dressing room.

-Not at all! You are very welcome here – sit down – you are my guest! Have you just arrived?

-All the way from the moors of glorious Yorkshire. I left in the middle of a blizzard, and I appear to have landed right in the middle of another one.

He looked at me blankly.

-A drink, perhaps?

He gestured to an array of bottles on a low table to his left, and with the same sweeping hand motion he surreptitiously closed the lid on the laptop, banishing the two-dimensional dancing porno-girls from the room.

-I normally take a gin and tonic around this hour – can I fix you one?

I agreed, already feeling welcome and perhaps a shade too at ease, all too soon.

He handed me an icy glass of gin, and fixing me with a warm smile, clinked his own glass with mine.

-What an extraordinary theatre this is

-It was once a Nazi headquarters, hence why its walls are six foot of concrete. Bombproof, bulletproof, deathproof, and timeproof.

He rolled his eyes sharply left to right.

–Well let's hope they're not songproof too?, I added, instantly wincing at my own inanity.

-Yes, let us hope, Mr Leonard. Let us hope.

He flashed a dead smile, reigniting his pipe with a glinting steel Zippo as he did so. He then seemed momentarily distracted, peering sternly into the ambient shadows. There perhaps was a sly rustling sound coming from one of the far corners of the room.

-I'm glad you could join me for this run of shows. They're intended to be very special shows, the culmination of a lot of - as you Brits would say - *Bloody work*. He continued snapping his focus back on me and emptying his glass. I've been following your career, your existential output. There is that one song in particular that I am exceptionally keen on.

I smiled politely and guardedly, feeling ever-so-slightly preyed   upon. I sipped my gin and glanced at the candled recesses of the cavernous and curiously ornamented room. It had the heady air of an exotic Eastern brothel curated by a lunatic.

Tiberius' eyes, glowing in the embers from his pipe, as blue as the enamel on the statues of Osiris, fixed onto mine once more. Something mischievous yet disarmingly earnest played across their impassive surface.

-Yes, there's that one song in particular.

Thes word relit the uneasy arc welder in my mind.

-May I ask which one? I ventured, my eyes not leaving his. I had the feeling that some arcane game had just commenced.

His gaze never faltered. Not even a flicker of doubt. He posed like some deviant model upon a runway, incrementally adjusting the angular position of his pipe to his lips. I was about to enquire again, when there was a perceptible shift of both the physical and psychic climate of the room. There was a swift, violent movement to my left and turning around I saw to my surprise a young woman with tresses of shoulder-length champagne blonde hair, reclining on a capacious velvet chaise longue. Her carmine red halter dress contrasting sharply the reptilian green of her eyes, an unignorably sensual threat reared its arrestingly beautiful head, veiled in the auric shroud of the room's golden gloom. That I had not noticed her presence before seemed an impossibility. She was looking directly at me, her face shadowed in a theatrical sidelight, entirely expressionless, her eyes blinking synchronously in a studied manner. An almost overpowering arrogance and an imperious chill emanating from her cut-glass, but not quite crystalline features. Without taking her Nile green eyes from mine she spoke, in a supernal purr;

-It is almost time.

The word time hung in the air with a precision that caused my mind to melt, thaw and resolve itself into a dew, albeit just for a moment.

Tiberius clapped his talon-like hands.

-Oh of course - we should be preparing ourselves, there's so very much to do. My apologies Mr Leonard, I neglected to introduce my...(he paused selecting the word) - *associate*... Miss Pinky Capote. But there is indeed no *time* for all that now.

Clasping my shoulder he ushered me politely but firmly from the room. The bombproof door shut behind me with a resounding, tomblike thud.

VI

I strode down the grim corridor that led to my own dressing room, my thoughts refusing to be rallied into any comprehensible arrangement. I felt a vague panic racketing through me. Tiberius and Pinky, what a pair of fucking weirdos. So appoline and vital mere seconds ago, they were already fading into vague mythic shapes that I groped at like obscene statues in the dark.

Stepping into my far less eccentrically-decorated room, I rifled through my bag for my notebook and tarot deck. Sitting at the dressing table, bathed in a pool of light from the opalescent lamps, I sketched down some unmediated impressions.

After a time, I noticed a tray with what appeared to be some kind of vegetable stew and a stack of warm irregular shaped breads on the side to my left. The evaporating spices gently scenting the air did little to arouse my appetite. There was also now a bottle of rare Yamazaki Japanese whisky on the counter that had definitely not been there before. I eyed these things warily. I assumed that Higgs had made sure they were present prior to stepping out. Wherever he had gone. There was a sudden pervading menace to the place that I had to work hard to push from my mind.

The presence of the stew and whisky had a quieting effect on my nervous system even without me having to actually ingest either of them. I stared at the page, and then at my tarot deck. I placed the deck upright before me on the desk like an acolyte called to attention, awaiting clairvoyant authorial direction.

Something about the initial encounter with Tiberius and the unexpected presence of Pinky Capote had unseamed me. I don't know what I had been expecting, but it was precisely not that. For a moment I wondered wildly if Tiberius had slipped something in my gin and tonic, but that was a lagoon of madness come all too soon, into which I was unwilling to plunge.

There had, I felt, been a metaphysical shuffling of cards under the table during our meeting. There was definitely a weasel beneath the cocktail cabinet, a great white circling in the waters, something whispering in the woodshed. There was something definitely going on. A strange game set in motion. The phrase strange game reminded me of some of the more misguided and sybaritic evenings at the already-very-distant-feeling church. I should never ever have read tarot on the altar.

As I was writing, I saw Higgs enter the room behind me. He paused, looking directly back at me, inverted in the looking glass, then he sat down on the long leather couch. I thought I detected a shadow of concern passing over his countenance, but I looked away, back to the spidery words on the page, before I could ascertain whether something was actually the matter. Maybe he was just in a mood.

I returned to my writing, trying to capture as much detail as I was able to excavate of the exchange just passed. I couldn't shake the feeling of its significance. Scottish Sophie taught me a particular word for thoughts such as these, and that word is *dree*. It means to endure, to bear with fortitude that which is wearisome, to last out, as the Scots say. A *dree* is both a hard task and also a long, drawn-out melody. To *dree* one's weird is, unforgettably, to endure one's fate, and suffer the consequences of one's actions.

Which I have now evidently done, I have lived my dree. Now you are in the paper-white autopsy room with me. (Are we trying to establish if it really was death by misadventure?) That's a curious thought. Only the entropic movement of time has really occurred. That time has only moved in your mind as you are reading this, and in my mind writing it. We are in different time zones. I haven't moved for the last six hours since I started setting these words down out here on the porch in Nashville. I can never be sure if it's a small mercy that as a species we have such poor understanding of deep, entropic time.

Only my mind has moved. The spidery squiggles on the page have set our stage. Your eyes are now following and decoding the alphabetic telemetry of this bit of my life.

Time. There was that word again. I added it to the other words on the page of my black diary back in Hamburg. Time is the first word Pinky ever said to me. The details of this first encounter felt like they may contain some kind of gestating germ, the snaking DNA of the virus that might follow our first encounter. I now know some things should be left alone, some hunches should remain unchased, some stones should be left unturned, and certain tombs left respectfully undisturbed.

After a quiet moment, intruded upon only by the scratching nib of my pen moving across the papyrus page, Higgs stood and helped himself to some of the stew, and on finding it agreeable to his taste suggested that I do the same. He did so while pouring two tumblers of whiskey.

-You should really eat, they want you on stage at 8.

-What time is it now?

-6.15. Is everything alright, Leonard?

-Yes, it's all as clear to me as a bell on a bright frosty morning, Higgs, at least I think it is. I just met Tiberius and Pinky.

- Pinky?

- Pinky Capote. I didn't know she was even on the tour. I didn't see her name in any of the correspondence. Anyway, she was as bizarre as the name suggests. I couldn't really say what it was for certain, but there is definitely something odd about her. Well, about both of them. Very fucking odd.

Higgs turned slightly on his heel,

-Come on, have something to eat, and drink this. We can talk about this Pinky Capote later.

VII

That night Hamburg would have a few more recherche revelations up its sleeve, none of which seemed to have much significance at the time. But as I sit here now by a flickering hurricane lamp, my typewriter balanced on my knees in this insect-chattering Nashville night, eighteen months and nine lives later, I realise just how much the entire universe pivoted on the events of that evening. I still hear the distant grinding of wheels turning within wheels. The pipe organ plays on.

The first show of a tour is either absolutely extraordinary or extremely difficult. That night in Hamburg, in those repurposed horror vaults, I walked out on stage to a heaving full house...The goddesses in the tower of song smiled beneficently down upon me.

I fumbled my way through seven uncertain, unsteady, under-rehearsed songs, occasionally pausing between numbers to engage with the audience. To my surprise they were riveted to each musical moment; each beat was timed entirely to their liking; each lyrical image perfectly framed... Or so it seemed. I had not, in fact, played a concert for several months. The grandiosity of this blag did not escape me. It seemed hardly possible that I was even standing so stalwart on my two hind legs, let alone able to express anything of artistic esteem. I left the stage bowing to a staggeringly warm response. I had for a fleeting moment been transformed into a minor god.

I felt so very alive. A palpable opening night success. A laurel-wreathed deity steeped in self-congratulatory locomotion. I drank gluttonously from that brimming chalice of dopamine, serotonin and adrenaline sloshing around in my skull. O The one true cocktail of the gods.

The backstage was unusually dark as I blinked my way out of the halogen halos of the stage lights. Applause dying away in my ears, I stumbled, my guitar clanging metallically into what I assumed to be a huge fire extinguisher – or perhaps it was a piece of a Panzer tank, or a suit of armour.

There was no one else lurking around the labyrinthine corridors; not a soul. Normally, this area would be thronging with road crew and musicians preparing to take the stage. Retracing my steps back to my dressing room, more by memory than sight, it occurred to me that it was also far too quiet. No intermission music had come on over the speakers after I had left the stage. I thought of that look that had lingered in the narrowed eyes of Tiberius as he had enquired about that *one particular song*.

I stepped into the glow of light at the doorway to my dressing room, gently leaning my guitar against the near wall as I entered. Everything was as it had been   when I left. My notebook and tarot deck there on the desk; the whiskey tumblers remained exactly where they had been placed down.

My eyes fixed directly into the eyes reflected in the mirror before me. My situation seemed vaguely impossible, or at least highly improbable, for so much had changed in such a small space of time. From a Yorkshire church to a Nazi rock and roll bunker overnight. *Space and time, space and time, space and time*; that phrase had been repeating like a chorus since I had departed from the church. *Perhaps all we needed was a little space and time*. The ancient word *theurgy* sprung to mind, I reached for my notebook:

noun: **theurgy**

1. *the operation or effect of a supernatural or divine agency in human affairs.*

o *a system of white magic practised by the early Neoplatonists.*

Theurgy describes the practice of rituals, sometimes seen as magical in nature, performed with the intention of invoking the action or evoking the presence of one or more deities, especially with the goal of achieving henosis and perfecting oneself.

I noticed that, in fact, all was not quite as I had left it. My tarot deck had been moved. An ebb of alarm pulsed in my throat. Yes it had definitely been disturbed ever so slightly. I was sure of it.

In accordance with my tried and tested pre-show ritual, just before leaving my dressing room I had selected a single tarot card from the deck, placing it carefully to one side, after a brief moment's meditation on the character (drawn at random) of The Hanged Man. Not the most auspicious of cards to draw prior to a performance, but I had felt oddly pleased to see his upside down form. He was a subtle recognition of the dramatic upheaval in my timeline. Everything had indeed been turned upside down. I felt willingly suspended. Upended. Well, The Hanged Man was nowhere to be seen. He had been moved, and two other cards haphazardly dropped in his place. The Queen of Cups and The Wheel of fortune.

It was then that she spoke from the shadows for the second time that night.

-I do hope you don't mind but I simply couldn't help myself. I am just helplessly drawn to those cards. It's the colours, the iconography, those veiled symbols, they make me feel so...

She trailed off expertly, clearly adept at getting away with things.

I was speechless. In this golden silence she took a step forward into the pool of matchless lights.

-Oh,   I exhaled, finding my voice in the far reaches of the aether: That's fine.

I paused, wondering if she could detect my lie. A transgression, a filigree of sensual trespass, a silent alarm triggered by her deliberate violation. All of this went unremarked. Why had she let herself in here, and how did she even know I had the tarot cards with me? Why had I welcomed her and lied to her with my first breath? I would have time enough to ruminate upon the malign ascension of our first meeting.

She stepped forward, again the insolence in her verdigris eyes meeting mine with the fervour of a raging inferno.

-I do *know* you are not supposed to touch someone else's tarot cards. I really do hope you don't mind.

I could hear a violin string of venom behind her words. I couldn't place her accent either, certainly American, certainly of the West Coast, but certainly something else still. Some grandiloquent and archaic flavour to her intonation.

-Perhaps you would like a reading one evening?

-That would be nice. I actually came to ask you something.

She turned and ebbed coolly towards the door. She wore her physical capriciousness like a shimmering golden shield, or perhaps it was a glamorous veil. Her walk was her own personal dance of the ten deaths of desire. An air of designed disengagement thronged about her. It obfuscated her motives in a way that I assumed allowed her to behave precisely as she wished, invariably in precise accordance to her innermost desires and adamantine will. As she moved –

I assumed she was leaving, once again without the courtesy of explanation – she paused and posed, lingering on the threshold, and, turning back, said:

-Leonard, my darling, can I borrow your guitar for just a little while?

-Is that what you came here to ask me?

She laughed, slightly spitefully.

-Well what else would I be here for? Yes, I need to practise something.

-Well yes of course, be my guest. I said hating myself for my obsequiousness and outraged at her insolence. I moved to offer her the guitar leant up against the wall, but before I could take a step, she had already seized the guitar and vanished into the shadows.

VIII

The next morning, as I boarded the fast train to Berlin, I did not have my guitar.

After my sycophantic complicity in its abduction from my dressing room the evening had descended into a haze of heady self-loathing, grim recrimination and clouds of sweet Turkish tobacco smoke. I went in hard on the bars of the Reeperbahn, finding comfort amidst the miasma of degeneracy. I was muttering curses under my breath. Hamburg is the perfect place to indulge such an impulse, my declamations of outrage punctuated by the clink of crystalline cups of Jameson.

At some phase in the evening Higgs and I ensconced ourselves in a corner bar of the opulent St George Hotel barroom on Barcastrasse. I was by this point being distinctly uncommunicative, feeling entirely confounded by the events of the evening. The spirit of the city was upon me, but Pinky was still playing on my mind. Between the rounds of Schnapps and Steiners I thought of my kittens, I thought of my fiancée returning to an empty church, and I wondered about the whereabouts of my delicate, perfectly-fretted rosewood guitar. Oh my god, where was she? Somewhere, out there in the Hamburg night...in the custody of Pinky Capote.

Higgs maintained a fine temper all evening, ebullient and pleased with how the first show had been received. Just to dampen the mood, towards the end of the night I coolly related to him what had occurred with the disturbance of my tarot cards and the 'theft' of my guitar. He nodded silently and sagely. We finished our drinks and, with little more to be said, retired to our well-made German beds. I didn't even unscrew the fire alarm in my room as is customary before commencing a dedicated chain smoke, ashing out the window, necking Spätburgunder wine from a coffee mug while listening to Van Morrison's Astral Weeks from the tiny speaker on my phone. I slept fitfully, realising at around 3 AM that I had not telephoned my fiancée as I'd sworn to. First thing I would do is attend to that. I made a solemn oath staring down at the milling prostitutes on the strasse below.

***

But then, when I came to, sobering up on the train out of Hamburg, I was in a crowded carriage, surrounded by friendly frauleins equipped with beautifully-designed pneumatic backsides, knowingly bended within tight-fit fascistic A -line skirts. Mascara and Kohl-drenched dark eyes everywhere. It really was a very cosy train carriage and I realised that I really didn't feel like calling my fiancée at all. Who knew how she would have reacted to my absence? I didn't think that this carriage was the correct setting for such a complex and potentially volatile conversation. I would call her as soon as I got to my dressing room in Berlin. Decision made, I flashed a smile at a cute young blonde girl in tight blue jeans who was looking directly at me, her shapely Bavarian farmgirl head cocked playfully to one side. I opened my copy of Zola's *La Bete Humaine*. In this version of reality the perfectly engineered Teutonic train carried me further into the metaphysical derailing of my life.

IX

An hour later we arrived at Berlin Hauptbahnhof and took a cab directly to the venue, which had formerly been a pornographic cinema. I stood outside, gazing at my name in lights, beneath the headline (TIBERIUS RED & PINKY CAPOTE : FOR ONE NIGHT ONLY) , in smaller letters it read SAINT LEONARD. I smiled. This blended with the expectation of seeing Pinky and demanding she return my guitar. Yes, demanding she explained herself to me; she was going to get the dressing-down of a lifetime from me. I looked back once more at my name in lights, and Berlin gaped its gaudy maw, and welcomed me into its tit-wanking bosom.

I had neglected to watch Tiberius' performance the previous night, as I had obviously been enraged by the sly theft of my guitar, so I had chosen instead to become obscenely drunk. I hoped my absence had gone unnoticed by Tiberius, as that could well have been perceived as some premeditated first-night slight, deleteriously gauche.

I was determined to watch his performance this evening and furthermore to be witnessed doing so very conspicuously. I was intrigued as to what his act, whether it be musical or occult, actually involved. I wanted to see Pinky's role in all this and to get to the bottom of my purloined guitar. There remained the unresolved question of the song. *My song*. The song in my catalogue that had so intrigued him. Was it possible that this one song could have led to my invitation to tour with him? But which one? I had the feeling that I was indeed playing a game. A game to which I clearly did not know the rules.

On entering the foyer, leaning against a picture frame I saw my precious guitar. Intact, unharmed, yet purposefully abandoned.

X

That evening, as Tiberius took to the stage, a profound silence rippled over the expectant throng. A spotlight followed him, guitar harnessed over his shoulder, his flowing sequined stage gown glittering like a map of the constellations.

He began with a lilting ballad that seemed to relate the hunt for long-lost treasure, dextrously strumming the sonorous ebony guitar with a manicured thumbnail as he sang. Song after strange song followed. Each one grew in length and narrative complexity, until they all blended into one vast melodic tapestry; songs stretching forward and backward in time like the warp of some elasticising memory.

The audience were hypnotised – or were they mesmerised? I couldn't be sure. I was standing in the shadows to the left of the stage and had barely moved for over an hour. I was transfixed by this remarkable performance. It was so oddly familiar.

While I was drinking deep of this meditative reverie, I sensed Pinky standing beside me. I had no idea how long she had been standing there, but before I could react, she strode out of the shadows onto the stage to join Tiberius. Her motions were brazen, open, exposing but not vulnerable, her black gown denying all. She stood statuesque, taking in her audience at the distinctive chrome microphone. They began a slow undulating duet detailing the waxing and waning of a complex tryst. It did not leave me feeling at all that romantic. I felt hollowed out, drained, and mildly panicked.

What kind of rock and roll show was this? Were they playing their hits? Perhaps I should politely excuse myself and leave the tour tonight before I get any more involved.

I could always just grab my bag and vanish into the Berlin night, disappear back into the oblivion of Low Moor.

The stage lighting plunged into a pulsating chocolate cosmos red. Tiberius was joined by several other musicians on stage. A drummer, an electric guitarist, a bassist and piano player. A stark shift in tempo and style occurred and a raucous squall was unleashed upon the auditorium. The previously pliant and hypnagogic audience were at once on their feet waving, flailing and cavorting to the pulsing, filthily writhing back beat. The intensity appeared to be building exponentially. Tiberius whirled around the stage, his golden robe twisting and glistening with sweat.

He now seemed to be incanting rather than merely singing. The arc-welding flame of the electric guitar licked at the edges of these ravishing carnal images. Scorching and searing lyrical descriptions of obscene lusting rituals and sacrilegious perversities. The lights – yellow, green, red, and somehow black – beamed out over the stage and onto the writhing audience. I caught glimpses of naked flesh dancing and moving; sometimes seemingly as one. I was certain a group sex act was actually occurring amidst the circling throng.

Tiberius was on his knees at centre stage, thrashing and wailing and screaming into the microphone as Pinky cavorted around him. She was singing a chillingly high countermelody, rising and falling beneath the sea of sound. I swore I glimpsed a thin trickle of bright red blood running from the edge of her tumescent lips, down her jaw to her décolletage. But before I could be certain, she had arabesqued over to the other side of the stage and cloaked herself in a velvet vermillion gown.

I felt the bile rising in my throat. I tore my eyes away. The performance was still building in animal vigour, but I could not stand to witness its profane conclusion. Not now. I staggered into the darkened corridor that led to my dressing room.

Gulping cool draughts of air conditioning I turned the lights up full, poured myself a tumbler of Japanese whisky and collapsed onto the couch. Moments later the door opened and Higgs entered. He leant heavily against the wall and limply shook his head like a beaten boxer. The freshly-broken sweat on his brow glistened like lurid arachnid eyes in the lamplight.

-My fucking god Leonard. What is happening here? What is this?

-I don't know.

Silence settled on the room. We could hear the distant tremulations of Tiberius's performance still gaining in bizarre and bestial momentum. Neither of us spoke further...We both started laughing hysterically.

XI

We laughed for quite a long time. The laughter seemed to dissipate the unease that threatened to overwhelm us. I rifled through my leather bag for Mother's rosary and placed it round my neck.

-Just in case...I mean, you never know.

Higgs stared at the rosary.

-The first ten of these are called a decade, the second refers to the mysteries, it goes on from there, I said, holding up the beads.

He smiled a hollow smile and returned to scrolling through a vast timetable on his laptop. He was trying to navigate our way to Oslo, where we were scheduled to perform the following night. I already knew it was a long journey from Berlin to Oslo.

-It's looking like a train, another train, a coach, a ferry and then possibly a very long taxi to get to the venue in time for the show tomorrow.

-Higgs, do you think perhaps we should just go home?

He paused, angulating the screen of the laptop and casting a liquid crystal pallor over his features.

-I mean, I can't say I am not enjoying it, he said softly, almost to himself.

-Yes. I suppose it beats rotting away for eternity in the Church of the Horses, doesn't it? We should proceed with extreme caution, Higgs.

-Well what's the worst that could happen?

He looked at me, the traces of his smile fading.

- But, yes, I see what you're saying.

-Good. Now that all the debauchery has finished out there, shall we head back to the hotel? I could do with a duck a l'orange, a bottle of rioja and a bath.

-Sadly not tonight, Leonard. We have to get the train in an hour from Berlin Hauptbahnhof to Neumünster. Then it's Neumunster to Flensburg, Flensburg to Fredericia,

Fredericia to Copenhagen Central, Copenhagen Central, to Gothenburg, Gothenburg to Halden, and then, if we have any luck, a 4-hour cab through the frozen fjords and rolling icy mountains to Oslo.

-Right. Oh good. I suppose I'd better pack up and have a nice big drink then.

-I have a final blow to deliver upon your bruises this evening Leonard. We have entirely run out of whisky.

I was out the door of the dressing room and halfway down the pink velour-walled hallway before Higgs could speak. My Spanish leather riding boots sparked on the baby blue linoleum as I belted towards the promoter's office. I knew he had a case of the stuff in there as I had spied it earlier when signing the relevant papers for payment. I should have requested another bottle on the spot there and then. There was no way I was even considering a twenty hour train journey without a bottle of Jameson. Arriving at the office, I was, by the grace of the great goddess, in luck. Herman was still cashing up the ticket sales as I entered without knocking. A few transactional moments later I was wandering back along the corridor, triumphantly clasping my glassy green whiskey bottle baby. It was then that something truly terrifying happened.

I was passing Tiberius' dressing room. The door was ever-so slightly ajar, allowing me just enough of an aperture to peer in. Tiberius and Pinky were both sitting in a circle of red candles in the dead centre of the room on two low bone-white stools. Their backs pressed against each other, Tiberius' arm and the fingers of Pinky's respective left and right hands entwined around her neck. In this perverse choking posture they were singing softly as Tiberius strummed his crude oil black guitar. It was not this that was terrifying. It was what they were singing:

I sent three lovers to the wilderness
And one came back
She had blood in her eyes and carried in her arms
A strange-looking sack
As I laid her down, she never made a sound, save for these words of misery...
So I looked inside the sack
Then I said my prayers, changed my name and never looked back...

The whisky bottle slipped from my fingers. I remember it cartwheeling through the air in front of me in smooth slow motion and then exploding in a violent shower of gold and green shards as the water of life gushed over the linoleum, splashing against the brown leather of my boots. The door of Tiberius' dressing room slammed shut instantly. For a dreadful moment I had caught a glimpse of his cruel cerulean eyes glowering at me. His black-as-a-starless-Egyptian-night beard bristling with rage at my eavesdropping. It was then that I passed out.

XII

-I don't understand, Higgs said. You look like you've seen a ghost.

We were ensconced in the sleeper carriage of the 1.20 AM express from Berlin to Gothenburg. We had requested the sleeper, despite the inordinate expense, as there were so many stops and connections we felt it was for the best, what with me succumbing to a full-blown mental breakdown. I had come to an hour previously, on the floor of the converted porno cinema, surrounded by the emerald green bottle shards, with Higgs standing over me looking deeply concerned. From my fitted leather seat I could see my reflection in the glass of the carriage as the nocturnal German countryside flowed superimposed over my face. I had seen the ghost of a song. A spectral symphony. A perversion of the laws of not only time but space. I'd heard a long low banshee's wail.

-Higgs...Something very, very strange happened backstage in that porno cinema in Berlin tonight.

-Yes I was there. You collapsed in a corridor and woke up ranting about holy guardian angels and the many hidden instruments of Lucifer.

-No, there was something else. Something much worse.I overheard Tiberius and Capote singing a song in their dressing room.

-Two musicians, on tour, singing a song in their own dressing room? How immensely inexplicable, how utterly terrifying.

- Yes it is.... You see, it was a song I hadn't heard for quite some time. It is also a song that doesn't exist.

With this Higgs clutched at his head with his hands.

-What are you talking about?

-Oh this is an odd one, Higgs. I can't really explain it at all. It's a queer and uncomfortable story.

-Well we've got 19 hours and 11 minutes until we get to Oslo and you have my undivided attention.

Leaning back into the leather seat, and with his free hand pouring two slugs of whisky into the tumblers, he exhaled heavily.

-Leonard, everything that has ever happened to you, near you or around you has been consistently strange. Every memory I have of you is strange. Even this very moment now is strange. It's the first time I've ever seen you waste whiskey so it had better be good.

XIII

'Where to begin. A few years ago, my fiancée's mother was residing in a converted mediaeval nunnery in the West Riding of Yorkshire known as Kirklees Hall. It was about thirty miles north of the Church of the Horses. It's a relatively well-known location amongst English folklorists for apparently being the historic resting place of Robin Hood. And there have over the centuries been dozens of fairly well-documented sightings of the so-called 'Kirklees Vampire' in and around the bleak region of moorland where her mother's house stands.

My fiancée and I decided to spend a long weekend with her mother at Kirklees Hall in the remoteness of the rolling grey-green countryside, surrounded by the dense elm thickets of ancient Saxon hunting grounds. This was sometime before we moved to the church and the area still held some strange fascination for us. Certainly at the time; in stark contrast to our frenetic existence in London, it was an incredibly appealing proposal of isolation and peace. If only for a few days.

Fifty metres in front of the imposing main estate there is a small stone game house, where in the past pheasants, wild boars, hares and pretty much any local animal would be left to 'drain' after they had been hunted to death on the grounds. You see, you have to thoroughly exsanguinate a carcass before you can butcher it for the table. This grim structure had been converted into a very ill-thought-through and uninviting summer house. It was, for obvious reasons, virtually never used.

At the time however, the game house had caught my attention, as it was made of huge blocks of Pennine granite stone, and, being about twenty-foot square and tall, the acoustics in it were bright, with cathedral-like reverberations. I had recently acquired an old four-track tape recorder and had brought some very hard-to-find cassette tapes and microphones along with me with the half-minded intention of recording some new songs in this weird building, away from the prying ears of the main house. Away from anyone at all, really.

On this particular Saturday evening we had dinner with her family in the main house. During the meal a storm began to roll in, and before too long the exposed house was being battered by howling winds and relentless sheeting rain. After dinner, I made it clear that I intended to go out to the game house to attempt some recording. This was met with palpable surprise and a certain derision. However I wasn't to be swayed, and, donning a macintosh, clutching my guitar and the ungainly recording equipment, I strode out into the storm and down across the lawn to the game house.

Once I was inside, closing the heavy hinged oak door, I lit several candles and commenced setting up the tape recorder. Grappling to suspend the microphones from the ceiling beams, where they dangled above my head by their own immensely long intestinal leads, hanging in much the same way, it struck me at the time, as the animal carcasses would have once. I was only able to grab very long mic leads from the studio before I left. So I had two bundles of cables, each twenty feet in length, which are really cumbersome to carry or move, having to be tightly coiled and slung over the shoulder. Another important detail of the game house is that, despite it being almost perfectly 20 square feet, the only windows are four very narrow slit windows no more than two inches wide, one on each of the four walls. These slits afford very little view of the surrounding environs.

So I settled down, sipping wine, and started to play around with a sequence of blues songs that I had, for no particular reason, been working on at the time. The storm soon blossomed but the acoustics in the space kept me distracted and totally absorbed in my work. I was pleased with the first few hours of recording but something quite unexplained occurred in the process.

Perhaps it was the anonymity of the environment or the storm outside, but at around midnight I found myself singing, or rather incanting...some very strange songs. Songs, I didn't recall composing at all but appeared to know every word to. Peculiar chords and weird melodic non-metrical phrasings, meandering structures, and howling harpy choruses, sometimes screamed, sometimes crooned with sweeping vibratos ringing off the ancient stone walls surrounding me and assuaging the baying of the storm outside. Some of the songs seemed to be in a true blues form, but again, altered in ways I had never studied or even heard of previously. Can you imagine that Higgs? I was strumming chord shapes and singing countermelodies I didn't even know existed, let alone where I might have acquired any knowledge of them. I lost all track of time as each new song followed the other, as if preordained by some unknown composer. The tape recorder kept faithfully whirring next to me and thank God I had it there to capture these perverse ballads that I seemed to be plucking straight from the cimmerian night air. The contents of these ballads were...unsettling and troubling, but compelling. It must have been around half one when I was struck by a feeling of absolute dread. A nebulous, idiopathic, chest-tightening tension, accompanied by notes of pure anxiety...something akin to the clinical heebie-jeebies. There was a sensation of being closely watched, but, with no real windows, and given that Kirklees Hall was situated at least ten miles from any other human habitation, this notion seemed unlikely, if not impossible.

I tried in vain to dismiss the thought, but I simply could not shake it; if anything, it seemed to increase in amplitude with each passing candle flickering moment. The storm raged, lightning forked, strobing across the moorland and treetops. In these split seconds of brilliant illumination I saw not a soul. No monstrous figure loomed outside silhouetted in those flashes, there was, I was certain, no one watching me.

But still that sickening feeling of dread persisted. I had to fight the urge to bolt from the building back to the main house. The feeling that had begun as an aching dread began to rapidly crescendo into pure terror. What amplified this sensation and made it more acutely disturbing was that there was no apparent reason for me to feel this way. I had seen nothing, heard nothing. Nothing had disturbed the room. I peered through the narrow slit windows again and could see nothing save the storm savaging the moorland and the distant line of trees bowing to the will of the wind. With my heart hammering in my chest, I clicked on my torch and blew out the candles. In the dark my blood was up and I rushed to open the heavy oak door. Just before running out into the night, I turned back and grabbed my guitar. I didn't bother gathering up the recording equipment as I felt certain it would be safe to leave it overnight. Given its ungainly weight, the remoteness of the locale, and it having no inherent value to anyone at all, I barely gave it a second thought.

Back in the house and warming up in front of the open fireplace, nursing a restorative glass, my composure returned. Watching the storm roll away, I began to feel a little foolish for panicking and fleeing the game house. I laughed out loud at my ability to spook myself so thoroughly. I had been absolutely terrified. Dispatching the last drops of my dram,

I went to bed as the clock struck three. The next morning I awoke to a commotion in the house. I descended the stairs to find my fiancée and her mother at the kitchen table and my fiancée's stepfather stood by the kitchen door, solemnly shaking his head.

-What happened out there, lad? Down at the game house?' He said in his broad Yorkshire accent.

I replied that I had no idea what he was referring to and that all had been fine when I left last night, aside from my having spooked myself, perhaps by staying up a little too late alone in a candlelit room, and maybe by having one glass of wine too many. 'Why?' I asked.

Without answering, he motioned me to follow him as he walked out the door. As we approached the game house, in the bright light of the morning, it was clear there had been a disturbance.

Slowing as we approached, a few steps from the structure my heart stuck in my throat. The lawn all around the outside perimeter of the game house had been churned up in the sodden rain last night by what was unmistakably the tracks of someone walking around and around the building. There were deeper patches of churned turf outside each of the narrow slit windows, obviously where someone had stood for quite some time looking through the window, moving from foot to foot to get a better view through the slit before moving around to the next window. It was clear from the extent to which the lawn had been churned that this activity had gone on for quite some time. Someone had been watching me for hours.

I followed her stepfather into the game house. All my recording equipment was gone. The four-track recorder, the microphones and the two immensely long and heavy coils of leads were all gone. There was damp soil smeared on the floor, remnants from the thief's muddy shoes.

However, what struck me as totally baffling was that the iPad, the flat screen TV and expensive hi-fi in the corner had been left untouched. Why on Earth would an opportunist thief spend hours waiting in a raging storm, waiting and watching me, and then only steal the ungainly equipment that had clearly no real monetary value whatsoever, leaving all the far more valuable items untouched?

Later, back in the house, I re-voiced this question to the local policeman, who had been called to the house.

'Why would anyone do that, in a storm like last night's, for no real reason, miles and miles from anywhere?' I asked him. 'Who would be out there?'

The police officer had his back to me, looking out from the lounge windows. Slowly, deliberately, he put his cup of tea down on the table. He paused, squinting back out across the twilit moor and said,

'It's probably best not to dwell on that too long, lad.'

And I never have until tonight. I've attempted to erase the entire event from my mind, or I have chosen not to remember it.

But the thing is, that song I heard Tiberius and Pinky singing in their dressing room tonight was the demented song I was playing out in that game house that stormy night three years ago. The one that seemed to come to me from the aether, or the other end of the universe, or wherever.

The only existing version of which I recorded on that tape recorder, which apparently vanished untraceably. Stolen by God-knows-who on that dreadful evening. I never, ever thought I would hear it again. I couldn't even whistle a note of it until tonight. And... There is one final thing. I have never uttered a word of this to anyone. When I said before that there were muddy footprints on the stone floor of the game house, well, I went back to inspect them several times that day. I didn't care to mention this at the time, as everyone in the house was disturbed enough. But, well, they honestly didn't really look like a man's footprints at all. They looked more like something had been muddily slipping and sliding around on the tiled floor. And at one point they seemed to have run or slid almost halfway up the sheer stone wall. It brought to mind the image of something writhing and thrashing on an operating table, desperate to get away. I think that was the one thing I liked the least about the whole weekend.

XIV

After I concluded my story Higgs fixed me with a flinty inquisitor's gaze over the table.

The gentle lolling of the train caused the lights to shudder intermittently over his arching eyebrows. He leant forward and pressed the button to cease audio recording on his telephone. I couldn't imagine what he might actually be thinking. In the process of recounting the story I had myself realised how utterly incredulous the whole sequence of events sounded. I still felt sick from hearing the song again. The back of my head and the muscles around my eyes reported a dull ache, I assumed from my collision with the floor outside the dressing room. It was lucky I had not fallen directly onto the broken bottle shards.

'I think I'd like a cigarette,' Higgs said, standing and reaching for the packet of Gauloise in his suit jacket, and he stepped out the sliding doors.

I gazed at my doubled reflection in the black glass, and then allowed my focus to shift to the distant hazed lights of some indecipherable structures poised on the landscape several miles away. The stalking feeling of unreality came at me again. I took a large sip of my drink in an effort to banish it. Without knowing where the impulse arose from I was on my feet and rifling through my tour bag. Moments later I had retrieved my battered phone and pressed dial. My fiancée's phone rang several times, there was a soft click, and the line went dead. It didn't even go to the answerphone. My heart jumped. The total absence of contact and my hasty abandonment of the church didn't sit well in my mind. Something was definitely amiss. She hadn't tried to ring me either: no missed calls, no text messages. I pressed dial again. The process was replayed. Click and the line went dead.

The train had gathered speed. Not a great deal, but enough to exaggerate the rolling motion of the carriage over the tracks. The shadowy things that ceaselessly whipped past the windows seemed to have gained in ghostly velocity. I thought I saw a woman waving a white sheet from the window of a distant cottage, but then she was gone, whisked away into the night as we rapidly approached another day.

I took out my notebook and distractedly returned to
the diary. Looking down at the scrawled pages it occurred
to me that the diary was becoming a map of sorts, a map
of my thoughts. However the map was incomplete and
esoteric, too vague to reveal any meaningful psychological
landmarks. No coordinates of conviction, nor any reliable
means of finding a path through the wild and increasingly
hostile terrain of undulating interpersonal events and
canyons of psychic misadventure over which my wayfaring
mind rambled and roamed. Putting my pen to the page I
wrote 'Here Be Monsters'.

XV

We made a near-fatal mistake on our way to Oslo. We had
whiled away several hours of the journey locked into private
tasks and inner worlds. Barely a word had passed between
us since Higgs had returned from his recuperative cigarette.
I had spent several hours blackening the pages of my
notebook with impressions, textures, tableaus, brushstroke
moods, reflections, astrological and quasi-anthropological
interpretations of the events that were unfolding. As the
pages darkened, so did my mood.

At one point I had played Gustav Mahler's symphony
in D minor from the laptop, while gazing wistfully into
the tundra outside the window, until Higgs had politely
but firmly asked me to 'Turn it off, now'. I had a feeling
that he was as troubled and upset as I was about the song
Tiberius and Pinky had sung, and the implications of the

story I had just related to him, and what that meant for the trajectory of the tour. Or even perhaps what it all meant for the trajectory of our lives. There was a creeping sense of 'What the fuck next?' starting to manifest. Was he perhaps becoming concerned for my sanity? I could understand this concern. The events I had related to him may well have seemed like the crazed notions of a man well departed from the righteous path. Perhaps I was displaying the first symptoms of a degenerating mental state. The slight cast about the eyes, the furtive glance of one who had spent a little too long digging into the darker orphic corners of Bloomsbury bookshops? I reassured myself that he had seen with his own eyes what had happened during Tiberius's performance in Berlin.

The sky lightened, the air warmed not at all, the pale sun shone over rock faces and snow, as craggy and unforgiving as our mood. Breakfast was achieved through the timely ambushing of a buffet trolley. A salty bun filled with peculiar soft cheese and a cup of tar-black tea into which I deposited four sachets of sugar.

The day settled in around us with the repetitive clatter of wheel on rail. My mood was grey. Grey as the oppressive and unremitting tundra and alike in its profound absence of feature. Aside from the occasional cigarette break or to go to the toilet, neither of us moved. After a few brief and intensely boring moments the sky began to darken again, and before I had registered the passing of a day I was gazing at the yellow-lit reflection of my face illuminated against the night-time window pane once more. Night had returned so soon, we were indeed entering the land of the midnight sun.

The train suddenly shuddered and slowed. We pulled into a desolate looking station. For the last six hours we had barely stopped at all, so this event caught our attention like an iron key dropping onto a porcelain plate. Higgs shot up, opened the window and poked his head out. He narrowed his eyes. A moment later he was consulting his telephone with an air of urgency. It was at *exactly* this point that the near-fatal mistake was made.

-Right Leonard, grab your bag, I can't stand anymore of this.We can hop off here and catch the local ferry and sail into the bay of Oslo. It's easy and takes less time. My eyes traced the desolation of the platform outside. Apart from a solitary lamplight I could see nothing and no one populating the space. No sign of habitation, nor even the merest hints of human activity. The pool of chilly lamplight on the platform did not look at all inviting from my current, extremely comfortable seated position. I expressed this view very clearly to Higgs.

-Come on, let's get off. It's been unbearable in here for the last twelve hours.

To heighten the urgency of the scene the conductor's whistle blew long and shrill over the freezing night and the train lurched, engine chuffing, steel wheels slipping on icy rails.

-Come on! Higgs yelled, and exited through the compartment doors.

I gathered up my effects, threw them into my bag, grabbed my guitar and followed him. We jumped out of the nearest door and onto a silent blanket of virgin snow almost four inches deep. The train pulled away into the soundless night. Looking down at my feet at the undisturbed snowfall I knew, right then, we had made a terrible mistake.

Higgs had already made his way halfway down the platform, when turning back to face me, a pained expression broke on his brow, he did a suitcase-reeling rotation, clocking at precisely the same moment as I did the complete and utter desertion of the locale. An absolutely empty liminal space, as blank as an abandoned theatre. Nothing. Not a thing.

-Oh dear

I looked up in time to catch the distant lights of our warm Oslo-bound train evaporating into the vanishing point of the night.

XVI

I know, you can see this scene. (As you are reading it, wherever you are, some years later, this page connects us telepathically across time and space)

You can see the pool of light from the solitary lamp which extended a few metres over the platform before all dropped away to total darkness.

-So, when's the next train due? My voice sounded small and anechoic.

-Well. That is possibly an issue.

-Go on

-Well you see, this is the express line we're on. The express line is reserved for the express train.

-Right. So, how often does the express train run from Gothenburg to Oslo?

-Every 24 hours.

-Every 24 hours?

-Once every 24 hours.

A heavy silence settled on us. The temperature must have been around minus thirteen.

-Come on, there must be something around here. Higgs trudged off up the platform.

-Where exactly did you think we were?

- I thought this was FJELLSTRAND! Higgs yelled, several metres ahead in the dark. I caught up to where he had stopped. He was standing next to a large sign with the name of the station written on it in large white letters FAGERSTRAND.

-It's an easy mistake to make, I said. But Higgs, this really is quite far from ideal.

-It's quite far from Oslo too.

-How far, would you say?

-About 37 miles, over those mountains, and across that bay in the distance.

- Oh right...Just over those mountains and across that little bit of fucking sea.

He set off again down the platform before either of us could allow the grave implications to settle in. I followed his footsteps, straining to make out his form as we moved away from the solitary lamplight. I looked up and, just to help matters, started hallucinating. Higgs was there one moment and gone the next.

-Oh Jesus fucking Christ.

There was absolutely no ambient light at all now, just the background radiation of ancient star light reflecting off the freshly-laundered, brilliant-white ice.

Tentatively I took a step forward.

-Higgs?

No reply came, but then a smiling face and the top half of a torso loomed over me, hovering perfectly there in the fine gauze of the freezing air. I staggered back, almost falling, but in that instant the illusion began to unravel. There was, you see, a long, thin three-sided bus shelter-type structure, so densely surrounded by compacted snow as to render it perfectly camouflaged against the horizon. A platform shelter.

Striding out of the shelter, arms aloft, he said irritatingly:

-It's not much, but it's something.

I pushed past him to look into the interior of the icy mirage. There was a single thin bench. I doubted its designers had speculated that it might one day be utilised for an unscheduled and probably fatal overnight stay. Despite the absence of an ensuite, massage table or walk-in wet room, it might, I thought, just about save our lives. If need be we could seal the entrance and construct an igloo-like interior, and just about stave off death from exposure. I flashed back to the image of Pinky rifling through my tarot deck.

I scraped a layer of blizzard from the bench and sat down. Higgs joined me. From within the sepulchral gloom of the cavelike construction I could just about make out the distant shimmering lights of Oslo. It felt as if we may as well have been on the moon.

-We should stay here for a moment and collect our thoughts, Higgs said

-We may perhaps just stay here forever. It's probably for the best if we make our last will and testament and come to peace with the wretched world we have inflicted ourselves upon. By the way, where did you disappear to last night? Might as well tell me the truth now.

Higgs shot me that particular look he reserves for very special moments to alert me to the fact that he was on the verge of losing his temper. I thought I would let it drop. A purgatorial silence settled upon us.

-I'm so glad you insisted we get off the train here.

Higgs kicked a snow drift.

I stood up and walked out of the igloo. I gazed up, and there was the red orb of Mars. It was the clearest and most menacingly vermillion that I had ever seen it.

-Behold, mighty Mars. The god of war bears down upon us, Higgs. We must have angered him and brought this malevolence down upon ourselves.

I was beginning to feel really cold. The true cold of an uncaring universe. I turned back to look at Higgs, who had not responded to me for some time. Perhaps he was already dead. I sat down next to him on the bench, nudging into him. He adjusted his posture with a grunt. The lights of Oslo had if anything become more distantly tantalising since I last looked.

-I was just reading a fascinating article in a science magazine I found on the train.

-Oh really? Higgs muttered

 -It was about the new science of quantum processing.

-Right

-It appears that in a couple of years they will have switched on the first one of these quantum computers in either California or Beijing, or possibly even Swindon, depending on who wins the tech race first. Now, the thing is, the moment they switch one of these things on, it will be able to process more bits of information than there are actual particles in the observable universe.

Higgs turned to look at me, his breath hanging in the air in rhythmical exhalations. I tried to ignore the fine sheen of frost that was coalescing on the sweat from his brow.

-Now what that means is, instantly this machine would be able to generate an artificial reality as complex as the one we are currently in, and immediately generate consciousness as complex as our own to populate it. As in, self-aware, thinking, feeling, experiential entities just like us. A perfect simulation totally indistinguishable from reality as we currently know it.

Higgs extracted a Gauloises from his pocket and lit it, his hands trembling.

-The thing is, the moment the first one of these quantum simulations comes online, the chances of there not already being many more of these simulations already running within it, reduces to a tiny fractional number. Something to do with the quantum probability model. Once one exists, well, an infinite number of them exist within it. Like mirrors pointing at each other.

-Mirrors within mirrors, creating an infinite wilderness of mirrors?

He gazed at the glowing red tip of the cigarette, which was as red and fuming as mighty Mars shining down upon us.

-It would essentially be like living within a multi-layered video game. Within each simulation, there would be one sole character, a godlike character who had set that simulation in process, and in each layer of the game above, there would be another god of that simulation, who in turn is curating the events in the simulation below.

Higgs inhaled on the cigarette.

-Sort of like the many gods in Hinduism, or the Kabbalistic tree of life. Each simulation contains a caretaker or author of his or her own level.

-Leonard.

-So it occurred to me earlier on the train that in that scenario the only thing it would be necessary to do is *not to be boring*.

- What do you mean?

-Well, as in any story, film or book it's always the boring characters that get killed off first. The more interesting you were behaving, the more outlandish, weird, eccentric, challenging, engaging you acted in your simulation, the less likely the god curator would be to kill you off. Because you would be providing experimentally valuable data. Or more simply you would be quite entertaining to them, or at least amusing, thus more worthwhile, and more valuable to keep around.So whatever you do, just don't be boring. That almost guarantees survival.

With this Higgs stood up and ran out of the igloo shaking his fists and screaming wildly at the sky.

XVII

I was quite touched at how quickly and literally he had taken my pseudoscientific hypothesis to heart. He was already a long way down the platform still raving and howling, emitting great plumes of vaporous exhalation into the night air. I cautiously followed after him, keeping a wary distance just in case his mind had snapped. Then I realised he wasn't waving at the sky but at something directly across the gaping expanse of the train tracks, at something moving on the far platform. I gazed into the monochromatic void. Was it possible Higgs was experiencing some kind of desert mirage delusion? I had heard of people losing their wits in extreme scenarios, but we had only been off the train for about twenty minutes. No...I too could see something moving. It was a very large grey lumbering thing, swinging a strangely familiar oblong-shaped object under one of its arms.

Whatever it was, it was moving lugubriously along the far platform, away from the trainline, towards the steep bank of rocks to the right hand side. It stopped and turned, and for the first time I was aware of its consciousness recognising our gaze. It lifted the oblong shape it held to its side aloft in an unmistakable threat; it was bearing arms at us. I realised it was a Yeti. It raised its other burly arm and waved...Oh god, it waved, it waved. It waved an unexpectedly cheerful wave.

It strode directly to the edge of the platform, paused, sizing up the jump, and then leapt down onto the tracks below, vanishing into the void of darkness. A bony white hand planted itself in front of us on our edge of the platform, a clawlike extension emerging from the thick grey seal-like skin. It was followed by the swinging oblong object - a skateboard.

It raised itself from the train tracks, heaving exactly like a seal, but then I realised this was a human, clad head to foot in a traditional Scandinavian fisherman's seal-skin coat and huge waders. He pulled himself and his capacious oily trousers up onto the platform and the hood down revealing the close-cropped blonde hair and rugged angular features of a Norwegian man in his early thirties. He extended a large hand to Higgs.

-My name is Krupp!

-Krupp?

-Krupp. I am Krupp. He slapped himself on the chest.

- Well, it's very nice to meet you, Krupp. I clasped his hand.

-What are you two doing here?

- Well Krupp, this is Higgs and I'm Leonard. We are lost. We are very lost.

-But there is nothing here? Why are you here?

-We made a miscalculation, quite a serious one.

-Well you are not lost anymore, you are with Krupp.

-I see you are a skateboarder Krupp?

-This is what I do, this is why I am on my way to Oslo. I have an important competition.

- So you were on the train? Higgs enquired.
-Yes. Krupp nodded.
-So why did you get off here then? asked Higgs, offering him the Gauloises.

Krupp smiled and took one and leaned in as Higgs lit the end of it for him, the flame animating his corticated features.
-It is a trick. You see, the express train is very expensive. 300 krona at least. I do not have that kind of money, but I do have the great wealth of my wits. I know that they only check the tickets when you arrive at Oslo Station – or if they come through the train during the journey, and then I just hide in the toilets.
-I see.
- I get off here, two stops before Oslo, where there is nothing and there are no ticket inspectors or barriers, and I take my boat from the little bay just below here for the last stretch of the journey into the harbour over there.

He smiled triumphantly, and gestured to the distant twinkling lights.
-Your boat? I asked.
-Yes, I have a small fishing boat. Perhaps you say a skiff. It was my uncle's, as were these sealskins. He left them to me, but I do not fish. I am a pacifist...and I skateboard.

He took a long drag on the cigarette, and beamed a broad and alarming smile at Higgs.

-Mr Krupp, is there any chance we could hitch a ride on your boat with you to Oslo?

-Of course, of course, you cannot stay here. You will die! he laughed. There are no houses or anything for miles of here, it is an old depot, not a good place to be. You will die a horrible, horrible death. You'd best come with me.

He started off in the direction of a cliff edge. There was a single stark and blasted tree clinging to the crested ridge. He paused, turning back and rifled deep inside his sealskin pocket. Higgs and I froze. I expected him to produce a serrated hunting knife. I held my breath, waiting to be gutted alive. But my concern was ill-founded, as he grunted and proffered a large tin of lager.

-Can I offer you an Elephant beer, my friends?

I glanced at the black and silver tin adorned with the crude image of a demonic-looking red elephant rearing up on its hind legs, its silver tusks glinting in the starlight. It said ELEPHANT and below that, in large red letters, EXTRA STRONG LAGER. I shrugged and took it from him. I cracked the ring pull as we continued on towards the cliff edge.

XVIII

We stumbled, slid, and came to a precarious stop as the incline levelled out, dropping precipitously away to a pebbled beach. The whisper-lapping sea shimmered silver under the moonlight. A gentle flurry of snow had started falling, a biting wind gusted around us.

-Well done gentlemen, that is a tricky descent, the boat is just along here, mind your step, these stones are very slippery...I took a long draught of the iron and ethanol-tasting Elephant beer and steeled myself for the voyage ahead. In a few paces Krupp had stopped and was pulling on a heavy black tarpaulin revealing a boat that was much smaller than I had been expecting. I shot a sideways glance to Higgs. It was no bigger than the sort of thing I had taken out on the Hyde Park boating lake. It constituted two narrow planks in the centre to sit on and a small perch next to an outboard motor.

I looked out at the thirty miles of freezing water between us and Oslo.

-Climb aboard, gentlemen. I will deliver you safely to Oslo.

Krupp unwound the rope anchoring us to the shoreline and stepped into the stern. We tipped backwards, but he deftly re-adjusted to compensate and sat down neatly next to the knackered-looking outboard motor.

-Please hold on very firmly, gentlemen. It will be a choppy crossing tonight

With this caveat he drew the starter cord and the engine roared to life in a single stroke. He let out the clutch and we were propelled out into the bay, the small boat bobbing like a cork across the black and white rimy waters.

As we rounded the outlet of the bay I turned from the headwind to face Krupp.

He had cracked another can of Elephant beer and he had one hand on the rudder. He looked utterly relaxed and at peace; a wide beatific smile was spread across his face.

-Krupp?

-Yes, my friend?

-Is The Scream still in Oslo?

-The Scream?

-The painting by Munch.

- Oh yes...*Skirik*. He nodded vigorously. I will tell you where it is when we arrive, my friend.

I turned my gaze back to the harbour lights as the tiny boat cut its uncertain course and all was dark. As dark as one that wastes by a sorcerous art and knows not whence he withers.

XIX

I am currently in hiding. I fled the Hollywood Hills at high speed. Only one person knows I'm here and I trust her implicitly. In fact I will be entrusting this manuscript to her when I leave. I have one, maybe two more hideouts up my sleeve before this whole thing is finished.

Who am I running from? Well the truth is, you already know. In time all things will become clear, perhaps clearer than you want them to be. Events accelerate quickly when I get to Oslo. Things gather their own wild momentum, like some unseen hand flailing out of control, or a mad automaton working of its own accord.

From where I am sitting on the porch there is a wooden support beam that holds up the sloping roof above my head. There are two Polaroid photographs tacked one above the other to that post directly at my seated eye level. The one I want to tell you about is the topmost one. There are several reasons why this image is of great interest.

Firstly, I have just received it. It was stashed in the mailbox at the end of the drive yesterday afternoon, with no mailing address nor stamp on the envelope. The second reason it is of great interest is that it is a photo of Pinky Capote. She is standing in the pagoda in the back garden of her bungalow in the Hollywood Hills. There's the tell-tale glimpse of her personal effects on the low cocktail table to the left of the image. A bottle of Stolichnaya vodka, a pack of Marlboro and what appears to be a thumbed copy of a red-covered paperback book that I can't quite make out. She is wearing one of her beloved green Dior dresses and it is split at the thigh to reveal her posed, Junoesque leg. This photo in itself is not that remarkable. What is remarkable is what she is holding in her hands, clutched to her breast, by the plunge of the dress. In the photograph she is herself holding another large format Polaroid photograph. It is a photograph of me, sitting where I am now. It seems to have been taken last night, as I am wearing the same clothes, and staring intently into the typewriter balanced on my knees.

This photograph is deeply unsettling. If you lean in close, and peer into the photo tacked to my post, look into the photo that's a photo itself, you will see in the background a silhouette in the doorway directly to my left – the doorway is just there, empty and bare, as I write these words now– do you see, in the photo, it's the silhouette of a woman, possibly a girl, she's in a pose of insouciance and her head is poised perfectly to one side, there's a lightness to her posture, but no real form meets the eye, the presence of a woman, or is it a girl, she wasn't there last night as I wrote these words into this world, the presence of something, I am all alone, here, can't you see, *what is it exactly that you are accusing me of?* It's the photographic evidence, the echo you say, *but there's nobody here and I never saw her I swear,* but there's the presence of something, it must be a shadow of something else, the presence of the girl or a woman I love, or is it the terrifying presence of me haunting myself, which does beg the question – is it he or she or I or her, which one of us is really this sensuous ghost? Oh my darling, my darling, it really depends, it really and truly depends, on which fiction that you love the most.

XX

Oslo at dawn. The nudge of the boat against the harbour wall, the look of surprise on the faces that spied us as our tiny vessel chugged into port. Krupp threw a line onto land and smiled at me.

-We didn't sink!

We hauled ourselves onto *terra firma*. I had the inclination to prostrate myself, bowing in thanks to mighty Poseidon. The small group of intrigued onlookers dissipated.

-Krupp, can you point me in the direction of The Scream?

He laughed heartily and slapped my back.

-Your appetite for angst has not been satiated by our crossing. Good man, good man, my uncle would be proud.

He launched into lengthy and complex directions towards Munch Museum, where I would find one of the great prides of Norway, a true treasure of the universe.

Higgs said he was going to find a hotel for us, and then head to the venue in preparation for this evening's show. I said my goodbyes to Krupp, assuring that I would see him again, and wandered off up the narrow path that wound its way to the harbour front. I never did see Krupp again, apart from of course when I meet him in my mind, in the eternal realm that opens up just before sleep, now carved into these pages. Long may he sail.

XXIII

There was no one on the desk as I walked through the heavy double doors of the Edvard Munch museum. It was strip-lit, clinical and not at all the appropriate environment for his life's work to be displayed. The one way into the gallery was through the gift shop. I had the immediate feeling that that saintly Norwegian painter would have loathed the place.

The first room was vast, about the size of a school gymnasium, with a dozen people milling around despite the early hour. There were four paintings on each of the four walls. It took me a moment to adjust to the low lighting pooled about the paintings.

I gazed at the painting closest to me. A maudlin woman holding her baby in bed; to her side her mother, presumably, comforting them both. It is entitled *The Sick Child*. Simple, linear, and absurdly affecting. I stood there, letting the image seep from my retina into my bloodstream. I thought of the extraordinary efforts applied to this canvas. I thought of the individual lives and events that he had witnessed and presented. It held my attention completely. I was for a brief moment suspended from all quotidian concerns: from my incommunicado fiancée, from the terrifying visions and vaguely troubling events of the tour so far. Free of the mind games and wheels within wheels whirring around Tiberius and Pinky. The oil painted image conquered all and held me enthralled, silenced and thoroughly intoxicated on this wet Wednesday morning.

-Mr Leonard! boomed a sonorous voice approximately one foot from my right ear. The room swam around the sound, rippling as if it was but a film or etheric veil through which the vibration moved. I whirled around and there, directly beside me, was Tiberius. He was wearing his large-brimmed black fedora, panda coat and a large pair of red patent leather riding boots. He smiled at me and threw both his furry arms up, smothering me in a bearish hug.

-So good to see you here, you know...*I thought I might*.

He said this, rattling my slight frame, which he clasped in both his outstretched hands, rhythmically shaking me to accentuate the stress on the words 'good to see you'. His brilliant blue eyes flashing warmly, possibly too warmly, directly into mine.

-Tiberius, how unexpected. Why did you think you would see me here?

-I don't know, just something about you made me think, yes, I bet you'll wander over to the Munch Museum before tonight's show. I thought about it in my scalding hot shower this morning, yes yes – and here you are – did you get here alright?'

- Let's just say we got here.

-And now we are both here! Psychically aligned and vibrationally united before *The Sick Child* - how timely, how becoming, how utterly perfect for our souls to be in this precise space time location together.

-Yes.

A not entirely comfortable silence settled. We were staring at the moody Munch before us. I shifted my weight from side to side, consciously weighing up the protocols of politeness in this situation. I was wondering if I should now spend the rest of my visit to the museum accompanying Tiberius. There was some great unspoken issue, something sitting between us, some sort of matter, a dark matter, I suspected. I still had no idea what I was really doing on this tour. Before I could consider my next move Tiberius turned sharply to face me and said:

-The tour is going well eh? Enjoying it?

-Very much. I enjoyed your show a great deal the other evening in Berlin.

Tiberius's eyes flickered for a moment, scanning left to right and then back to my eyes. He leaned in closer still, a smile cracked his face, glacial white against the black of his beard. He turned his gaze back to the painting, and then as he started to stroll leisurely towards the next gallery room he continued:

-Touring is in itself an anthropological and social marvel. The lengths people will go to encounter live music. It demonstrates how fundamental, how essential music is to the human experience, don't you think Mr Leonard?

I nodded politely.

-Music is the earliest of human technology, predating written language. It probably predates spoken language, which opens an extraordinary can of psycholinguistic worms. Did you know they've found flutes in the Giza de Costello caves in Spain that are 40thousand years old. The oldest records of written language date to 3300 BC, some 40 thousand years later. For thousands and thousands of years, before anyone even had a written alphabet, our species was playing music, singing and playing songs. We were just rocking out across the planet. All tribes, creeds and colours.

I stared at him blankly.

-Music was the first language our species was capable of using because it was able to exhibit complexity, nuance, and universality. This universality is something which remains very prescient to my own work, you see.

He paused, eyeing me sideways

-And I am sure in your own work, too Mr Leonard! The argument that still rages as to why major tones tend to elicit similar emotions to all peoples across the planet, usually more positive emotions. Whereas minor tones seem to conjure sadness and the blues? This is very real magic, wouldn't you say?

He took a breath and then paused again.

By now we had wandered through several of the smaller gallery rooms. I had been glancing at the canvases as he spoke, but the bubbling loquacity of his speech had somewhat beguiled me. He paused before another painting.

-This is quite aptly titled.

Stark reds, gaudy yellows, savage blacks and dreary blues combined with the maudlin aspect of the faces gazing back at us, entirely in keeping with the sentiment of its title: Anxiety. It was to my mind clearly a prototype or run-up to Munch's most famous work. The painting that had attracted me to this museum this morning. I suddenly felt like I could...

Tiberius's eyes scanned the surface of the painting in a metered rhythm, as if he was trying to pick out a particular face from that crowd. He continued speaking to me in a low purr.

-So even now, at the height of the Anthropocene, music remains the primary universal language in existence. It is so ubiquitous, truly everywhere.

He paused for a second as if weighing up which direction to turn, before selecting one to the right that led to a further corridor. I felt a rising in my blood, I was going to demand an explanation:

How were you and Pinky singing that song the other night? The song that I sang only once two years ago. A song that didn't exist, that doesn't exist, the song I made up in the middle of a

*moor in a howling gale, a song that the only recording of was
on a tape machine stolen in nefarious circumstances.*

But I didn't say anything. Instead I stared at a canvas that
we were walking past. *The Dance Of Life.*

- I can absolutely guarantee, Mr Leonard, that in the last
two hours you will have heard a song. And I can guarantee
that you will hear at least one more song in the next two
hours. Maybe a song that you sing to yourself, maybe
something you heard from a passing car radio, or some
piped muzak you hear when you go to the toilet, or step
into a lift. Music surrounds us, always. It is inescapable.

With this he turned to me, smiling, and ceremoniously
held up his arms.

-Here we are, the main event. The great statement.

He gestured to the painting directly before us. Softly lit,
and emanating a potent energy of unease. I exhaled audibly,
which I suspected played as a tad melodramatic. I had of
course seen it countless times in reproduction, I think it had
first registered with me as something I should know about
when I was around thirteen and stumbled across it while
leafing through an encyclopaedia of 20th century art, on a
long car ride to some destination that had nothing to do
with me, but everything to do with my mother. Since then
I have seen it at least four or five times a year. One of those
images that has become universal, ubiquitous. Tiberius
took a step towards the canvas.

-*The Scream* is the Mona Lisa of our time. If da Vinci
evoked the renaissance ideals of serenity and self-control,
well, Edvard Munch defined how we see our current age,
wracked with insecurity, anxiety and uncertainty.

-Ok...thanks...I *definitely* never thought about it like
that before.

He paused either not detecting or pointedly ignoring my
dripping sarcasm. He then leaned closer to the picture, and
appeared to be examining a particular stroke of brushwork.
-Almost his complete autobiography in one image, you
see?
I cleared my throat.
-He was clearly feeling something in his surroundings
that he sought to express so viscerally. The rising up of
dread, the terror, the overwhelming this-ness of everyday
experience.
I said this nonchalantly, trying to make it sound world-
weary and slightly dismissive. I took a step towards him.
-I certainly have felt these moments in my own music,
or have had the briefest sensation   of something similar
within me.
I spoke these words slowly and deliberately. I was thinking
of the dark melody I had sung that night in that stone room
on the moor. The same song he too had somehow sung in a
dressing room in Berlin two nights ago. Surely he knew that
I knew that he knew what all this was really about.
He didn't reply. He stepped to the right and examined
the distorted screaming face of the painting.
-Yes...Yes I hear you old boy. I hear you loud and clear.
He was nodding slowly. I wasn't sure who he was talking
to.
-You read the tarot, don't you? Pinky told me you
offered her a reading the other night?

He made lingering eye contact with me.

-You offered her a reading after her own indiscretion of rifling through your personal tarot deck.

A smile skirted across his fleshy red lips.

-So you are a reader of signs and symbols? A student of the ancient laws, Mr. Leonard? I assume you too have undoubtedly heard the silent scream that reverberates through nature from time to time?

He turned back to the painting. There was no one else in the room with us, not even a security guard. Just he and I, and the screaming face on the canvas. My two-day-old shirt clung to the small of my back.

-This painting is based on Munch's actual experience of a piercing scream that he heard while he was out walking near Oslo harbour one day. Those two fellows you can see in the background are his friends. They had walked ahead and left him. He was momentarily alone amidst a group... and that's when it struck him, the great existential scream.

-I can relate.

-Oh?

- Isn't that the point? We can all relate to it, hence its fame??

Tiberius appeared to ignore me. He pulled a smallish object from his pocket and glanced at it intently. He hastily replaced it after a moment's consultation and turned back to the painting. His proximity to the wailing black orifice was but a whisker now.

-His mind must have been in a most abnormal state when he heard that sound.

He let out a queer whistling tone from between his parted lips. For a moment I thought he might lean forward and actually kiss the open screaming mouth. He continued, his voice now hoarse and guttural.

-Edvard choses to render it in such a style—.

He gestured at the curved brushstrokes, millimetres from his fingertips.

-—as could, if pushed to extremes, destroy all human integrity. These flowing curves represent a subjective modern linear vision imposed upon Mother Nature herself. In doing so, in blending the curves he thereby finds a way of making the multiplicity of particulars unified into a totality of organic suggestion. It is, in short, *ripe with feminine overtones*.

He let out another discordant whistle. He was still but a breath away from the canvas. He continued, the bristles of his beard so close to brushing the painting itself as he spoke.

-Yet in fixing his own masculine, albeit deformed image in the centre foreground of the painting, he is reminding us that man is part of nature and his complete absorption in such a totality of existence liquidates the idea of the individual. Previous to this, as in the other lesser paintings, he had just dabbled with the idea of the line.

At this moment the Scandinavian sun seared through the overcast grey clouds, and the room was suddenly irradiated with yellow light. The tall reinforced window to my right casting a long crucifying shadow of Tiberius' onto the oak floor. I stepped into the shadow, drawing closer to the painting, and closer to Tiberius. He took this, I felt, as a sign of interest in what he was saying. As if I were leaning conspiratorially closer. In truth, I was very keen to get away from him and the painting.

-But, Leonard. Man is always a part of Nature. Schopenhauer taught us very well that no man can escape his own personal storm.

He turned to me, grinning toothily.

Storm.

-He has immersed his subject, and himself in a maelstrom of expressive lines. A total absorption into the implied emotional resonances of the scene, an attempt to totally liquidate the individual. He is reaching out to the viewer, he is desperately attempting to depict his own morbid experience, he has *let go of everything...*

Tiberius indulged himself in an archly dramatic moment. He threw his hands out wide in a prayer-like gesture and prostrated himself in devotion before the canvas. It was a little too much. He continued in a booming voice:

-He has allowed himself to become distorted by the flow of nature. The scream that he is hearing, that he is experiencing, that he is expressing, could well be interpreted as the agony of obliteration of human personality by this overriding and unstoppable unifying force of nature!

He was now standing so close to the painting I was amazed an alarm had not sounded.

-Despite it being a portrait of Munch the man, the creator of this painting who underwent the experience depicted, the portrait bears no true resemblance to himself or to anyone else he knew. The creature in the foreground has been depersonalised, ground down and crushed into sexlessness!

He rubbed his index fingers and thumbs slowly together, forming circular, Hinduistic gestures in the air before the canvas.

-He has stamped a trace of the underlying femininity into the monstrous form gazing back at us from the centre of the canvas. A femininity that is close to absorbing, or assimilating the entire goddamn scene, the entire fucking world Mr. Leonard!

I cleared my throat nervously. I had a horrible premonition that he was about to desecrate one of the greatest paintings in the history of the world in front of me.

-As far as we know, he never painted like this again.

He took a step to directly face me, close enough for me to feel his spiced breath on my face. His face had devolved into a grotesquely carved mask. His heavy gaze settled on mine. I had the suspicion that this showman knew exactly what he was doing. He spoke in a perfect stage whisper.

-You know, Leonard, at the top of *another version* of this painting – one that was indeed stolen from this museum several years ago – well, above that version Edvard Munch had written, in his own hand, 'Can only have been painted by a madman'.

I started to edge backwards and he placed both hands heavily on my shoulders,

-You see, with your own eyes, no? That within this picture, the picture you made a significant effort to come and see this morning, that the artist has set up a special defence. A defence in the form of the plunging perspective of the red road and the yellow fence that preserves the rational world of three dimensions. The fence is holding at bay the nightmarish swell of expressive psychological curves surrounding the harbour scene. Safe in this rational world, the two men in the distance remain, unequivocally masculine. Strong, fine men. But...

Here his left hand shot out, his fingers halted, millimetres from the uninsurable value of its surface.

-Here in the foreground, grasping *unified nature* is so very close to crossing the fence and devouring him. It is close enough to distort the very form and personality of the painter himself. It is that fence, just that humble wooden fence that protects him from total absorption into the subjective madness he is confronted by.

XXIV

Seven hours later and the footlights dimmed. I was stage left of the darkened auditorium in Oslo. There was an expectant hush emanating from the congregated audience.

I walked the twelve steps to the microphone in pin drop silence. The spotlight above ebbed and aureolised to life, isolating me in a blinding pool of tungsten light. I leant down to plug in my acoustic guitar and a smatter of restrained applause rippled across the audience. The first few seconds of the first song were the tightrope of taste which I nightly traversed. Always hoping to win the trust and precious attention of the audience. I didn't introduce myself, preferring to simply step forward and strike the first chord of my first song. The minor suspended cadence echoed over the auditorium and allowed my mind to slip effortlessly into the twilight demi-monde of that lovelorn ballad. A world within became a world without, carried on a song.

By the time I had sung my way to the first chorus I could feel the audience becoming ensnared in a shared realm of imagination. Just as this reverie of words and melody was becoming intoxicating, I became suddenly aware of something amiss with my guitar. It felt weirdly bottom-heavy and I noticed the strap was slipping on my left shoulder. I was concentrating so hard on the peculiarities of my guitar I was losing the thread of my song. I felt the melody falter for a second. I was also becoming aware of an unusual vibration; a dreadful rattle was emanating from the lower body of the instrument itself. As I reached the final line of the chorus my mind was racing through all the possible causes for this, and a thought struck me: Pinky's abduction of the guitar two nights ago.

I struggled on with the show and during my penultimate song the stage lighting gradually changed, and I saw for the first time that the crowd before me were all dressed in identical long black cloaks and all of them were female. 800 cloaked women. Not a single man in sight. These cloaked ladies were all totally silent, their attention wrapt on my singing. Three disorientating minutes later I bowed to oddly synchronised clapping and then hurried off the stage.

-What the fuck is going on here, Higgs? I said, striding into the dimly lit dressing room.

-What? He started up from a doze he was having on the couch.

-Well, firstly, there's something in this guitar – it's heavy and it's rattling. Secondly, why is the entire audience women, all wearing weird cloaks?

-Really? All women? That's interesting. Higgs smiled and a wistful dreamy look passed over his eyes

-It is interesting. Do you think the cloaks are some kind of fan thing?

-I'll have a word with the promoter. Can't really complain though, can you Leonard? All those ladies breathlessly hanging off your every word?

He laughed and turned to pour a little whisky into a tumbler. Turning back and handing me the glass, he toasted.

-Here's to the cloaked and mysterious ladies of Norway.

I clinked glasses but immediately set mine down on the dressing table. I placed my guitar on the floor and knelt down over it peering into the sound hole to see if I could see what was in there. It was too gloomy within the body of the guitar for me to see anything at all. I was going to have to gain access to the internals of the instrument. I rolled up my sleeves like a field surgeon and I started to unwind the strings, discarding them on the floor next to me. In a few moments the sound hole was exposed, the guitar looking oddly naked, unstrung, laying bare its gaping orifice.

I glanced up at Higgs on the couch watching me, a perturbed expression on his face. I plunged my hand into the bowels of the guitar. My hand clasped onto a round heavy dampish thing and I pulled it out. I held it up to the light. It was a clay sculpture of a cat's head, almost to scale and exquisitely detailed in design.

I stood up and moved to the glowing row of lamps in front of the mirror. There I could see that the cat sculpture was really quite accomplished. A chill ran up my spine as I noticed something in the detail of the face. It was my cat, Harold, who I had buried my first night in Yorkshire. I looked more closely and tried to dismiss this resemblance, but there was no refuting it, the likeness was uncanny. Higgs was standing by my side, looking intently at the thing.

-I don't like this at all, Higgs. I can only assume this is a bizarre prank by Pinky and Tiberius, to what end I don't know...but I don't like it. I've got a good mind to go and confront her about it right now, before she goes on stage, mess her fucking *vibe* up a bit.

-Hold on for a moment, Higgs replied, reaching for the clay cat head that seemed to now be cruelly smiling up at me. I blinked hard, trying to dismiss this trick of the light.

He turned the thing over in his hand, and peered closely at the back of its skull.

-What's this? he handed the thing back to me. There was some small script carved into the clay at the back of the cat's head.

Priests in black gowns are doing the rounds, binding with briars my joys and desires

LEONARD MEET WITH ME TOMORROW AT 11PM at THE KAVALIER BAR AT THE HOTEL IMPERIAL, VIENNA. COME TO ME ALONE.

Below this was a small star-shaped symbol that I didn't recognise.

-A message from Pinky Capote, I assume.

-Couldn't she have just sent you a text?

I ran my hands through my greasy hair. I couldn't take my eyes off the sculpture.

-I have a feeling there is another message encoded within this message. Obviously, she was trying to get my attention.

-The priests in gowns?

- William Blake. *The Divine Image*.

She certainly knows what she's doing. Did you tell her you were a Blake freak?

-Of course I didn't, we've barely spoken.

-A coincidence then?

-Maybe pure chance, or maybe a message within a message. There *are* about a thousand women in black cloaks in the auditorium right now...*doing the rounds.*

-Well you shall have your answers tomorrow evening in Vienna. Perhaps she is just sweet on you, Leonard? You've caught Pinky's eye and she's looking for a little romance on the road? This cat's head is just an extraordinarily niche kink?

- I forgot to ring my fiancée again. I rifled through the pockets looking for my battered phone. Finding it, I cursed that it was dead.

-Have you got a charger, Higgs? I have to get hold of her right now, this is quite serious. I haven't spoken to her for days and you know what she's like, she won't be reacting well to this.

Higgs raised an eyebrow and passed me his mobile phone from his pocket.

-Use mine, but be quick, we're booked on the midnight flight from Oslo Airport, which is at least an hour out of town. We're flying direct to Vienna tonight, otherwise we won't get there – and if we don't get there, we won't get paid, and if we don't paid, I don't know what will happen. God knows who routed this tour but I have never seen a more impractical travel itinerary in my life. We're essentially going back in the direction we just spent two days travelling from. It's utterly daft.

I was, however, not paying attention. I had started pacing around as I waited for the phone to connect. It rang in long unfamiliar rings, Norwegian telecoms I presumed – it rang three times, then clicked, and the line went dead. I looked at the screen and the No Signal symbol was showing.

-Fuck this, this is fucking ridiculous. It feels like something is actively preventing me speaking to her.

-Come on, try her again at the airport, our cab will be outside any moment. Don't get too worked up, she'll be fine.

I snatched up my travel bag and strode out to find the cab.

XXV

An hour later we were wincing in bitter wind, striding across the tarmac of Oslo airport. I was surprised to see a small bright silver propeller plane awaiting us, a set of rickety wheeled steps leading to the cabin door. Turning to Higgs, I gestured towards the plane, my sleeve billowing in the fierce cross-wind:

-Higgs, why are we flying to Vienna on a plane from 1932? What airline exactly did you book this with?

-There were no regular commercial flights available, so I spoke with Tiberius' tour manager and he recommended this private charter company. It's just us, a few businessmen and some of Tiberius' road crew on this flight. I thought you'd enjoy it. Just order several large drinks, smoke an inflight fag and fall asleep alright?

He gave me a thumbs up and we ascended the steps of the Boeing 307 Stratoliner. I couldn't help giving the engines a lingering once over as I climbed aboard.

The cabin stewardess who greeted us was platinum blonde, crisply uniformed and nordically striking. She directed us to our seats with a sensuous, inviting, borderline unprofessional smile. The plane only had two rows of seats and was far narrower than the cabin of modern airliners. It felt sort of like being sat in a very dilapidated, very dated and very dangerous bus that was just about to take off. I was sitting on the left, Higgs took his seat to the right, the waist-width gangway between us. There were in fact only 20 seats in the whole aircraft, and ours were exactly halfway down, adjacent to the wings, which also looked alarmingly small. There were only two other passengers, a pair of surly looking men who I didn't recognise from Tiberius' touring party. Both were heavyset and hunkered down, wedged into their seats directly in front of us.

I settled down into my seat, considering the thousands of souls who had nuzzled into the very same spot. I thought of them and their unknowable lives and backsides, and gazed at the small oval of the window next to me. It really did look very glassy, like the sort of glass you have in a terrace kitchen window. I shivered as I hunted around for a blanket. I noticed that it did not quite smell like any aircraft I'd ever been on, either. It had the distinct bouquet of a Soho nightclub. Clicking my antique, neckbreak-guaranteed seatbelt I found myself thinking about my life, how destabilised, fractious and contingent it had become. I thought of my now estranged fiancée, from whom I had essentially vanished overnight. That was certainly how it must have felt to her.

With an uneasy stirring, my mind found its way to Pinky Capote and her weird invitation awaiting me tomorrow evening. What did she want? I found myself thinking of what she might be trying to manipulate out of this situation, what she wanted from me, and how far I would be prepared to go – how far would I allow myself to be led? I thought of her in bed for a flickering pornographic moment, of undressing her from that astonishing vermillion gown, the honey-and-Chanel smell of her neck (somehow I knew this would be her scent), her expensive sluttish underwear, her legs unwinding, those green reptilian eyes, lidded, glowering and alluring. For some reason I suddenly started humming an Elvis song.

I don't wanna be a tiger
Cause tigers play too rough
I don't wanna be a lion
'Cause lions ain't the kind
You love enough

I just wanna be
Your teddy bear

Put a chain around my neck
And lead me anywhere
Oh let me be (oh let him be)
Your teddy bear

I was singing quite loudly and gazing out of the cabin window as the torrential rain sheeted onto the runway outside when I looked forward and was surprised to see both the burly men seated in front of me craning around in their seats, their shiny grey suits straining at the seams. They were staring intently at me, their faces blank and expressionless, and their eyes glassy as great whites. I promptly stopped singing.

I rifled in the bag by my feet for my William Blake, as they thankfully pivoted back around in their seats. I wanted to read *The Divine Image*.

Priests in black gowns are doing the rounds... I accidentally said this out loud as well, and instantly sensed the burly men's eyes on me again. Steroid pumped pricks.

Priests in black gowns are doing the rounds...

I was in a queue in a derelict train station, I was queuing for coffee alongside an older couple, a grey haired and wiry framed man in a dishevelled puce suit, the suit looked as worn as his complexion, his wife was perhaps in her late fifties with a shock of frizzy auburn hair and that particular, peculiar paper white thin skin. I had reached the front of the line and it was apparently my turn to be served; as I ordered a coffee the auburn haired woman turned and quite forcibly barged into me. I was taken off guard, I staggered into the counter, and then turned and naturally apologised to her, even though it was her own mistake. In response to this she tutted loudly, her gaudy lipstick-smeared lips smacking together disgustingly... she promptly hurled herself into me again, harder this time, hard enough to knock me into the display counter of cakes and pastries. I twisted round, trying to right myself, my hands squeaking loudly against the glass of the display as I did so. The barista was in this moment placing a large cup of takeaway coffee onto the counter, the auburn haired old woman stepped forward, seized the coffee cup from his hand and dashed it into his face. Now he staggers, screaming and scolded; I step forward to try to intervene, but she grabs my throat in a talonlike cold hand, I am momentarily paralyzed by surprise, a horrible second of recognition passes as I gaze into her reeling rheumy blue eyes, and then I started struggling to free myself of her grasp. I fall backwards and over the counter behind me, my legs take the entire display of cakes and confectionery with them as I fall, they shower down over me, croissants and buns bouncing off my head, but at least I am free of the clutches of that demonic old crone. I stagger to my feet, for the moment relatively safe behind the coffee counter, crouching behind the broken displays I witness the unfolding scene as people are now running to and fro around the coffee shop, the train station staff seem to have cottoned onto the weird crime scene unfolding. Alarmingly the old auburn haired witch has somehow leapt up onto the far end of the coffee counter, near a row of sinks, she is scattering dishes, crockery and coffee cups all over, she then steps into the sink and reaches forward with long leathery arms, with superhuman strength she seizes the bald headed barista and *lifts him up into the air with one hand, his legs thrashing animally, the dishwater in the sink is sloshing around her feet in a rising frothing maelstrom as she lifts him higher and higher, his bald head glinting obscenely with sweat as he tries with all his might to break free of her grip, from her clutch handbag swinging wildly at her side, with her free hand she draws a long glimmering dreadful Liston knife, the kind I have only seen in the Hunterian medical museum, designed for removing limbs as quickly and efficiently as possible from wounded soldiers in the Crimea, and here locked in the terrible instance my visual timeline seems to start to lag, stutter and freeze like a poorly buffered internet video, but despite this I still feel so present in the moment, as if my body is recording the horror unfolding, it's just ghastly and too well-lit from the strip lighting everywhere, rendered almost too real, a hyperreality from which I cannot look away. Slowly, dreadfully, the auburn witch applies the knife to the poor man's scalp and his bald head opens like a crimson egg. The collected onlookers scream and fall over each other to flee, and I too find myself running from the place.*

I am somehow teleported, half running, half tumbling down a derelict alleyway, replete with bulging dumpster bins and cardboard boxes strewn about, snatches of what appears to be a sprawling grey cityscape can be seen through the narrow aperture between two rows of buildings. The scene feels curiously unfinished, like it has been hastily cobbled together, as in an unfinished videogame. At the end of the alleyway I find myself at a crossroads, more grey buildings on all four sides, the windows and doors look as if painted like stage sets. Gazing around it appears that even the streetlights are glowing grey, onto the heavily overcast scene. This feels like London, but a demonic reimagining of it where all the colour and vitality has been washed out, leaving nothing but oppressive, dreary authoritarian inhumanity. Just like London, actually. I select the road to my left and find a labyrinthine stretch of closed shops sprawling before me, the light is now constantly shifting and changing, bringing out different textures. No people to be seen anywhere. This absence begins to worry me. I feel now uncertain of where to turn. I decide to retrace my steps back to the scene of the scalping.

I am expecting that the police will be there dealing with the witch when I arrive, however I found the coffee shop abandoned entirely. The space has been cleared and disturbingly rearranged, the counters and tables have been repositioned to resemble some sort of church. Stepping forward into this gloomy temple, a very real sense of disgust and dread begins to pervade my mind, the scalped head of the coffee man lolls against a makeshift crucifix constructed crudely from two menu placards. I look down at my feet and vomit catches in my throat; I force myself to turn my watery gaze back to the scene, and as I do so a young, entirely naked woman, a brunette, steps delicately out from behind the coffee counter altar, her body daubed in strange symbols painted with the slain man's blood. Something ritualistic about her dance movements. I turn on my heels and once again run from that place.

The concrete of the street concourse outside begins to disintegrate beneath my feet, becoming first clay-like and then thick moss and then grassy turf, my surroundings have morphed into dense meadows and thickets of woodland. I am totally disoriented but continue running, the light shifts again into a long frequency predusk brilliance which warmly settles on the space I am running through headlong, I am on a downward pastoral descent, rocks and sticks and stones, branches scratching my face, I am now pelting down a steep hill, I have that little boy feeling of running beyond my limits, I am leaning forward into gravity's pull, my feet feel light, I am stumbling madly out of control. I force my gaze away from the ground immediately before my feet and see that, at the bottom of the steep decline, rising rapidly before me is a tower, a perfectly proportioned medieval tower, grey and mighty stone redolent of all that is traditionally associated with the realm of fantasy and fairytale. My feet continue to carry me of their own accord towards it when another young woman dances out from a nearby pink and purple flowered clearing, she is wearing a nymph-like gown of translucent material, light and gauze-like, barely covering her tits and torso; its colour shifts from a deep verdant green to a hot vermillion as she scampers playfully towards me and seizes my hand, which from the earnest pleading look in her light grey eyes she expects me to take, which I do so willingly...I am now feeling utterly lost, bereft of all meaning or volition, and what is worse is that I know I am dreaming, I know I am... but somehow the depths of enchantment propel me forwards and deeper, and further downwards, in spite of her beauty, and in spite of her strong kind eyes.

XXVII

I awoke with a gasp, my legs kicking out and colliding with the chair in front of me. The William Blake paperback fell from my lap onto the cabin floor. Despite the chilly climate my brow is spritzed with sweat. I reel my eyes to the right and see Higgs is hunched over, scrutinising a map of Europe. I leant in a little closer and could make out a complex criss-cross pattern of geometric lines riddling the outline of a continent. I had a pang of recognition for the shape. I noticed that he was adding these lines himself with a black marker pen. He turned abruptly to me. The cabin light flickered in his irises. I wasn't sure if this was a question or a statement. He smiled at me thinly.

-You've been sound asleep since take off.

-How long have we been in the air?

-An hour, hour and a half. You alright?

-Yes, I just had another spectacularly weird dream. How much longer is this flight?

-I'd say two more hours at least

With this he bent forward and reached into his rucksack.

- I remembered to grab this for you,

He winked and passed me a two thirds-full bottle of whisky. Sometime later I awoke to a hard jolt reverberating through the aircraft. I opened my eyes and saw a brilliant white flashing thing whirling around the propeller blades outside of my window. It was gowned and magnificently bejewelled. Then a shower of red and white sparks erupted. The engine slowed, screeched and stuttered to a halt. There was a dreadful moment of yawning silence...but then, mercifully, the engine roared back to life. As the red and white sparks dissipated several of them fluttered by, sticking to the cabin window. In the half-light, some of those sparks were bloodied red, some were celestial white...and all, apparently, were not sparks at all...but long, lustrous, angelic feathers.

XXVIII

This must be Vienna.

I groaned to myself as the plane bounced its way down the runway and the empty bottle of whisky rattled around my feet. I wanted Versace sunglasses, three litres of sparkling water and no questions asked. I turned to Higgs, he had his jumper wrapped about his head like a shroud. The plane trundled towards the terminal and then something unexpected happened. Higgs stood up as the plane connected with the terminal point. The collision caused him to stagger forward at the exact same moment the two surly gentlemen in front of us also stood up sharply, and in precise motion, seized one end of the map that Higgs was still holding in his hands.

-We will be looking after this for you my friend, the taller man said in a thick Slavic accent.

I think Higgs considered resisting, but then with a shrug he relinquished the map. The smaller of the two gents (whom I now suspected to be KGB agents) tucked the map into his ill-fitting suit jacket, nodded curtly and stomped towards the exit.

Twenty minutes later we were in a cab, negotiating the inner city traffic, making our way to the hotel. Higgs sighed, leant over and handed his phone to me. On the screen there was a photograph of the map he had been poring over on the plane.

- I linked together all the points we have visited on this tour so far and it formed the same symbol that was embossed on the cat's head.

- It's an old symbol, really old. You may have seen one I had laying around the church.

-Is it witchcraft?

-No, not really, it's something else – far, far older, and possibly far worse.

***

Walking into my dressing room, I was confronted by Pinky. I had not been expecting to see her until the evening, and frankly I was not prepared. She seemed quite different, by day. Before I could say anything, she stepped forward and placed her hand directly on my chest.

-I absolutely *love* you in this sweater.

She ran her fingers down the tatty old jumper Higgs had leant me because I was complaining about the cold. I laughed, a little surprised.

-But I guess everyone compliments it.

Before I could reply, I saw Tiberius over her shoulder, deep in conversation with a very beautiful, dark haired and statuesque woman. Pinky seemed to notice me noticing.

She placed her hand firmly on my hip, and directed my attention towards a table strewn with bottles of booze. Positioning me precisely so that my back was to Tiberius, and allowing her a direct eyeline, she rapidly decanted two hefty slugs of Johnny Walker Black.

-So...I was gonna ask you something...Would you like to go see The Kiss painting with me? I know it's super touristy, but it's, like, just around the corner, and I've never seen it before.

-Well...Of course I will.

Instead of responding she gripped my collar-bone, and turned me so that I was facing her, sideways to Tiberius and the statuesque brunette. She tilted her head coquettishly, locked eyes with me, and began giggling in an unmistakably flirtatious manner.

***

On stepping onto the freezing Strasse, it soon became apparent she had absolutely no idea where we were going.

-Say, Leonard...you don't happen to know where this painting is, do you?

-The painting? I presume it's in the gallery.

I began to suspect that this was another of her arcane tests, but she seemed genuinely confused.

-Well...what's the name of the gallery?

I asked her, sensing an opportunity to prove myself capable of taking charge. I stopped a passing stranger and asked for directions.

-*Schloss Belvedere*, came the haughty and reluctant reply, accompanied by a vague gesture down the street.

***

25 minutes later we arrived out of breath, having taken the most inefficient and circuitous imaginable route to the gallery. We stood awkwardly in front of *The Kiss* for a minute, next to numerous other 'romantically' inclined tourists.

-Very nice, I said.

-Yeah...it is, like, stupidly cute.

It was impossible to ignore the palpable awkwardness between us. I could sense that she felt it too. She shifted her weight from foot to foot, and then suddenly emitted a yelp.

-Oh my God, Leonard, we're going to be late for the show!

***

For some reason, I couldn't bring myself to watch Tiberius' show that evening, surreptitiously exiting the stage door of the concert hall immediately after finishing my performance. Pulling up the collar of my greatcoat and glancing around furtively to ensure no one spotted me, I scurried down a side alley into the Viennese night.

Back at the hotel I showered, and changed into the last of my clean black shirts, and slipped into my antique Dior dinner jacket (a mysteriously generous gift from a promoter in Paris who claimed to be a close friend of the

Dior family. I haven't the faintest idea why he bestowed it upon me, but it is one of the few items of clothing I truly cherish. It always feels like I am stepping into a slither of some debonair duke's history). Gazing into the full length mirror, I considered a final cigarette, but remembering that expediency is sometimes the better part of valour, I turned and walked confidently into the biggest mistake of my life.

XXXI

The cocktail bar of the Hotel Imperial was empty and bathed in a low gloom. The only light emanated from discrete candles and the glittering emerald green Parthenon of booze at the far end of the room. A tear of sweat wriggled its way down my back as I clocked Pinky, sitting to my left at a circular table. It was as if my body saw her before my eyes did. The room itself seemed to be lounging around her.

I was more nervous than I'd predicted that I would be. Was I really expecting answers? Some kind of terrible psychic attack? Or the affirmation of my darkest suspicions? Perhaps, to be fair, I was just another horny monkey in the jungle thrilled to encounter a new potential mate with attractive behavioural traits and unusually vivacious markings? I must be tall and handsome and square-shouldered, a fatal male. Snippets of macho prose flashed portentously across my otherwise intensely feminine mind's eye. At the last moment of approach, I walked straight into the sofa. My left leg collided with enough force to give me a crippling dead leg.

-Good evening, Leonard. You didn't care to stay for our show?

-Good evening, Pinky. No, not tonight.

I couldn't tell if she had noticed my collision, or if she was otherwise engaged in generating an air of suffocating insouciance. Looking at her, my pulse quickened. Her dress, I could only assume, had been conjured by the spirit of Coco Chanel herself. Christ, I needed a drink.

Pinky's form is as slight as a swear word, but has all the coiled energy of an Old Testament commandment. She looked wonderful waiting for me at this table. Beautiful, yes, but with an unmistakable air of menace. Her eyeline bearing down severely onto the glinting face of her gold Givenchy watch.

I realised I was late.

She didn't stand. So I leant in like an ash tree bowing to a sudden wind. She smelt like ancient smouldering amber and relentless Marlboro Red cigarettes. The nape of her neck was warm as the flesh of an animal shaved for an operation. I lingered for a moment. Her face betrayed nothing of whether what she was experiencing was a sincere satisfaction or a studied sentiment. She snapped the celluloid moment shut by reaching for her cigarettes and a glinting white Zippo.

-What are we really doing here, Pinky?

She placed her lit cigarette into the cut glass ashtray.

-Or should I say – what am I doing here?

The bartender cleared his throat. It looked impeccably carved.

-Two vodka martinis, with a twist and an olive,

She flashed a smile I wasn't entirely sure I cared for.

I did however admire her arrogance, not even looking the waiter in the eye, nor enquiring as to what I wanted to drink. She had clearly made the decision for me before I sat down. Flashing her green eyes to the side in a cartoonish play of consideration, and conspiratorially leaning forward displaying her Rodinian carved décolletage, she said:

-Mozart, Brahms, Beethoven, Schubert, Mahler— and now me and you. We've all played Vienna, Mr. Leonard.

I winced at this absurdly pretentious opening gambit.

-A great city of art, ambition and intellectualism...not to mention a healthy dose of therapeutically developed sexual deviancy.

My cigarette smouldered, and a cobra of smoke danced in the thin membrane of air between us.

- Did they really all live here? I added, with a nauseating smile of my own.

She didn't reply. She simply let her fringe slip slightly across her left eye as she took a drag on her cigarette. Noticing her sensual intimations I glanced around, pretending to nod appreciatively at the tasteless excess of the décor that so clearly betrayed some horrific insecurity in the mind of its designers. The cocktails arrived. My suit now felt like it didn't fit me quite as well as I took my first sip of the martini.

I had the definite sensation of her eyes examining every exposed facet of my being, with the quality of a jeweller studying for some fatal flaw. I couldn't help feeling that she was assessing my worth.

-Don't you want your olive? She reached over and plucked the black, bobbing orb from my glass and popped it in her mouth. She reclined back into the furnished shadows. A content half smile danced around her mouth and she distractedly let the candle lights play over her irises as she chewed the oily fruit.

-I didn't entirely enjoy your invitation here. Where do you find time to sculpt cats' heads while you are on tour?

-I just wanted to get your attention.

I took another tooth-aching sip. The bite of the vodka. She had confessed to the cat. The game was afoot.

-It upset me. My cat died quite recently and it very much resembled him.

The martini felt exactly like being thrown through a plate glass window.

-How could I have known what your cat looked like?

-I don't assume you did, but it upset me nonetheless. The Blake quote is what really caught my attention.

She fingered her lighter, clicking its lid open and closed, a metronome struggling to catch a wayward time signature.

-Leonard, as you are a man who openly brags about living in a haunted church replete with a graveyard for a garden, I'm quite surprised that a cat's head could upset you so much. And anyway, don't all cats essentially look the same?

We both set down our cocktail glasses at precisely the same time. It broke the tension, we were both exposed, betrayed by our unconscious mechanical behaviour. The play had broken down; one of us had fluffed a line. I reached for a Gauloises to buy me time. She leant forward and lit the tip with her white Zippo.

I had lost all patience with her and her ridiculous, juvenile game...If it was indeed a game. I decided now was my moment to protest. I did this by standing, as if to leave.

-You really don't appreciate being challenged, do you? she snapped.

-You haven't given me much of a chance to challenge you.

I looked down at her, a little unsure. Her dress was without doubt a masterpiece, clinging to her delicate anatomy; small, pearllike and perfectly formed. She motioned to me to sit back down, which, after a brief and feeble protest, I did. Feigning resignation, I slammed my cigarette packet down on the marble table with an air I hoped would signal the finality of my grievous impatience.

-What is Tiberius up to? And how do you fit into all this? If something feels fucking weird, it usually is fucking weird.

-What are you talking about? We are on a rock and roll tour, you are the support act.

She let the word support linger, ever so slightly, ever so snidely.

-Ok – why am I here? Why am I playing these shows with you?

-Don't ask me. I didn't choose you.

She took a long sip. I suppose she thought she was a Countess.

-Tiberius likes you. He likes some of your songs.

-Pinky, you and I know there's more to this than just playing some songs. I've seen strange things. Things you also know I've seen. What were you doing in the dressing room the other night? That song you were singing - if you can call that singing - that's one of my songs. A song I've never recorded, I've never released. No one else alive has ever even heard it. I only sang it once...One night in the middle of nowhere in an abandoned slaughterhouse in Yorkshire.

-You sang it in a slaughterhouse? What are you talking about, Leonard? You are sounding alarming. She snorted horsishly into her martini.

-Where is Tiberius?

-He's visiting friends. He has family in Vienna.

-Friends or family?

-Both.

I paused. I had become angrier than I'd realised. I smoothed my hair back over my temples, which were now slick with freshly broken sweat. Pinky levelled her eyes onto me, making some silent judgement, appraising some unseen symbol I appeared to be flaunting in my rage. Her eyes were recording everything, every interplay of mind and matter. She placed her lighter back onto the marble tabletop with a theatrically timed click.

-There was a reason I invited you here tonight, yes, of course there was.

I didn't react. I just continued to meet her gaze, trying my hardest to repress any telltale expression on my face. Any atom of information she got a hold of, I knew she would split apart and unleash more destruction on my already shattered life.

-I wanted to get to know you...better. Since we are working so closely together now.

-What? A wayward note was rising in my voice.

-I thought it would be nice to talk some more. Somewhere alone, somewhere where we could come to understand each other on a different plane.

-Do you manufacture a cat's head effigy every time you suggest meeting someone for a drink?

She laughed, throwing her head back and letting the empty room feel the full force of her mirth. I felt my newly discovered disgust for her rise again, a dull pulse ebbing in the back of my neck.

-Now, about that church of yours – did you leave a *Little Miss Leonard* behind waiting for you?

She delivered this inquiry with the grace of a stiletto to my chest. I caught her eyes flicking down to the engagement ring glinting on my holy finger, wrapped around the stem of the cocktail glass. I admired the sickening vividity of their lizardlike verdigris. There was something else in them too.

-Is that what you invited me here to ask?

Another artillery ripple of laughter. I felt any fascination with her drain from me.

-Well, is there, Leonard? I am intrigued – does anyone really live in a church on their own?

-Yes and no.

She arched an eyebrow. Its delicate dark traced a curve against the rush of light and shade of her carefully unkempt blonde hair.

-I haven't spoken to her for days...Weeks now, actually. She was working away when I left, and then there was a blizzard, and then I was away on tour and I haven't been able to get hold of her. It's been...

-Difficult? she said firmly, finishing my sentence for me.

-Yes.

-I can only imagine it was hard for you both living in such a foreboding, frigid place, all alone. Just the two of you up on those rolling black and barren moors.

-How do you know it was on the moors?

-You told me yourself. You told me all about it, Leonard.

-When?

-One night recently, I think.

She rolled her eyes. My mind drifted.... Some aetheric current carried me from Vienna, back to the church, back to the coordinates of space and time through which I had inhabited those vaulting spaces with my fiancée; briefly, and perhaps not entirely happily. Pinky clicked her fingers. I glanced up, aware of my surroundings again.

-I am not sure I really wanted to move there, to be perfectly honest with you.

-Who could blame you, Leonard?

Her voice gently purred, and although she did not appear to have moved at all, I felt like she had edged imperceptibly closer to me.

-I think that our experience of reality is like a stylus moving over the grooves of a record. If we were to observe the minute undulations, peaks and troughs it would make little sense to us as music. It is only if we relax, let go and let the music play that we can have a sense of the whole piece, and truly experience the song. Otherwise it would all just appear as fragments of sound and vibration. It is the experience of the sequence of notes that generates the melody, and in turn it is the melody that creates the meaning, the emotion.

-Tell me something about you and Tiberius.

-What's the great mystery? I've known him for years, we sing, we write, we perform together. What more do you want to know?

-How did you meet him? I can't imagine he's the sort of person you just *bump into.*

She smiled.

-You'd be surprised. You really would. I met him in California; he was an associate of another musician who I am certain you are aware of. They were working on something together. I had left New York on my twentieth birthday to try and find a certain sound that I had been hearing in my head since I was a child. Arriving first in LA, the sweet sirens of Big Sur drew me up to the northern coast. I was playing at being a Kerouacian hippie for a summer. Somehow I fell in with some friendly beatniks, who looked after me, giving me rides and good times. I could barely play guitar and at that time I only had one song of my own, but it was one I had laboured at for hours, and it carried me further then perhaps it should have. People would smile when they heard it and offer me whisky, cigarettes, shelter and other things. The song was called *Aphrodite's Ass*.

One night we had lit a campfire on the beach just south of Monterey. That evening, as the gulls shuddered in the breaking surf, and the fire crackled with shimmering pine sparks, and the sand was hot, hotter than it was even during the day, I saw a lone man striding towards us. He had an ancient looking guitar in his hand. I could see it swinging in a pure silhouette against the wine-dark sea. No one seemed disturbed as his darkly bearded and heavy-cut presence joined our number. It was hard to make him out precisely in the flickering of our campfire, but I knew there was something about him, as if he contained a certain secret that, one suspected, he might impart if only we made him welcome...

Back in that grand Viennese bar, I became transfixed as she spoke. This was perhaps the most of her inner world she had ever shared. I sensed a potent truth ringing in her words, as if for a moment she had forgotten the childish game we were playing and was instead shaping the air around us into a world she had once known and loved with simply the sound of her voice and the colour of her words. I found her storytelling, in spite of myself, incredibly seductive. I attempted to find my own voice to express these sentiments, but with a vague and undulating snakelike movement of her body, she forbade any interruption, and continued her story.

-That night, as the fire began to die down and the merriment waned into concerns about whose van or place we were staying at tonight, this mysterious man leant forward towards the flames. I'm aware that this sounds melodramatic, Leonard, but, well – he swung his guitar over his shoulder and gently began to play such beautiful music...

At this moment I stifled a smirk. I absolutely loathe that particular sort of late-night mysterious wayfaring man on the beach with a guitar and wistful searching eyes...I felt compelled to tell her so...I found it hard to believe she would be taken in by such a character.

I looked up into her perfectly Apollonian face. She had, since I last glanced, surrendered her disaffected Elizabethan predeposition and had become much more like an earnest and wilful child. Her eyes rapt in the searing heat of a story.

-Go on, I nodded.

-Well, Leonard, he played me this song, it is one he performs on this tour now, but of course that night was the first time I had heard it. It was entirely unlike any music I had ever heard before; it was unlike anything I had ever felt before. It was as if the beach and the sea and the sky sort of evaporated around him as he sang, and left us all suspended in a seemingly infinite plain, where time felt flexible and you could will a thing, a thought or person into being, and there was no true causation, only the ever flowing and meandering rhythms and sublime vision of his words.

-Sounds like pretty good acid to me.

With this, her raptured expression broke, and she cast me a look. The kind of look I would later come to adore from her – a sort of withering, playful scorn. The corners of her mouth twitched briefly into a cherubic, self-admonishing smile.

-From that day on I never really left his side.

-So the man on the beach with the guitar was Tiberius?

-Well yes, obviously. Well, I just moved in with him, stayed with him at his...

She let out a sudden direct current of laughter.

-Well, that actually brings us right up to what I wanted to speak to you about.

-Hang on, I said. He plays you one song and that was it, you've been his. Well what are you to him exactly? His collaborator? His concubine? No...you're clearly more than that. So anyway...One song and that was it?

-As I said, it was a very special song. Songs are what this is all about...that's why you are here. I mean literally here right now. Forget any notions you may be harbouring about free will...

-Pinky, I must say, it's you who's beginning to sound.. alarming....

-Quite alarming, she continued. I mean, when did you choose to be here? Right now, in this exact spot, drinking these exact drinks, here exactly with me?

I paused, a little wrong-footed by her strange presupposition.

-Likewise, when did you really choose to join this tour? Did you make all the decisions, matter-of-factly, coolly, calmly, level-headedly? Entirely of your own volition? Your own inviolable free will?

-Well...

-No...obviously you didn't. What brought you here tonight were songs. Songs of all sizes and qualities, but songs nonetheless. They have been our chariots, Leonard.

Reaching for yet another cigarette, I didn't say anything, because I could see she had a point. Songs had brought us together, brought me to this place, to this moment –at least from her way of seeing things.

-We're intrigued by you and your songs, and, well, we were thinking of inviting you to join us at his retreat.

I laughed.

-You went to all this trouble to invite me for a threesome?

I laughed again but it sounded strained.

-If only it was that simple, Leonard.

She traced the condensation of her martini glass with her little finger.

-No. Not quite, young man. Tiberius has a retreat, a very, very special place where we work together, as a collective, on songs, music and art. We work at ways of experiencing all of *this*, you might say. She gestured delicately at apparently *everything*.

-Collective? There are more than just the two of you?

-Yes.

-How many?

-Well that depends...anyway, don't get caught up in the details. So yes, what I wanted to speak to you about tonight was after the end of the tour, about you joining us out in California, at the retreat, for say a month or so. You're welcome to stay as long as you like.

...

-Well, of course you don't have to decide right now, take a moment, we have still another ten nights to go on this tour, plenty of time for you to consider, and ask me anything you like about it, although I'd perhaps prefer it if you didn't mention our meeting to Tiberius yet.

I didn't like the sound of that condition she had slipped in. If I was invited to stay with Tiberius, why was I not allowed to mention the idea to him?

-Well, thank you for the invite...

-Think it over. She said, smiling. Sometimes when she smiled you had the impression she was considering doing something really awful to you.

-Now I really should think about retiring to my room.

She gestured languidly in the direction of the ceiling with her now empty martini glass.

-Yes, yes, I should do the same. I barely slept last night, this morning I mean, and we are playing Paris tomorrow night?

She rose and strode with unexpected pace in the direction of the exit.

I stared down at the table, the ashtray still smouldering and my mind reeling from the oddly quite moving music I had just been irradiated by. It felt like a symphony had just finished. Her stiletto footsteps halted. I turned around in my seat to see her standing, framed by the shimmering baroque brass doorway.

-Oh...She had a vaguely petulant look on her face, affronted by some unspoken slight.

-`Aren't you going to come up and read my tarot, as you promised?

I stood and followed her out the door.

XXXII

Ten days later, I was staring at the Irish sea from the porthole of the 'Ulysses' ferry, sitting in the 'James Joyce' bar. We had finished the tour. Higgs was sitting opposite me. He was bobbing rhythmically in time with the moiling sea and looking for all the world exhausted. As the sun set over the distant black rocks framed in the porthole, he was too light in conversation, not to be drawn. A foghorn lowed and the ferry yawed its way through the glaucous waters and over the tinny speakers came the sounds of Fleetwood Mac's *Rumours*.

-How are you?

-I loved Dublin, what a show, what a way to end this tour.

-The promoter was livid, you overran by twenty minutes.

-They loved it.

-They really didn't.

-What does it matter, the tour is over.

- Where are you going back to?

-The Church I suppose.

I looked fixedly out across the inverted horseshoe of the bar.

-Leonard, I spoke to your fiancé today. She's left you. She's left the Church, she says she never wants to see you again.

-What do you mean?

-I mean she's now your ex-fiancé.

-Ahh that's why you were being so weird.

-She said she's had enough.

-Enough of what?

I stood up staggering against the pitch of the boat.

-I'm going to the bar, would you like one?

-Leonard.

I had spent the last ten consecutive nights with Pinky. Ever since our fateful rendezvous in Vienna. That first supernova kiss in the lobby, the lift, the deliciously expectant walk along the corridor to her room. The room key sliding into a well-worn brass lock. The hinges clicking closed behind us like the mouths of angels tutting. She fumbled for the softest of lights, and our great love affair began.

Back on the ferry:

The wind whipped the heavy steel door away from my hand as I stepped out into the blooming seascape. The crepuscular sun was streaking through the clouds like spilt tea, waves crashed and my great coat flapped like a torn sail as I gripped the starboard rail, childhood memories of treasure island flashing over my feverish face.

-Well, what do you want to do now? Higgs yelled from somewhere behind me.

-I think I want to go to California.

-I knew this was coming.

-I've been invited, I said, squinting into the pale horizon.

-What do you mean you've been invited?

-Pinky and Tiberius have invited me to stay at their retreat.

Saying it out loud to Higgs over the howling wind, I realised with a throb of embarrassment how silly it sounded.

-What? What kind of retreat?

-To be honest I don't really know, she wouldn't tell me anything about it. But it sounded very nice.

Higgs gripped the deck railing beside me with both hands, his knuckles whitened.

I proffered a cigarette from my pack, and as he took it I shrugged and screamed over the gathering tempest.

XXXIII

Higgs organised a send-off party for me seven nights later in Notting Hill at a cocktail bar just off Portobello Road called 'A Can of Worms.' On returning to London, he had hastily made arrangements to place all my belongings in storage. I had then spent the next seven days and nights careening around the capital from friend to friend, foe to foe, bar to bar, defiantly announcing in an occasionally slurred voice, that I had 'Fallen head over heels in love with a drop-dead gorgeous chanteuse and was eloping to the West Coast of America' to everyone in earshot.

I did not want the send-off party and wasn't really sure who to invite, since I'd become estranged from my true friends in London during my self-imposed northern exile.

It boiled down to several hardy industry associates, people I knew purely from working or drinking, a handful of people who are essentially strangers, and my dear friend Jim and his wife Sara. Jim was an older collaborator, always reassuring, a big man with a sizable soul and a demeanour both terrifying and heartwarming to a beat. A New Yorker, he spoke with a deliberation and tenderness that belied an eviscerating wit and forensic humanity. I was so happy to see them that night before I left town.

The evening was sousing towards its gin-sodden end. I myself had sunk about six of Jim's preferred and strongly recommended cocktails of choice, *The Suffering Bastard*. We were leaning in at the table and talking softly over our vast skull-shaped glasses. We were navigating an infinite radial plain of easygoing conversation about everything from Edwardian architecture to outsider Estonian photography and the impenetrable meaning of the Voynich manuscript. Jim looked up at me, his grey eyes glistening.

-When do you fly?

-9 AM.

-Have you been to LA before?

-I have but only briefly, just for shows. As I said before, I am now in pursuit of true love.

He stared at me.

-It's a hard town and not for everyone. Sort of place that can squeeze you like a fist if you show it any sign of weakness.

I slugged on my suffering bastard.

-It'll yield to your will if you know what you truly want... and if you play by its rules....one piece of advice.

His cocktail glass rattled under his Brooklyn baritone.

-Just be cool.

I looked up. His face was as inscrutable as an Easter Island statue. I went to speak, and he held up his hand.

He took a long swig of his cocktail.

-Watch, observe, and record, but for the love of Christ, be cool.

Six hours later, as I settled into my seat onboard the airliner that was to carry me to California, Jim's words were still ringing in my ears. His advice would save my life, not once, not twice, but three times before the year was through.

A truth that's told with bad intent
Beats all the Lies you can invent.

It is right it should be so;
Man was made for Joy and Woe;
And when this we rightly know
Thro' the World we safely go

...

Every Night and every Morn
Some to Misery are Born.
Every Morn and every Night
Some are Born to sweet delight.
Some are Born to sweet delight,
Some are Born to Endless Night.

THE SCHOOL OF LIFE

I

Once upon a time in the United States of Forever Ago.

Pinky was, to my complete surprise, standing at the arrivals gate at the very front of the line of expectant faces, and, my word, if you must arrive drunk on inflight free champagne and half a bottle of Johnnie Walker sweating profusely, staggering under the weight of your leather bag containing the contents of your entire life, direct into Los Angeles airport at 4 PM one afternoon in June—let it be Pinky Capote waiting to greet you in a catsuit and a smile.

-You made it! Welcome to California, baby!

-Pinky Capote.

I threw up my arms and almost toppled over.

She stepped forward and kissed me. I wasn't in any way complaining but the French kiss was almost a little too intense, a shade too much like a romantic denouement from a nineties blockbuster. After a few too many seconds, I opened one eye halfway, expecting passerbys to be catcalling and whooping like in the movies, but no one was taking a blind bit of notice. We strode out the freon chill of the air-conditioned airport into the blinding white heat of Los Angeles. Pinky took my hand and gently perambulated me towards her emerald green Porsche Spyder, which, as we approached, shimmered as alluringly as a television advert.

I threw my bag in the back and slid onto the sizzling leather passenger seat. I was much closer to the ground than I was expecting. Pinky smiled and then turned the key and the twelve cylinders of the engine a few inches from my legs roared to life. She slipped on a pair of Cartier Panthere sunglasses and floored it, wheel-spinning out of the parking lot towards the freeway on-ramp.

The 405 Freeway, three minutes later, 87 mph. The narcotic scent of native honeysuckle blended in with the nicotine from her cigarette, against the roar of the wind's rush, infusing with the partially combusted hydrocarbons of the 6.5 million glowing exhaust pipes that call this city home. I gazed out at Los Angeles whizzing past at high speed. I was already lost in its impenetrable psychogeography. Pinky was glancing at me, a knowing smile on her face:

What do you think?

-I already fucking love it here.

-There's a bottle of Extra Añejo in the glove box if you fancy a swig

She turned off the freeway and a sign for Silverlake zinged past. She slowed a little in the more suburban streets and I saw my first close-up impressions of Los Angeles. The sky, the pacific, the concrete, all emerging from the 16:9 letterboxing; the city of endless potential and sensual temptations. From the imported palm trees to the space-age silhouettes of the buildings, the architecture and signage betrays the fact that this city needs you, it needs you to fulfil its function as the holy city of desire.

Pinky slowed in a queue of traffic at a stoplight. To our left was a huge white seven-story building behind an imposing wrought iron fence, upon which a gold-lettered sign declaimed,

'Hollywood Celebrity Centre.'

-What is *that* place?

Pinky glanced at the white building and then just shrugged.

-I dunno, some kind of clubhouse for really rich folks I guess.

I started to reply when she gestured with her cigarette to a bar on the right side of the road called 'The Bourgeois Pig.'

-Now that place is great, you will love it baby, it's a late, late place. I like going there to get breakfast for dinner at like two in the morning, we can go sometime.

The stoplight changed, and we sped off along Franklin Avenue. As we stopped and started according to the whims of the ebbing current of traffic, it occurred to me that in LA a car is not just a symbol of freedom, it is an absolute necessity, being the only way to navigate a city so vast and deliberately strung out that nobody even seriously considered fitting a functioning public transport system. A car was an extension of the self, and Pinky had her Spyder to traverse this web.

She took a right as we passed a 1920s hotel called the 'Villa Carlotta,' and as she changed gear, I spotted her unusual ring. I hadn't noticed it on our European travels. A small glinting Venetian poisoner's ring on the little finger of her left hand. I stared at its gilt crafting and wondered what to make of it. She noticed me notice, and, leaning over, took the tequila from my hand, winked, and took a pull from the bottle. I went to speak, but she just took another long drag and handed the bottle back to me.

A few minutes later, as we hit the long inclining curve of Vine Street, the start of the serpentine skyward climb into the hills, I discovered I was in quite a good mood, and just then as the Spyder swung northwards and upwards, between a gap in two buildings I saw for the first time the Hollywood sign. An unblinking hieroglyphic eye, a shrine to the demiurge, a piece of fakery held up on sticks.

The engine roared as we corkscrewed through the narrow roads, passing huge exotic mansions that triggered countless secondhand cinematic memories. Pinky had a different energy here in her native climes.

When we had been on tour together, she had either cast herself as my surrendering supplicant or masochistic tormentor. She had made herself a sacrificial gift to Eros on the flowery bedspread of the Four Seasons, on another night a mediaeval maiden receiving carnal knowledge while bent obscenely over a Marriott balcony table. I noticed that here in these hills, in command of a vehicle containing both our mortal souls, her demeanour was more assured – playful but more in control.

-Where are we going?

-To my house, of course. And tomorrow morning we drive upstate all the way to Big Sur.

-To the retreat?

-Well, actually we are going to a wedding first.

-Whose wedding is it?

-Two good friends of mine and everyone I know. It's going to be the best time, you'll love it. You'll really dig this couple.

-Who are they?

-I will tell you tomorrow.

-So when do we go to the retreat, is it near there?

-Tomorrow, mister.

I had the feeling that she was really enjoying being in control of every aspect of the situation. The car accelerated sharply as she throttled 200 horses with the delicate flexing of her shapely heel and toe. There was even a hint of control in her cadence as she commanded me to just relax, honey bunny.

She pulled a hard right and slammed on the brakes, screeching to a dead stop precisely in the narrow drive before a traditional hills bungalow.

It was a brown stucco with all the usual 70s adornments and kitsch trimmings right down to the Chinese style bamboo water garden gurgling by the front door. She hopped out and I watched her callipygian form flexing in the catsuit as she mounted the steps to the oriental doorway. She looked back, flashing a smile as she beckoned me to come hither.

I found this scribbled in my notebook a year later when I had gone into hiding in the desert:

I really only knew Pinky in the way that we meet those creatures that often populate our dreams. Those trickster halflings made from a collage of souls we have encountered in waking reality. Those chimaeras of cut-out friends and lovers. Later in the day, when I reflect upon my sleeping visions, I want to will them into existence, or to return to her half-light unconscious kingdom, to her embraces, to return to her odd love, to her timeless kindness, to sculpt her, unchanging as a statue, as a reminder of why life is worth the long lonely meander.

***

The more I had sex with her the more I knew that she was a servant to a higher power. When I licked her glistening cunt, she reacted by giggling like a debutante. On all fours she writhes and takes it screaming like a harpoon to her heart. All she really desires is for her sexuality to be unconditionally worshipped. Each reaching caress of the tongue is an affirmation of her sensual identity. To Pinky, sex is very much an extension of her artistic ambitions and she curates her quim as obsessionally as her wardrobe. Later, as I came upon her face, her expression made me feel like an all-powerful Aztec priest ripping out the heart of his millionth sacrificial victim and holding it aloft, still beating, to placate the god he murderously venerated. I shuddered and moaned at this strange and beautiful naked girl knelt before me in the blood red dusk.

-Welcome to the sunshine state, honey bunny, she beamed, licking her lips.

That evening she played the *White Album* as we sat out on the veranda of her house which was built, I assume, by a Star Wars set designer in between jobs in the seventies.

The same veranda I've already shown you in the polaroid photograph, the one I received in the post to the cabin in Nashville when I started writing all this a few months ago. I think all of my favourite memories of Pinky are located in this twilight, jasmine- and honeysuckle-scented midnight garden.

-More wine, baby?

She had slipped into a brightly patterned silk kimono after we left her bedroom. In the distance helicopters circled. Spotlights streaked the sky, the city was looking for one of its own. The Napa Valley wine was making me sick and volatile. I felt like my life was beginning again. I had made a break for it and surrendered to the music of chance. Never had I ever given anyone so much power over myself as I had granted to this dirty blonde chanteuse, who was refilling my glass and singing along to 'While my guitar Gently Weeps.' She leant back, her bare feet pressed coolly against the table top.

-When do we go to the retreat, Pinky? Where are you hiding Tiberius?

-We go to the retreat the day after the wedding, of course, it's not far down the road from the ceremony.

-So where's that?

A pique of annoyance played over her brow,

- Leonard, *please* just enjoy yourself. It's all going to be so much fun, trust me, you will see Tiberius again very soon!

She held up her little finger:

-I Pinky promise.

-I'm not sure if I trust you.

-You've trusted me this far, darling.

The only way to know if you can trust someone is to trust them.

She smiled her most slippery smile, the one I had previously numbered and catalogued it in my mind as Treacherous Smile no. 4.

I went to bed sometime later. I had sat out on the veranda smoking and thinking of all the possible ways in which this love affair could and probably would end. Watching the sky lighten I drank the last of that sickly sweet wine which had almost turned bad in the heat of the Hollywood night, and retired to make love to her once more.

II

The next morning looked precisely the same as every morning on this particular longitude and latitude: blue skies and 80 degrees on the nose by 11 AM. We were north by northwest in Pinky's Spyder somewhere on the 101 freeway, speeding out of the city. The landscape opened up as we left the city behind, the roaring Pacific Ocean appeared to our left and for the first time I saw miles of unbroken California stretching out ahead of us. We listened to Classic Rock radio stations and smoked Camel lights. Pinky would occasionally point out sights as they passed. I was just content to sit beside her, feeling pretty pleased with how everything had panned out.

An hour or so into the drive north, Pinky suddenly wanted to show me a place that was 'really special' to her childhood. I glanced at a passing sign that read *San Luis*

Obispo. What a beautiful name. A moment later she pulled off the highway onto a winding road that led down to the seafront. We got out of the car and walked over a hot gravel drive to a gaudy pink building in the style of a faux Bavarian guesthouse with a neon sign that read "The Hotel Madonna."

-When I was a kid we came here.

-Who?

-My Mom, Dad, my sister, and me...sort of for our vacations.

-That sounds nice...what did your Mum and Dad do?

-Oh, well I guess they were like conceptual artists...very much high-concept art.

-Right...I've no idea what that means, actually.

-It wasn't always that nice...the art always came first.

We walked over to the car and got back inside. She sat clutching the keys in her fist, looking back up to the pink hotel. She inhaled sharply, and I tensed, and for a moment expected her to start sobbing...but the sob never came. She started the engine and turned to me.

-I hope you write this little trip into a song or something one day.

III

The Fernwood Motel is just a little way down the coastal road from the Henry Miller Library in Big Sur. What a fine place, I thought, stepping out of the Spyder into the balm of its curiously Mediterranean climate to begin my life again.

When we checked in, Pinky leant forward and signed in as 'Miss Bambi Woods.'

In the 1950s ambience of our room, under a flickering yellow light bulb, Pinky slipped into her outfit for the wedding. I perched on the queen-size bed counting my cigarettes and wondering if I had enough. She slithered a vermillion Chanel dress over her simple white French underwear and tousled her champagne hair with her other hand. I looked down at my green camo shirt, dusty black trousers, and boots .

-Pinky, I really don't think I should turn up at a complete strangers wedding dressed like I've just walked off the set of *Apocalypse Now*.

She looked me over, cocking her head.

-I reckon you'll fit right in my handsome honey bunny.

***

A little while later we stepped out of our motel room and walked up the 101 with the roar of the Pacific to our right and the louring darkness of the redwoods on our left. We turned a gentle bend in the road and there was a rickety wooden sign that read 'The Henry Miller Library.' Pinky squeezed my hand in excitement. The sun was setting red behind us and we passed through those beautifully primitive gates.

IV

The library was much smaller than I was expecting. I'd been imagining a grand edifice hewn from marble and gold but it was, to my surprise, little bigger than a local garden centre. Its dilapidated structure nestled amongst the fragrant native pine trees with the occasional giant redwood towering overhead, creating a dappled, shadowy ambience. Here and there, scattered amongst the ancient trees, were abstract works of art. Sculptures of wrought steel, a dozen derelict television sets stacked flickering together, and a simple hengelike arrangement of rocks.

Pinky said 'hello cowboys' to a group of guests emerging from a tree-lined path. They flashed brilliant smiles that were so familiar that I almost said hello myself. I twigged cringingly a moment later upon realising they were a pair of famous film stars. Hardly that surprising I thought, they are an indigenous species to this part of the world. We emerged from the woods into a thronging clearing directly in front of the library. There were flickering flame torches around the periphery and dozens of candles illuminating a striking arrangement of tables. There were nine tables, each about nine feet long, criscrossing each other to form a pentagram pattern, with tall dripping red candles positioned at their outermost radial points. Wooden benches traversed either side of the tables, and at the head of each one stood an ornately carved throne-ish chair—none of these were currently occupied.

Some of the congregation were standing and moving towards the centre of this clearing where there was a majestic redwood soaring skyward several hundred feet above our heads. Its canopy is as vast, as reaching and heaven-bound, as a high church roof. In front of this stood a simple wooden altar, garlanded with wild flowers and adorned with coloured silks and several large leather books. Strewn around it were carved musical instruments the style of which I didn't recognise. Behind this scene was a small cluster of glimmering campfires and some weathered looking teepees, with one or two clearly narcotically twisted revellers wandering unsteadily amongst them.

The throng of guests began to gently swell forward to find their place before the altar preempting the beginning of the ceremony. This made me feel uneasy and a little exposed as I was, after all, the uninvited guest. I had a hot pang of shame. I was a bona fide wedding crasher. It was then that I realised I had lost Pinky.

Looking around sharply to face back into the glowing light emanating from the double doors of the library I saw, to my surprise, Tiberius Red, standing in a soft silhouette, a cigarette dangling from his lips. He was staring directly at me. I realised he had probably been watching me for some time, perhaps since I stumbled out from the wooded path with Pinky, wherever she was now. I threw up my hand in an instinctive, nervous wave. He didn't respond, aside from taking a long drag on his glowing cheroot. He exhaled a thick cerulean plume of smoke into the night air, and I found myself propelled towards him. In a moment I had traversed the twenty feet of scrub between us, and I was extending my hand to wave again when it was suddenly seized by Pinky.

-Darling, it's time we took our positions, she said breathlessly, her eyes flashing and betraying what I sensed was an unfamiliar emotion of stirring alarm.

-I was just about to...

- You can speak to him later. I want to get a good spot to watch my friends get married.

She planted a kiss firmly on my half open mouth. I looked back to the library as she started pulling me away, but Tiberius had vanished.

V

The soon to-be married Chevaliers, John and Charlotte, stepped forward from behind the great tree. They were followed by one of my favourite cult singer-songwriters. An artist famed as much for his reclusiveness, as his music. The kind of musician it's easy to believe doesn't really exist. And yet there he was, his bald head and ginger beard were unmistakable. He was wearing a capacious white gown, and he had a Grecian garland of flowers around his neck. His shining head adorned with a glinting laurel, he was the image of Bacchus himself. He was clearly the Priest of the proceedings. He stood behind John and Charlotte, who faced towards us, their arms by their sides, both palms facing out. John dressed simply in a white shirt and black tuxedo suit and trousers, his long hair rakishly slicked back. Charlotte was beautiful in a traditional cream fifties wedding dress. Her hair long dark and curled with a hint of playful glamour from the flash of brilliant red lipstick on her lips.

The air came alive. An uplifting C-sharp note rose resonantly from what must have been a score of silver trumpets muted with silk. Ten trumpets, twenty trumpets, a century of invisible trumpeters blowing pure paradise from the shadows. The note crescendoed in a tree-top rustling parabola and then died away into the gentle crash of the Pacific breakers just below the enchanted setting. The cult songwriter-cum- bacchanalian master of ceremonies stepped forward and spoke in a warm, authoritative voice:

-We are gathered here together today to celebrate the union of John and Charlotte.

I placed my arm around Pinky's small frame and pressed her close beside me. My head swam. How on earth had this happened? How was I here, in this place, witnessing this? Something had either gone terribly wrong, or terribly right.

The ceremony was beautiful. Gentle, thoughtful, and intensely intimate. Nothing at all like any other wedding I had ever attended. There was a slightly voyeuristic tone to the proceedings, caused in part by the complete absence of any light in the congregation. It felt more like we were a hushed audience to an opening night production, which only increased the theatrical vibration of their entwinement. We were all lucky witnesses to this one-night-only performance of the most primordial and sacred of ceremonies.

There was a group exhalation of breath, and a cathartic wave of giggling broke across the congregation as the priestly songwriter spoke the fated words, 'You may kiss the bride.' The deal was done.

Pinky looked as though she were about to speak and cry at the same time, it was the sort of thing she would do. But all she did was stare at me. An intense, bewitching half-light look dancing in her eyes that resolved firmly on mine—it did in fact remind me of the night we first met. But it had another energy of near-reproach, or was it regret? A twinge ran down my spine. Before I could find anything to say to her searching expression, a single electric guitar seared a magnesium flare E chord across the forest. Then, a pistol-shot of a snare drum heralded the opening of the dancefloor and the eruption of celebrations.

-Let's go get fucked up, said Pinky, and she darted away from me into the golden gloom. Her silhouette skittering in the direction of the makeshift bar now alive with the gushing activity of bacchanalia. Arriving several paces behind her, I could see the only two things being served were red wine and mezcal. It was going to be an evening of ferocious, celebratory excess. She slammed a glass tumbler into my hand, the fairy lights and candles in the trees swam in   its ethanoic depths.

-Here's to the Chevaliers, and here's to eternity!

She clinked my glass and downed at least four fingers of the sanity-slaying liquor. Mirroring her, I knocked mine back. It was the best mezcal I'd ever tasted, accompanied by a great rushing wave of euphoria. I spun around to take it all in. Pinky was doing some mad two-step dance to a raucous rendition of Dylan's 'Highway Sixty-One Revisited.' All around me were beautiful wild strangers in the night. I was in Big Sur, I was in love with a lunatic, but man could she dance. I was a long, long way from home but the night's fire felt good on my skin. I let all my senses play into themselves, amplifying and escalating their energies in a divine feedback loop. I couldn't help but feel so very welcome. I sashayed my way to the bar and sank another mezcal.

-Here's to the Chevaliers!

I howled again into the swirling throng of revellers beneath the trees. The campfires were all aglow and everyone was going in the same direction. Everyone had the same destination as we danced and writhed and revolved. I felt I could see the very mechanics of love in the universe moving in lustrous, rapturous flesh before my eyes, a great human hedonistic machine expressing itself collectively, joyously. We had all lost our self-aware solipsism and surrendered to the holy excess of emancipation from the prison of individuality. Tonight we moved to the tune of the oldest music in existence.

I think several hours passed in this reverie of dancing and frolicking and giddying exultant worship of the seraphims of derangement. There were all kinds of things happening in all kinds of places as figures and forms, nymphs and fawns, moved from campfire to campfire. Snatched moments of intimacy and intrigue arose and fell like minor symphonies every few minutes.

Some of the gathered guests had gravitated towards the pentagram arrangement of tables and were devouring many different kinds of fruits and local delicacies in between deep swigs of wine and the nectary nepenthe of flowered mescal.

Speeches were made, but they were impromptu, disordered, and unsolicited. Friends would rise and speak freely their true hearts in regard to the new union. These earnest salacious speeches were met with choruses of cheering acquiescence from a well-worn-in and well-won-over audience.

Someone dinged a glass, or a bell, or a glass bell, and who I believe to be John's best man stood on a table. The candles guttered in puddles of wine, hissing and spitting like vipers around his feet.

-Ladies and Gentlemen, thank you all so much for attending this remarkable evening, this the most beautiful marriage of our two most beautiful friends.

He stamped the table. Cheers erupted around the pines, as well as catcalls, whoops, and I believe someone even cracked a bullwhip.

-As you know, the Chevaliers have requested absolutely no wedding gifts. However, they have gone and got you all a gift to commemorate this special day. If when fancy takes, you wander towards the library, you may pick out *one* book of your choice from its shelves to remember this day by, courtesy of our supreme hosts, the happy couple, ladies and gentlemen, the Chevaliers.

A raucous cheer erupted. This thoughtful gesture somehow said everything about the two of them in one graceful symbolic act. Looking around, I could see many people eagerly winding their way towards the glowing yellow portal of the barn doors of the library. I appeared to have misplaced Pinky again.

I drew a cigarette from my jacket and lit it with a book of matches I'd taken from the desk at the Motel. I smoked alone, standing in the centre of the array of pentagram tables. I was alone, but I was happy. I could barely bring myself to think of the word let alone feel it, but its presence was persistent and undeniable. Happy. To the extent that I could almost reach into the night in front of me and embrace it like a forgotten friend. I finished the cigarette and glanced in the direction of the library. I quite fancied taking my newfound feeling of happiness with me over there and having a jolly good rummage around with it in Henry Miller's filthy stash of books.

A distant sound arose, carrying on the gentle sea breeze over the tops of the trees. It was the voice of a woman. A high seering, beseeching note, with mellifluent, enchanted words entwined in sonorous phrases flitting between gusts of the breeze. She was singing in a language I didn't immediately recognise, but it felt disconcertingly familiar, as if I had heard it before, perhaps in a dream. Had I perhaps once even heard this song back in the church? Before I could study its fine aching interplays, it died away with the wind, leaving but a trace of faint emotion resonating in my mind. A scent like gunpowder, mingled with the jasmine and honeysuckle all around.

I laughed at myself, at my incorrigible mind. I laughed to dismiss the sudden uneasiness that had arisen. I willed my newly reacquainted feeling of happiness to return. *There are places I'll remember all my life, though some have changed.*

I topped up my glass one-handedly and, I liked to think, quite suavely as I passed by the last of the pentagram tables and strode on towards the library. I whistled the tune as I walked. I did not know it then, but what I had just heard from the woods was in fact the dread song of a siren.

Whether it was a welcome or warning, even now, to this day, I could not say.

You were happy for a moment, were you?

Pity he who dares to dare the gods.

VI

I stepped into the library. A library I had been reading and thinking about since I was a teenager. It was a small wooden cabin, lined floor to ceiling with shelves on all sides. Bisecting the centre was a curving bookcase that created a yin and yang division point in the room. The small clattering room was already quite full of wedding revellers and hence far more raucous than a library normally is, but it was not by any means a *normal* library nor was this a *normal* time to be visiting one.

Politely excusing myself between garrulous roaming gangs of fellow drunken bibliophiles, each person aware of the other's seeking eyes. Everyone was out for a unique literary treasure. I began to peruse the chaotically well-stocked shelves. As you might imagine, it was a home to more arcane and oblique textual fare than your average outlet. Rare Erotica, tons of it, obviously. Stacks of unrecognisable yet clearly experimental modernist literature. Walls of impenetrable 19th and 20th century French semiotic philosophy, as was to be expected. Screeds of fiery and mostly forgotten political tracts. Vast swaths of bibliographic mystery confronted me.

There was something illicit about perusing a library with the express intention of stealing a book from its shelves. One of the only true and inviolable rules that my mother had ever taught me was thou shalt not steal from the library. It was a sacred lawsacrosanct. This invitation to rob was a small but knowing act of subversion from the Chevaliers. Their first act of giving back to their friends as a man and wife.

I glanced around at my fellow thieves. It was a glamorous den of iniquity, but the way that books were being seized and passed around and stuffed into bags, coats and bras, was really quite unsettling. Not quite as funny as you might imagine.

I continued to peruse. It occurred to me that whatever book I selected would say something about me to my fellow guests. It was a subtle test of one's taste, worldly outlook, psychological mettle. Everyone walked around clutching their one book from the library like a calling card.

Moving through the charged throng, I was being shoved and pushed aplenty. Imagine if libraries were always like this. Book after book flying off the shelves. I turned to witness a thing I had never seen before, two handsome men in suits close to actually fistfighting over a paperback. They were both wrestling furiously for it with their white knuckled hands. I noticed it was a copy of Harold Pinter's complete plays –I suppose a thing very much worth fighting for. Here, the pages and compendiums of knowledge were cherished and prized above all things else.

I was jostled by a young lady dressed in a silvery aquamarine jumpsuit. She was Japanese and leaned over me for a book, Psychogeographical maps of the outer Hebrides. I nodded politely and ducked below her arm that shimmered like a salmon, and found myself at the V section, precisely where I wanted to be.

V is for Vulnerable, Vulva, Vendetta, Vaccine, Valuation, Vibraphone, Vigorous, Virginity, Vibration, Validity, Verisimilitude, Verifiable, Veracity, Volume, Vociferous, Vestibule, Vocation, Vast, Variable, Vantage, Vanguard, Ventricle, Voyeurism, Vulgarity, Vicissitudes, Volition, Volleyball, Vulgar, Vespal, Verbal, Vixen.

But there at the end of the shelf, was V for Vonnegut. My eyes came to rest upon the book I had been looking for *Cat's Cradle* by Kurt Vonnegut.

I fought my way to the library check-out desk where I found a harassed-looking librarian observing the unfolding mayhem with a look of half-horror, half-bemusement on her face. As people pushed forward in the queue and presented their purloined book, she would take it from them, making a note of the title (I assumed to order a replacement) and then with a resigned, regretful air, stamped the frontispiece of the book.

There were three people in the queue ahead of me, and to my surprise one was the glamorous-looking, insouciant tall brunette whom I had seen with the film stars when I first arrived. She was standing waiting patiently to check her book out of the library forever. She seemed unphased by the unfolding chaos, if not a little distracted, dreamily lost in thought.

I found myself daydreaming as to who she really was and what her connection to the Chevaliers might be. I stared fixedly at the back of her head, into the sea of her dark tresses when, without warning, she suddenly turned around and locked her green eyes with mine. I was exposed. I felt that she sensed my surprise, an imperceptible smile flickered across her features. It was replaced by a sterner, more concerned look. It was then that I recognised her. In a flash of recognition I knew exactly who she was, and it explained immediately what she was doing here. She was a popstar. Not one that I had paid any particular attention to, but nonetheless she had caused quite a commotion with her debut album a year or so earlier. This process of recognition lasted a fleeting moment, I smiled at her. And then, for reasons that shall forever remain a mystery, I gave her a double thumbs-up.

Oh god. Her look turned to a frown on her sharp aquiline features, and she whirled around to face the librarian. Moments later she had checked her book and exited briskly out the door of the library.

The frazzled red-headed librarian took the copy of Cat's Cradle from my hands and dutifully noted its title in a small black register, stamped it and handed it back to me, gesturing towards the door. Stepping outside, I opened the front page of the book to read the freshly inked page:

Lovingly Stolen from the Henry Miller Library, at the kind behest and gift of the Newlywed Chevaliers.

I smiled into the night. The scene in front of me was in full swing. Silhouettes darting amongst the trees, dancing figures picked out in the backlight of the several roaring campfires. Music emanated from three or four locations dotted around the encampment. The sounds of acoustic guitars, violins, and roaring rhythm and blues intermingled in the night. Well-dressed and well-embraced guests stumbled in and out of the shadows. I stepped towards the edge of the pool of yellow light from the open library doors. I lit a cigarette and began to consider how I was to find Pinky in this adult never-neverland.

There was a rustle of fabric in the shadows to my left and the mysterious popstar brunette stepped into the island of light on the edge of the night. I almost dropped my book and cigarette, she gracefully extended a long thin wristed hand to catch the falling volume and, glancing at the cover, handed it back to me.

-Vonnegut, good choice stranger, she purred in an expensively schooled North American accent. Before I could reply she continued,

-We've got something in common.

-What's that? I said in a slightly offhand and defensive way. I actually surprised myself with the brusqueness of my tone. She held up her own book in yellow half-light,

SlapStick by Kurt Vonnegut.

I laughed in recognition.

-So we do...

-Strange book for a strange night. She fixed me with a disconcerting gaze. For the second time in recent evenings, I felt like I was being assessed and judged by some unfathomable scale.

-Are you a friend of the Chevaliers?

-No, not at all really. I'm aware of his music...I like it a lot, but no, I was invited through someone ...

I cleared my throat, unsure exactly as to how best to describe my relationship.

-Well I'm with Pinky, she was invited, and sort of insisted I came.

The mysterious popstar smiled a chilly half-smile, replaced by a look I couldn't immediately decode, but I was certain I had seen it before.

-Pinky Capote? she said the two words with an accented pause.

-Yes. I cleared my throat, the night felt like it had ever so slightly closed in around me.

I took a drag on the stub of my cigarette.

-Sorry I didn't catch your name - I'm Leonard. I extended a moist palm.

She took my hand, clutching it like a clairvoyant and closing her eyes. Her head rolled back. I was just beginning to speculate as to what sort of marvellous drugs she may be taking when she snapped her eyes open and pulled me close to her. I was overwhelmed by her musky perfume. Nuzzling her mouth to my ear as she whispered her name to me. She let go of me, a small droplet of her newly liberated spittle cooling in my ear.

-Do you want to play hide and seek?

-What do you mean?

-Count to ten Leonard.

She darted into the night, her high heels clickety-clacking like a highwayman's horse.

I reeled, my eyes swimming up into the sky. The entirety of Orion's belt glowed and glistened from the distant past over the millennia and down onto this moment. I counted to ten quite quickly.

VII

The following morning Pinky and I's motel room looked like it had been carefully redesigned by a thoughtful murderer with a taste for feng shui. A puddle of crimson sick on the beige carpet was my eye-rubbing welcome to the day. I knew it wasn't mine, so I glanced around looking for the perpetrator.

Pinky was sidesaddle on a chair. Her dress coiled around her waist like a boa constrictor. The air was opaque with steam. I heard the shower running. I got up and found a bottle of water and tried to rouse Pinky. She groaned and said 'I really think Pet Sounds is the greatest record of all time' and promptly vomited more red stuff onto my legs. I looked at the sick and looked at this weird woman whom I now loved. I wondered about the shower. Had it been running all night, or was someone in there? Tentatively, I stepped towards the half-open door of the bathroom.

-Hello?

No reply, I stepped inside. The radio was blaring a country and western song, something about 'Satan We Serve.'

-Hello? I called again, looking past the clouds of steam liberated from the roaring showerhead behind the drawn curtain. There was no reply, but I could, straining my bleary eyes, make out what appeared to be a somewhat misshapen form in silhouette behind the flapping curtain. It seemed too short, too slight, too squat to be a person.

My pulse quickened, I called out again to no reply. There was nothing for it, so I screwed my courage to the sticking place and approached the shower. The deformed silhouette looked even more nightmarish the closer I got. What the fuck was in there? Whatever it was appeared to be standing stock-still, not moving at all in the scalding torrent of water gushing down from the showerhead.

The morning had taken a terrible turn. I had no recollection whatsoever of the end of last night, or even how we had got back to the motel, let alone who or what was in the shower. For a sickening moment, I remembered the distant vision of the demonic flaming dog I had seen months ago standing on its hind legs in the graveyard of the church...Could it possibly be that the hound had followed me all the way to California and for reasons impossible to comprehend had finally decided to extinguish its eternally tormenting flames in the en suite shower of my motel room?

I could barely breathe as I took a final step towards the curtain. At the last moment I considered it might be pertinent to arm myself, there was after all no knowing how this thing in the shower may react to having its morning ablutions interrupted. I spied a wire coat hanger and seizing it, I stepped towards the shower holding it aloft before me. I took a breath and ripped the curtain asunder.

There was a four foot tall cactus in a pot, with a battered, sodden Spanish guitar nuzzling against it. A selection of watermelons and grapefruit and six empty bottles of wine surrounded it, and what appeared to have once been a large wheel of camembert. Worn like a crown on top of the cowboy hat that was positioned on the neck of the guitar. The camembert had melted in the boiling deluge, and coagulated into long stringy strands like thick viscous cobwebs over the entire ensemble. It was truly a monstrous installation, quickened from the tail end of last night's excesses. Why had we done this? What arcane purpose did it serve? It was very hard to say. I felt it was a bad omen of things to come. After a while, I turned off the shower.

There was a shuffling in the doorway behind me, it was Pinky. She had her Chanel dress pulled around her like the survivor of a glamorous shipwreck.

-Is everything ok, Leonard?

I looked at her, placing the coat hanger softly onto the sink.

-I think so.

VIII

Not the best of breakfasts. We staggered out of our motel room and wandered past the rows of parked cars. I had barely any recollection of last night after I'd disappeared into its stygian shadows, hunting the brunette pop star who liked Vonnegut. I felt it best not to mention her to Pinky just yet.

Pinky didn't speak much as we found a corner table in the motel diner that had not altered at all since 1955. As we perused the menu and gulped glasses of ice water, I considered how our sudden intimacy, living together, sharing a life together, being a sort of odd couple, had in no way diminished the air of intrigue that permeated her being. It was like being in a relationship with a very attractive, very wilful cat that could occasionally talk and drive a car. We ate breakfast and downed a half dozen coffee cups between us in almost unbroken silence.

-Pinky, do we head to the retreat today?

-Yeah. About fifteen minutes' drive from here.

-How long are we going to be there?

-I should say about six to seven months.

I laughed.

-Six to seven months?

I put my coffee cup down slowly.

-What? What kind of artistic retreat takes six to seven months?

-Well, Tiberius is trying to write his way around death.

She looked directly into my eyes, her innocent expression suggesting I should not be surprised by this news.

-Write his way around death? I said it once in my head and once out loud: *write his way around death*? I had taken quite a lot of strange on this trip so far. I had withstood many peculiar turns, but the brazen nonchalance of Pinky reporting to me that the reason we were about to embark on a six month retreat was so that Tiberius could *write his way around death* seemed a tad much. I actually felt fibres in my mind rend and tear. I stood up and walked out into the carpark.

I felt lost, in the freefalling way that one can only truly feel when one has surrendered everything to love and then, realised, perhaps too late, that a grave amorous miscalculation had occurred.

Apparently I had sacrificed everything; my fiancé, the life I had worked hard for in the godforsaken church, my career, the kittens, my entire record collection, purely so Tiberius could drag me to the woods north east of the global entertainment capital, so that he could *write his way around death*. How had I fallen for this utter madness? How had I fallen for her? I felt a sharp tang of bile rise in my throat. I heaved.

Once the show began, there was no stopping it. I was startled by the sheer volume of liquid I contained. I didn't even have time to bend over before it started pumping out of me like a fire hydrant. Before too long, I was on the tarmac on my hands and knees, expunging every fluid ounce in my body. I had evaded. I had lied. I had said 'yes' too many times instead of 'no,' and now came the hammer's blow. Workers of the soul rise up, you have nothing to lose but your shame.

I shuddered into the hot tarmac. I saw a pair of converse all-stars shimmering before my eyes. They shuffled around the dredge of curiously clear vomit. I looked up. A brilliant Big Sur sunbeam lens-flared through my teary right eye and I could see a man in his eighties, dressed as if he was in his twenties. I looked down at the sneakers again, at the pooling fluids that I'd ejected. I tried desperately to read my fate in the tea leaves of my own gastronomic debris.

-Son...son...How are you doing down there son?

-How does it... Look Like I am doing? I heaved again.

- I've made a terrible mistake, and I don't know who I am anymore

His converse shuffled in the chunderous flow, but to be fair to him, he did not retreat.

-Well, we all know how that feels, lord knows I've felt that creeping sensation every few years since I can ever remember feeling things.

I didn't believe him, how could he possibly know this feeling? His voice had the soothing qualities of an old-time Christmas movie.

-Let me help you up, you sure have made a mess of something.

He was tall, quite large, and grey-haired.

-Son, why don't you relax for a second.

He extended his hand and proffered me a battered CD. Elton John's *Goodbye Yellow Brick Road*.

-I've been listening to this recently, and it's been making me feel really good.

I stared at the CD, then to his warm eyes encouraging me to take it.

I tried to speak but my voice was gone.

-Take it, I've been listening to it all week and it's like he just really gets me. It will help you out son, trust me.

I took the CD. The stranger seemed very pleased, he waved and walked off towards a battered white Ford pickup truck.

I looked back at the diner. Pinky was standing at the doorway. Her hands once again on her hips, a position where they spent a lot of time residing in our relationship. Thankfully, the other diners had moved away from the windows. Pinky walked slowly towards me, politely stepping around my pool of vomit. I wiped my eyes and looked at her. There was to my surprise a playful smile ghosting around her mouth.

-I think we should walk down to the beach, I think you could do with some sea air. You look a little green about the gills.

I nodded. I didn't actually feel so bad, certainly a little lighter on my feet, physically and perhaps even emotionally. I had purged something, or everything, I was dazed but ok. I tucked the CD into my back pocket.

We walked around the side of the motel, following the beckoning roar of the pacific, and found a narrow path that snaked down into a dark descent of pine trees and scrub. It really didn't feel necessary to speak as we seemed to be communicating to each other in another sort of way. After a few slips and stumbles, we emerged onto a brilliant white and deserted beach, ranged in on either side by stark cliffs that seemed unchanged since the dawn of time.

There was something quite disquieting about the intensity of the waves breaking on the oblique incline of the shore. Wave after wave of chaos broke before me. Waveforms that had begun 1500 miles away across the ocean finally wrecked themselves here on these sands. Pinky was busy admiring the golden sand on her feet. Time passed, we stood there, watching the relentless waves.

-Tiberius is trying to write his way around death, because he thinks he has spotted a loophole in an eternal cosmic clause, the holiest of laws.

She said this matter of factly.

-He's been at it for years. Occasionally making breakthroughs, sometimes setting himself back a long way in the interstellar time map. That is, the interstellar time map inside his mind. He is charting his own exploration of inner space.

-Right, cheers for clearing that up.

The wind that had started to rag around and gather in intensity.

-It has a lot to do with songs and music and a bit to do with some weird Grecian rituals he's uncovered. There's also these self-help exercises based on witchcraft and sorcery. You'll see. It's not actually so strange when Tiberius explains it.

I turned to look at her. She looked away, unable to hold my gaze.

-Not so strange?

The sun slid behind a grey flank of clouds. A squall was arriving in timely, emotionally attuned triteness.

Tiberius is trying to write his way around death.

I sensed Pinky wanted to speak further, no doubt to assuage my worries, to convince me that everything was still ok.

The wind grew fiercer, blowing my hair into my face. The ionically charged tension crackled and the air was electric and close. I started towards the sea. In a few paces I had reached the breaking tide, foam rushing over my boots. I kept walking. The sky was closing in. I could hear Pinky screaming behind me. I tasted the sharp tang of iodine in the air. I honestly had no idea what I was doing. I was at the mercy of an impulse, an urge. I was almost waist-deep, and my trousers were starting to feel the heavy tug of the current. A wave slammed into my face, making my eyes sting and taking the breath from my lungs, but I continued to wade into the raging maelstrom. My feet began to slip. Another step and I felt the sea floor drop away, my head bobbed under the water. I surfaced, spluttering and swimming, unmoored from the land. I felt the current seize me. Wave after wave came crashing, and I felt a dreadful embrace begin to pull me into the depths as I began to sink. I thrashed in the water, as a jolt of overriding self-preservation kicked in. I tried to rotate my body against the clawing of the current, the water cold, black, and blinding. I began to fight the sea with all of my strength, hoping to angle myself back in towards the shore. I was spending more and more time under the waves, barely breaking the surface for long enough to seize a breath. I couldn't tell which way was up or down, let alone if I was swimming towards the beach. I felt sharp fatigue and a horrible throbbing in my limbs. With the last of my reserves I kicked out in futility against the sea, heaving my arms. A wave caught me and threw me deeper down. I felt my fingertips scrape the seabed. Rolling weightless in the surging water, I realised that I was drowning. I thrashed. The stupidity of what I had done flashed before my eyes, the final gargling tale told by an idiot. The throbbing of my heartbeat in my ears was joined by a high arpeggio note, as if some distant underwater violin was being played by a mermaid. The ascending note grew louder, and I began to feel a terrifying release. My lungs burnt as if I was actually on fire, but it was an odd comfort in the freezing watery blackness, and as a crescendo rose, the heat in my lungs burst into a hypnotic flickering pattern of brilliant red flames dancing and tessellating out across the infernal water as all of it began to fade.

A cold hand suddenly seized my arm from below. It was dragging me down, down further still, to what would be my final watery resting place. The cold vice-like grip kept dragging me down, impossible to resist, and all about me was still the fiery, watery haze. I didn't fight it, I let it haul me through the churning waters. In my final moments of mortal consciousness, I felt the darkness rising.

And then my head broke the surface, and I was gasping and heaving fresh air into my smouldering lungs. Daylight hit my eyes, refracting into a trillion watery shards. The hand kept tugging, and I felt the sand on my back. I was out of the sea, gulping in huge lungfuls of air, the flames in my eyes and chest dying down, I was looking up into the azure blue skies above. Pinky standing over me, her mouth moving like an opera singer and her fine hands cleaving the air. The timpani ringing in my ears subsided, my hearing returned, and I could hear her screaming at me.

-You stupid, stupid fucking cunt.

I rolled into a kneeling position, coughing up huge gobbets. She herself was stripped down to her underwear, wisely she had removed her clothes, before entering the raging waters to retrieve me. It was doubtless this decision and her surprising prowess as a swimmer that had just saved my life.

She was still screaming at me. An immense flowing and florid diatribe of well-aimed expletives, outlining my failures as a human being.

-Fucker. She concluded.

She slapped me so hard it made me see stars and my ears started ringing again. Reaching in my pocket, my fingers found a mulched watery mass wrapped around a spastically vibrating plastic block. I pulled the waterlogged contents from my pocket. Not only had I almost lost my life, I had also destroyed my phone and my passport. I was not having the best of mornings.

I stood up slowly, still catching my breath, and glanced back at the now-glassy sea. The storm had passed as quickly as it had arrived. I squinted, I thought I saw something glistening out there just above the waves. I peered, shielding the sun from my eyes, and saw what looked like a golden trident wreathed with seaweed and clutched by a scaly grey hand, waving wildly, and then slipping beneath the waves. I turned, seeing Pinky's footprints in the sand sloping back up the beach. Entirely unsure of anything at all, I decided to follow them.

IX

I am going to tell you about the twilight drive on the twisting road heading towards the retreat. The retreat I was now dreading.

But first I am going to return us for a moment back to the porch of my cabin in Nashville, where I am writing these words. I've been sitting here on the porch for quite a while writing all this down. The hurricane lamp flickers, my ashtray smouldering, and all around me the Tennessee forest is alive with waltzing ghosts.

I am the solitary nocturnal accountant of love, half-drunk, with my head down, going through the bittersweet receipts of yesterday's phantasmal dances.

Writing. Sitting in a silence that is only disturbed by the clitter-clatter of typewriter keys, occasionally glancing up into the stars I can see framed by the trees, or to the pool of lamplight aureoled around me. What I am really doing here is engaging deeply with my imagination.

Engaging with the imagination is not always just sitting making things up. It can be a lot more pure and potent than that.

There is nothing like sitting up in the dead of the night, in a swirl of cigarette smoke and coffee cups and wine glasses, holy amulets, roadmaps, paperbacks, photographs, record stacks and sinking deep into a story which you are partly writing, but is also partly writing you. Things are coming alive before your eyes. Sometimes the ones you love the most appear, their faces framed perfectly between the lines on the page.

When you sink into the sacred place where it's no longer strictly your personal invention or private fantasy, you sink into a Daemonic realm. A borderland.

You see they come from within, they are really your closest friends. *It's not so much that you have a thought, but that the thought is having you.* You can usually trust them, these inner beings, and in time you can come to rely upon their insights and the gifts, some glistening, some not so glistening, that they bring to your door. Or that lay shuddering and twitching on your midnight page.

Nowadays, when I hear stories of people encountering angels or elves, fairies and aliens on lonely rural roads it no longer strikes me as outlandish, indulgent, or even insane.

Sometimes believing is seeing.

The Japanese have a fine concept, Kotodama, which means 'Word Spirit.' The idea that mystical powers reside in words, lurking within names. *Haunted Words*.

I looked up a second ago to see that Terence, the youngest and wisest of the dogs I'm surrounded by, had just started digging a hole next to the oak tree that stands about twenty feet away from me, directly in front of my cabin. There is something about the ferocity with which he is pawing at the soil that chills my marrow. It has given me cause to stop typing for a second.

I light a cigarette from the packet sitting on top of the twenty typed sheets of writing that constitute my efforts this evening. I glance at my watch. It's 3.33 AM. I can hear only the endless whirring of the cicadas and the hoot of an owl. The wick in the hurricane lamp sizzles.

Terence can obviously see something that I cannot see. I begin to suspect that the universe has paid close attention to the cosmic monologue I've just been typing and sent me a sign. I glance at the page in my typewriter, reading it back:

In the dismantling of consensus reality, we must first examine a closer definition: The domestication of dogs is the greatest conspiracy theory of them all. Or dear DOG almighty.

I take a meditative drag, sip my tequila and consider that maybe I have been out here too long. My eyes come to rest on Terence's insistent digging. Now only his hind legs and furiously wagging tail are visible protruding from the mound of soil.

Don't dismiss this bit as a writerly device deliberately intended to subvert the auto-novelistic form. There's a reason I've brought you, like spirit in a seance, to sit with me here on the porch. So sit tight and listen close, and, whatever you do, don't move my glass.

What happens to me at the retreat is really fucking weird. So fucking weird in fact it took me a long time to live it all down, to process and deal with it. I travelled endlessly after the event in order to distance myself from that moment. To put it in perspective and, in doing so, draw closer to its dark heart. I had to develop certain aspects of myself so I could even write it down and take some responsibility for it all.

I am working on a theory that imagination can work reflexively. That it has a permeable membrane. The imagination can flow both ways, into and out of reality, from one realm to another. I mean, if it's possible to sit down, open a book and sink into a whole other universe it's equally possible that the imaginative world can somehow push back and manifest itself of its own accord into the real world. It can imagine itself into being. It can cross the abyss. Appearing as coincidence, spontaneous emanations, late night phenomena, supernatural occurrences, or spectral visions. Ghosts passing through a two-way mirror. Strutting and fretting their way between the hemispheres of the brain. I no longer dismiss tales of elves and angels, because their existence only depends upon which way you turn your attention. *They told me that night & day were all that I could see; / They told me that I had five senses to inclose me up. / And they inclos'd my infinite brain into a narrow circle* Terence is still digging away as I stub out my cigarette. I am feeling uneasy. I am here all alone. I reach for the lamp and take two steps towards the hole. It has only been a few months since I received the polaroid of Pinky in the post. It is hard, at times, to escape the sensation of being watched, of being under surveillance. *Not so much you having the thought as the thought having you.*

The dog was digging amongst the roots of the tree. I held the lamp aloft. The hole was much deeper than I had expected. I teetered on its brink, struggling to understand how the dog's paws could have possibly dug so deep, so quickly.

Terence stopped digging as I leaned further over feeling a twinge of vertigo. The dog had dug six feet down into the ground and the network of the tree's veins (perhaps these were its brains) were exposed and glistening, twisted in the light of the lamp. I was about to turn and walk back to the porch when I heard the sound of feathers fluttering and wings flapping. I heard a screeching. It screeched again. A bird.

What?

Terence nuzzled philosophically into my legs. The lamp in my hand was quivering, I leant in, extending it further before me. Another screech came from the hole. I gazed deeper.

*The loop of time can either be a golden loom or a very
unkind mill and the imaginative mind can be a relentless
firing kiln.*

The soil is pitch black. I could see a black thing squirming
amongst the black. I say see, but it was more like a feeling,
a big sharp feeling, a slow-moving feeling, it was hard to
know if it was coming from the ground or from me. But it
began to rotate, slowly, rhythmically, it was a needle finding
a groove. But this needle didn't skip and the tempo built
and I leant further in to see the black thing that was black
moving against a black abyss. There was a sense of relentless
rotation, and it shifted from 45 rpm to 33. A form began
to emerge, it was taking a sort of shape, but seemed to be
struggling as if the resolution of the world was too much
for it to bear. It was oleaginous and slippery yet somehow
ephemeral and diaphanous. A crow, a great black bird,
emerged from a nest that was deep in the earth.

*Earth, I read somewhere, is a word with no origin, no one
knows who named the Earth.*

Its eyes came to life. I witnessed its first ever blink and the
flash of its oily iris described to my mind that it possessed a
consciousness. The crow was recording raw data about its
newfound murky surroundings.

Very hard to relate precisely what this moment felt like.
What it truly looked like. Negative Capability. A temporary
world on the borderlands of sanity.

*With a book in your hands, you are alone, but not alone,
the wind at your window is your wife, the stars in the sky are
your children.*

Looking at this crow taking form before my eyes, I wanted to run, drop the lamp, and flee back to the cabin, however, the dog stood firm by my side. Another option was to seize this thing, whatever it was, and drag it scrawling and screeching and begging and beseeching from the page, stamp on its newly made mind in rage, or capture it and put it into a cage, and then write it well out of existence. The third was to not move. To let the originality of life take its own course, to let life write its own narrative and impose nothing authorial on the unfolding events.

I had felt this dilemma before, one evening months ago, while looking out in extraordinarily sad circumstances over the city of Los Angeles.

The bird that looked as if it had been torn from an oil slick. To fill the void of my inaction, the creature flapped its wings free of the soil as any self-respecting chimaera would do, and rose like a horrible idea from my unconscious.

The black bird wheeled and swooped about my head, the dog started barking and reared up on his hind legs. I swung the lantern at it, the air seemed to be alive with ringing tinnitus, but it was a tinnitus of wings and feathers. I staggered back from the hole. The thing was screeching, and I felt a cold bony beak brush against the curve of my cheek. I swung out at it again, I screamed, and the lantern fell from my hands. It shattered as it hit the ground, spilling fuel which exploded in a flash. Flames now seemed to be all around me, both from the earth and the air. I realised I was trapped in the purgatorial space between two realms. The bird had started circling a few feet above my head but was entirely hidden by the night. I screamed at it, and the dog ran back to the open screen door of the porch. The crow followed it, emitting a horrid strafing sound like a fighter plane running him down. Terence made it into the house and never looked back. The bird, not giving up, arced through the air and alighted on my writing table. It struck a stately pose, more representation than real. And then nonchalantly shirking the last of the earth from its wings, looked about it, like it owned the place, and then it looked directly back at me. The portholes of its eyes still haunt me like full stops.

The fire from the lantern had exhausted itself, just a few last flickering willow the wisps of flames remained. I glanced back in the direction of the bird, desperately trying to formulate a plan; I was very scared. Scared in much the same way I had been the bright frosty morning in Yorkshire when I saw that something had stolen my tape recorder with those weird songs. A fear of something that lies beyond.

All reality is but a paper mask, push push push at it and you may perhaps see the truth.

As if the crow had heard my thinking it flapped its wings, disturbing the neatly typed pages of this manuscript, the pages I had left on the table. There was something goading about that.

Before I knew what I was doing I was striding towards it, my arms outstretched. I started making a horrendous screeching cawing sound. My strategy was to mirror its own terrorising behaviour. In a second I was upon it and my approach appeared to be having the desired effect. The bird seemed afraid, if it's possible for a bird to seem scared. My foot struck the step of the porch, and the bird reared up emitting a sound that seemed to shimmer in the air. I froze, now unsure what to do, it cocked its head and blinked petulantly at me.

It started to peck up my pages, the bastard thing. Two pages, a mouthful of pages, it looked up at me, its eyes unblinking, blind, mindless like black marbles. With a squawk it took the pages between its beak, flew right at me. I leapt at it, missing it by the finest of margins, my fist returned to my side with a single feather in my clenched fist. The bird, the crow, the thing, this monstrosity from the earth that had now stolen precious pages of my novel and was circling around my head like all the millions of ideas I had previously considered but not written down. I decided to fucking kill it. I decided to chase it, chase it to the ends of the earth, to chase it to the crack of doom, to chase it at least as far as the main road. I was running headlong into some woods pursuing a bird that as far as I could tell existed only in my mind. As I staggered into the night, I felt very, very alone. The crow flew unhurriedly as if it knew I would always pursue it. I had to get those pages back, these very pages. I noticed there were other things running about the woods too, there were things that were definitely not animals, they were shapely and graceful, dancing and darting amidst the shadowy pine trees. I caught glimpses from the corner of my eye as I hurtled beneath branches and swerved around tree trunks. The crow had alighted onto a low hanging branch twenty metres away. I slowed to a halt. Eye to eye as it gleefully sucked upon my manuscript pages as if they were fresh tobacco wads.

-Give me those back you fucking bastard.

This time there would be no escape. I threw myself at the infernal feathered thing, the crow's body connected with my outstretched palms. An impossible catch, but the bird was in my hands. I squeezed down on it and extracted my pages from its maw. It spat and hissed like a fire onto which I had pissed. It was writhing, trying to peck its way out of grasp, but I had my pages back. I let the thing drop from my hands, it flapped to the ground and then rose like a balloon and started circling again about my head. It let out a bloodcurdling 'cawwwwwwww,' but I no longer cared. I walked away from the clearing as the sun chose a cinematic moment to hit the horizon, and the woods turned an ultramarine blue. I walked triumphantly back to the cabin.

***

I locked the door and took a precautionary measure, an occult practice that I had discovered months earlier in leather bound books in the Church of the Horses. I seized a salt shaker from next to the cooker and poured out a wide salt circle from the front door to the seat in which I sat, encircling me and Terrence completely. The dog was huffling to himself and glancing towards the door. I could tell by the rhythmic thwack of his tail against my leg that he was glad I had returned. I straightened the pages out before me, massaging out the creased palmistry lines of the crow's beak, rubbing them against my thigh. I read over each page, not really sure what I was looking for. Perhaps just to check if anything I had been writing correlated to what had just happened with the crow, to ascertain if I had accidentally conjured it.

These were the pages of exegesis detailing my time on tour with Tiberius and Pinky. I stared at the words typed on the page. It occurred to me that they were like road markings. The symbols that all good drivers oblige. To obey the painted shapes on the road. I opened another bottle of tequila and lit a cigarette. 30 minutes later, I was satisfied that all was present and correct. Terrence stood and growled grimly at the night outside. The sky shifted from black to blue. The distant diffident cawing of a crow. The salt circle was my seal of spiritual security. I glanced around for the tumbler of tequila and turned the final page. There were things there I had not written. There were sentences I didn't recognise. Nine pages that I had not set down. Nine new pages. Inserted after I had written about the night in Berlin where Pinky had purloined my guitar. Nine pages. Terence howled. I leapt up knocking over my tequila, there was a rustling sound and light, bare feet moving on the porch outside. I recalled the dancing figures I had just seen in the woods.

Later I would burn those nine pages when I was out in the desert of Joshua tree. All will be revealed.

I moved towards the door, terrified but desirous to see who was on the other side, to see who was waiting there on the porch.

One scorched fragment of those nine pages remains - It fluttered out the back of my notebook one afternoon years later in Highgate, I am holding it in my hand now, still trying to decipher it.

X

I climbed into the passenger seat of her Porsche. I was still soaking wet and wheezing sea-water. Pinky didn't even wait for the door to close before she accelerated out of the motel parking lot and onto the 101 heading north at high speed.

She had slipped on a beige driving mac and was looking surprisingly well put together. A flash of -Rouge Coco lipstick setting off the 'French resistance' look perfectly, but there was something about the way she was driving (slightly slipping gears) that alerted me that a nasty weather front of passive aggression had settled in.

The redwoods blurred by on either side of the road, and the last of the sun stroboscopes through the branches, a trace of the threading rain splattered against the windshield. I realised that despite my narrow escape from Poseidon, I was still in paradise, with the girl of my dreams, and, knowing my dreams, that was really saying something. She looked moody and cute and even more like an agent provocateur on an undercover mission.

- What you did back there could have got us both killed.

I looked out the window at the shapeless blurring shadows.

-You had just told me that Tiberius is writing his way around death. Perhaps I was just putting it to the test.

I opened the window and the air roared like a banshee.

-I am sorry, I really am sorry.

She glanced sidewards at me, the hint of a smile flashed over her face and I thought all might be saved.

-Could you just put a record on or something please?

I rifled in my back pocket and retrieved the copy of the Elton John album the old man had given me, it had survived the sea. I slipped the CD into the player and as the bankrupting string section of 'Goodbye Yellow Brick Road' kicked in I saw distant lights of the approaching town of Big Sur up ahead, blurred by the rain but still brightly viridescent.

-Pink, would you mind if we pulled over when you see a shop?

-Why?

-I just want to get something.

-What?

-Cigarettes, I left mine in the sea, maybe a bottle of Mateus or something.

-Ok, fine. She said with another sideways glance.

We passed a handful of big houses at the edge of town until the red neon of a local store appeared a few hundred feet away. Pinky slowed and we pulled up with a squeal of brakes and thrumming rain on tarmac. Opening the door on the now torrential downpour, I asked if she wanted anything.

-A few packets of Marlboro and some water. We gotta long way to go. Maybe a Baby Ruth bar.

She stuck out her tongue.

I smiled as the Elton John song swelled and I slammed the door, scampering towards the glow of the convenience store. Nodding to the clerk behind the counter and perusing the shelves I was thinking: She just said...A long way to go...I thought she said the retreat was about fifteen minutes away.

I stopped at a rack of postcards and selected a gaudy 70s rendering of Big Sur's coastline. Putting the card, a Baby Ruth, and two large bottles of water on the desk I said,
    -Can I get four packets of Marlboro Red, and do you sell postage stamps?
    The clerk nodded and reached under the desk and placed a pack of stamps before me. He then added the cigarettes to them and rang up the price. Handing him a twenty dollar bill, I remembered something else,
    -Do you have a pen I could borrow by any chance?
    Handing me back my change he nodded and placed a black ballpoint on the desk. I scurried to the back of the store shoving the cigarette boxes in my pockets. I leant against a half-empty shelf, it was to write this postcard for which I had engineered this detour.
    DEAR HIGGS, I AM AT A CONVENIENCE STORE NEAR BIG SUR. I AM WITH PINKY. GOING TO STAY WITH HER AND TIBERIUS AT THE RETREAT I MENTIONED. I HAVE NO IDEA WHERE IT IS OR HOW LONG I WILL BE THERE. IT IS ALL A BIT ODD. THERE IS NO WAY OF CONTACTING ME (POSEIDON CLAIMED MY PHONE) BUT IF I DON'T SURFACE IN TWO MONTHS PLEASE SEND HELP.
    ALL MY BEST, LEONARD.
    I dated it and addressed it to a bar in New York owned by a friend where I knew Higgs would receive it, bars are always very particular about mail. I affixed a couple of stamps and then as casually as I could returned to the clerk.
    -Is there a post box around here?

He eyed me, then gestured to a small yellow fixture on the wall.

-The mail gets collected twice a week, next collection Wednesday.

-That's fine, I said, dropping the postcard into it and smiling. I clutched the bottles to my chest and exited into the rain.

XI

She, I suspected, knew that I was up to something. Elton John was still playing on the stereo, but instead of being a comfort, his ballads of 70s excess had started to sound more like a warning or possibly even a veiled threat. I lurched back in the deep leather seat. We passed through Big Sur in a snare hit. I didn't recognise a single place-name on the passing signs. The winding wooded roads, our growing intimacy. Two people who were entirely on their own but also unspeakably close. I looked at the glowing lights of the dashboard. I glanced occasionally at the beautiful woman beside me, she was chain-smoking and driving like it was the last hour of the last ever Le Mans.

-Pinky, if you could go back in time before there were cameras and you could take a snapshot of someone, a polaroid to catch them as they really were, who would you photograph?

She turned the record down and rifled for a cigarette eyeing me suspiciously, pushing her thumbs into the steering wheel with enough force to make her cuticles flash white.

-William Blake. What about you, Honey Bunny?

I thought about a photograph of William Blake, capturing him not in gentle pliable oil paint, but snapping him there as he really was, in all his visionary glory, with the tools of creation at hand.

-Well...who would you photograph, darling?

-I would love to get a colour shot of D. H. Lawrence.

Pinky let out a little laugh,

- Why's colour so important?

- All his portraits would enrage him because he would say, 'I don't know who that man in the photographs is. No one ever recognises me!'

-Why not?

-Because his red bushy beard would always come out black in monochrome. So when people saw him in real life they never recognised him. It infuriated him. I would love to go back and get a snap of his bushy red bead, if only for his eternal peace of mind.

We drove on for a few more minutes in contemplative silence.

-I'd love to photograph Charles Bonnet too.

Pinky glanced sideways at me, a smile forming around her curled lips

-You know, the luminary French psychologist?

- Vaguely, yes, what was he known for again?

-Well, people with significant vision loss often experience vivid, complex recurrent visual hallucinations. These are known as fictive visual precepts. One characteristic of these hallucinations is that they usually are 'lilliputian,' you know like in Gulliver's travels, honey bunny?

I nodded.

-They are hallucinations in which the characters or objects appear smaller than normal, or in some way horribly deformed or demonic. I think of you in the bathroom this morning about to murder a potted plant, remember?

She laughed.

-You know that the most common hallucination is of mask-like faces or cartoons, usually childhood cartoons.

She glanced up into the rearview mirror.

-Sufferers understand that the hallucinations are not real and the hallucinations are only visual, but most are afraid to discuss their symptoms out of fear that they will be labelled totally insane.

I laughed.

-People suffering from Charles Bonnet Syndrome may experience a wide variety of hallucinations. Swirling complex coloured patterns alongside images of aliens and ghostly figures are most common, followed by weird animals, plants, or trees and sometimes simple inanimate objects. The hallucinations also often fit neatly into the person's surroundings and general state of mind. I find it fascinating.

As if to emphasise this thought she flexed her heel and toe softly against the pedal propelling us even faster along the rain-drenched road.

-Hold on, we are taking a sharp right.

The car wheeled starboard, I let my head loll on the seat, for a moment the car headlights flashed over a wall of trees and then we were careening down an even narrower road.

-Have you heard of paper streets? She said wrestling the vehicle back under control, having narrowly avoided a head-on collision with a line of trees.

-Paper streets? No but, I can imagine that there is a 'paper street' somewhere in the world.

-Paper streets are streets that *only exist on paper*. Deliberately put in by map makers or property developers in order to demarcate land that belongs to someone but hasn't yet had a road or something built on it. Other times they are made up to protect the copyright of the map, to ensure that if that particular paper street name appears in another map they can prove a rival cartographer copied it from their original map. Also called 'trap streets'.

-Trap streets? I asked, not liking the sound of where this was going.

-They're rarely acknowledged by publishers.

I eyed the road and reached for my seatbelt.

-There's whole towns named and mapped that don't actually exist. Sometimes people try to find them. Even more weirdly towns appear at the made-up place-name, as if they were magically brought to life from off the page.

-What? What are you going on about, my dear?

-Well, what happens is that someone has seen the map and gone out there looking for the town and not found it, and then decided to build a town in the exact spot named on the map. A magnificent example of reverse engineering reality. I think there's one of those towns somewhere in rural England come to think of it.

Another sharp right turn had delivered us now onto an even narrower road that had no reassuring xenon yellow streetlights. There were now just the car headlamps, lighting up the streak of double gold thread running relentlessly down the centre of the night ahead.

-Right, does this have anything to do with anything Pinky?

-Yes it does. Tiberius's retreat is in a place known as Mountweazel.

-Mountweazel?

-Mountweazel, well the place near it, it's just beyond the start of the Big Sur River. It was once going to be the town Mountweazel, well that was the name of the 'trap street' on the map that named it so.

-It was once going to be Mountweazel...

She looked back at the road. I turned to look out at the terrible reaching tree tendrils that were grazing the outside of the car, reaching out from the woodland beyond.

XII

-We are on our way there now, Leonard.

-Ok, so we are on our way to Mountweazel in order to write our way around death.

-Yes.

-You told me earlier it was fifteen minutes away. That was three hours ago.

-I may have misspoke. I can never be quite sure how long it takes to get there, what with all this.

She gestured at the night-cloaked road ahead and tapped her ash from her cigarette deftly into the tray at the same time.

-All what? *What's all this?*

-All this. All these meandering un-signposted side roads and dead-end lover's lanes.

-How far away would you say we are now?

-Hard to say, but no more than an hour or so, if this rain doesn't get any worse.

I looked out my window as the rain immediately worsened.

Why did I keep placing myself in total helpless isolation with my beautiful lovers? Women of irresistible qualities, unquantifiable capacities, insatiable appetites, incorrigible tenacities? Women who seemed willing to breathe me in like pale fire and exhale fine ash. Ash that I would later mix with whisky on lonely late nights and overwrought writing to formulate a bright brutal ink with which I will make my gilded confession on the page. It occurred to me that there was objectively very little difference in the actual experience, in the actual atmosphere, inside this Porsche, from that of the stone silent Church on the moors. You can leave, but you always take yourself with you, I thought, is a line from a song I would never ever want to write.

-What?

I turned my head to see Pinky staring at me.

-What the fuck were you just saying?

-Did I just say that out loud?

-You're being weird.

That's fucking unbelievable coming from you – I thought, making very sure this time that I was thinking it, keeping my lips firmly shut. Pinky shot me another look and turned the radio back up.

***

I awoke with my head hitting the dashboard, there was a terrible squealing sound. The interior of the car was thrashing and shuddering. Pinky was screaming, and then she stopped screaming, then the car stopped, and I rebounded back into my seat hard enough to make every unstowed thought swim for a second. The car had come to a dead halt. Pinky was hurt. There was a smell in the air that reminded me of my childhood. Iron, gasoline, and abraded rubber.

Pinky was sprawled out onto my lap, a fine gossamer string of spit and blood connecting her head to my right leg. There is always a siren to alert you to shipwrecks, in this case there was the ringing in my ears. I put my hand tentatively, onto her shoulder, *please don't be dead*.

-We hit a snake.

She groaned.

The stereo was still playing Elton John. I looked out the bleary windows, we were, thank god, still on the road. Pinky was coming around.

-I think we hit a giant snake.

She slurred while easing herself up. I gently held her head in my hands and examined her face. The bleeding was not that serious, she had a small split in her lower lip. I rifled around the seats and found a box of tissues and gave her one, her eyes met mine, a dazed distant look drifted over her irises. She sat back in the seat heavily, and rubbed the side of her head with the other hand while dabbing at her lip.

-Ouch, she said.

-We are not having a good day, sweetheart, I smiled and brushed the stray strands of hair from her face.

-What happened? I was asleep.

-A massive fucking snake was suddenly crossing the road, I swerved to avoid it and the car spun.

-Well, we are still on the road, luckily, we could have gone straight into the trees.

She didn't reply, just peered forward at the headlamps that were beaming into the woods. Clearly processing the thought that if we had gone into the trees, we would both be dead right now.

-I am going to check the car. Give me a moment.

I opened the car door and stepped out. The rain had eased off, but the air was thick and felt as wet as the tropics. We were a very long way into the woods by now. The car was at a 45 degree angle, sprawled across both lanes of the road. The gently idling engine was the only sound apart from the murmurs of the breeze in the trees.

I walked around the front of the Porsche to check for damage. I crouched down near the wheel arch and was relieved to see that the axles were intact. I then did a complete circuit kicking each of the tyres in turn and then walked to the front of the car and squinted into the headlamps. Yes, I was fairly sure the car was still road-worthy. I walked around to the passenger side and was just about to open the door when I remembered the snake. I stopped and peered back down the road past the black scrawls where the tyres had zigzagged over the road. Beyond these demarcations there was, just visible in the starlight and the red glow of the rear taillights, a huge black snake sprawled across the road. I froze. Pinky was right, we had really hit a huge black snake at high speed. It was bigger than any snake I thought indigenous to California. It was bigger than any snake I thought indigenous to the world. It must have been nineteen feet long and as thick as an undersea power cable.

Breathing slowly and steadying my nerves, I walked very softly towards it. I was possessed by morbid curiosity. I walked past the car, and in a few deep breaths I was standing just in front of it. Was it dead? It hadn't moved at all, but it was hard to be sure. It seemed more irregularly shaped than a normal snake, and it was of a scale unprecedented in the animal kingdom. It had an oddly knotted body covered with many small horned protuberances and it was much thicker at one end than the other. It was absolutely monstrous, grotesque. I shuddered. The thing I should do is turn around and get back into the car immediately, but I was captivated by its horrible dimensions, by its sheer perverse scale. I felt my heart pumping adrenaline because for the third time today I was confronting a monster, I stepped closer, and leant forward to get a better look.

I blinked hard and peered intently at the snake, seeking out its head to try and assess if it was still alive. I just wanted to see the creature's eyes.

I let out a peel of laughter. Straightening up I took a step forward and kicked the snake in its belly as hard as I could. It skittered inanimately down the road a few feet. It was a fallen tree branch.

Shaking my head and laughing, I walked back to the car. It was an eerie scene, but all the danger had drained away and the adrenaline converted itself to a head rush of joie de vivre. I climbed back into my seat.

-Well, the snake is dead. And the car is fine, Pinky.

-Good, what kind of snake was it?

-A Branch Snake darling, lesser spotted in this part of the world.

-What?

-It was just a tree branch, Pinky, and it's fine.

She laughed a small laugh and looked at me.

-We could have died.

-Second time today for me, so to be honest I am feeling rather lucky. Two fateful escapes in one rotation of the earth. Hopping over fatal destiny like a hurdler.

I lit a cigarette and peered out the window.

-We should move the car, if anything comes along they will wipe us out.

Pinky put her hands on the wheel. Her bottom lip was a little swollen but looked rather succulent, I leant over and kissed her. We actually kissed for quite a long time, a surge of stinging serotonin flooding our shaken souls, a tang of blood mingled with lust for a trembling moment.

-Also, how far are we now from Mountweazel?

-I don't think I can drive Leonard. My eyes aren't working right. You will have to drive.

I smiled and took a drag on my cigarette.

-I am really not sure that's a good idea. We'd really be pushing our luck, if after everything that has happened today, I got behind the wheel of a sports car.

-You're going to have to, Leonard, we can't stay here, it really, really isn't a good idea, it's not safe. The retreat is only a few more miles.

-I've only driven three times in my life, and one of those was a go kart when I was six.

She opened the door and walked slowly, unsteadily around the front of the car. I saw her eyes flash red as they turned to look at me in full beam. She opened my door, and said,

-Get out, you have to drive.

XI

I got the hang of driving pretty quick, the car was automatic so it felt just like playing a video game. In this level of the game, I was tasked with driving Pinky Capote towards a place that doesn't really exist. A mythical place in the mountains where a magician awaits.

-How am I doing?

-You are doing brilliantly. You are my very own Steve Mcqueen, honey bunny.

46 minutes passed. There hadn't been a signpost or turning since well before we hit the snake. Pinky had put on the Rolling Stones, and I had taken to driving, like a duck to crack cocaine. It was actually quite relaxing. The road was

getting narrower and the whirlpool of branches overhead had become like a ghostly tunnel of love, and I had become intoxicated by the speed.

-Follow the curve to the left here, and lay off the gas a little.

I was negotiating the curves like they were the flowing patterns of speech in an easygoing conversation. It was like my many anxiety dreams about driving, just without the anxiety, and I somehow knew this time even when I woke up, I would still be driving. I glanced to my right, Pinky was smiling at me dreamily, with her feet up on the dashboard. She seemed totally relaxed and trusting in my dilettante driving abilities.

-Pinky, you know the snake back there, the snake that almost killed us, the snake that wasn't really a snake, the snake that was in fact a fallen tree branch, the snake that is the reason that I am now driving this car?

- I remember.

-In one sense it really was a snake in the road.

-I thought you said it was a branch.

-And you know you said the one person you would like to photograph is William Blake, well...

She laughed and wiggled her foot in front of my face.

-Slow down here, where the road bears right, we have to look for the turning. It's a single-lane dirt track, it's the only way of finding Mountweazel.

I nodded and slowed the car. Sure enough there was a very narrow turning, a barely noticeable gap in the relentless run of trees next to the road. It was amazing she had spotted it, or remembered where it was. I slowed the car to a halt, craning my neck to get a better look at the worryingly steep drop from the tarmac onto the dirt track.

-Are you sure this is the place? Are you sure this car can take it?

Pinky nodded.

-This is the place, and I've done this drive many times.

I turned the wheel and we pulled off the road and turned sharply onto the dirt track that dropped away into the forest. The headlights barely made a dint on the caliginous darkness. It was unwise to drive any faster than twenty miles per hour in these conditions. My foot was constantly hovering over the brake pedal, in case of anything, be it real or imaginary, appearing ahead. After a few minutes, the track opened up. The trees on either side began to thin a little and it was suddenly possible to see the start of a meadow. And there too, shimmering silver and white in the sylvan moonlight, was a fast-flowing river, winding its way along next to us.

-There we go, there's the river, it's not far now.

She gazed out her window at the river.

The automatic gearbox dropped down into second as we hit a patch of gravel, the car jolted, and Pinky and I bounced out of our seats. The road inclined so steeply upwards that there was a glimpse of the gibbous moon and a few stars, before it angled sharply left and down. A magnificent vista opened up before us. An oval meadow surrounded by miles of unbroken redwood forest canopy that rippled in the moonlight. A thick carpet of trees, rising along a cresting range of mountains, ascending to one mighty peak that towered above the landscape. Wisps of nimbus clouds slithered around its summit.

In the centre of the meadow stood a stately house. The many windows of its facade gazed blindly back at us. The glimmering lights of its thrusting porch picked out the elaborate gothic rococo architecture.

I let out an audible, slightly melodramatic exhalation.

-There she is. Pinky said softly,

- She?

- Hecate House, - it's a she.

I eased my foot down, and we accelerated over the gravel drive towards her.

XII

There was a small car park that was full of cars. At least twenty, parked haphazardly all over the place. There was something about that I didn't like. We rolled to a stop by the steep steps up to the porch. I turned off the engine. The evening air had the sweetness of honeysuckle   upon it, but there was also another scent that I could not immediately place. A pungent floral bouquet with an acrid, almost swinish, undernote, like something's flesh had recently been badly burnt. I walked to the boot to retrieve our bags. Pinky was already at the top of the stairs and stood glamorously in the amber light of the gas lamps.

-Welcome to Hecate House, you are here at last.

I followed her up the stairs, across the wide-roofed porch that encircled the house on three sides.

-What is this place, Pinky?

-It was built in the late 1920s by Randolph Hearst, you know, the weirdo millionaire famous for setting up RKO broadcasting and also war profiteering. Well known for being a total freak. He built Hecate House for his favourite mistress. It was supposed to be a hunting lodge and bolt hole far from prying eyes. But he must have ended the affair before getting much use out of it, or out of the mistress for that matter. No one knows what really happened. Anyway, by the time Tiberius acquired it, it had been shut up and abandoned for years. It hasn't changed at all from the day it was built. Just the way we like it.

The planking of the porch creaked beneath my feet. The silence of the night was broken by the screech of an owl. I looked back at the river. Pinky rummaged in her handbag for something. With a flourish she produced a large set of keys, so ornate and shapely that for a moment I mistook them for jewellery. She glanced back at me, flashing a grin, and I followed her in.

The glowing single bulb of a grand Tiffany lamp illuminated a spacious oak hallway bedecked with antlers and hunting ephemera. Stepping over the threshold of the house had a definite sense of stepping back a century. Pinky bent to remove her ankle boots and placed them neatly in a rack that contained a wide array of shoes. It looked like a gathering of an eccentric large family. Cowboy boots, climbing boots, a pair of handmade Parisian high heels, a pair of brogues, some Armani slip ons. I added my battered Doc Martens to their number.

-Do you want anything?

-No, no, I think all I need is to sleep right now.

-I will show you to your room.

Your room...not our room.

She was halfway up the thick-carpeted stairs, one hand on the balustrade.

-Coming?

The first flight of stairs opened onto a large landing, there another ornate lamp emitting an orange hazy light, just enough to make out the array of dusty antiques dotted here and there. A huge stuffed bear loomed grotesquely out of the far end of the corridor. Oil paintings of young women in various states of undress, soft erotica which would have been scandalous at the time they were first hung upon these walls. There were several oak doors on this landing, all of them closed. Pinky was already on her way up a second flight of stairs.

The second landing was much the same, but this one had a large copper vase at the far end instead of a stuffed bear. This huge vase was covered in cuneiform, it looked vaguely Greek. Pinky paused by a door waiting for me to catch up.

-Your chamber, Mr. Leonard...

She pushed open the heavy oak door revealing a well-proportioned room, illuminated by the moonlight falling through the tall casement window on the far side. The plush Tudor bed, replete with scarlet velvet bedspread glowing under the bedside lamp. I stepped in, placing my bag down softly on the worn rug that covered the creaking floorboards. I turned to Pinky. She had lingered at the threshold.

-Are you not coming in?

-Not tonight, baby.

-Where are you going to sleep? Are we not sleeping together here?

-Another night. Tonight you've got your room and your bed all to yourself. Tiberius prefers us to work this way. I have my own room, but you will see me first thing in the morning, bright and early.

Before I could react to this annoying new stipulation, she had closed the door sharply. I heard her bare feet crossing the landing, the stairs creaking beneath them.

I stood still, feeling a little unnerved by the new arrangements. My weary eyes settled on the baroque writing table by the window. I heard footsteps, and the door opened. Pinky came in without a word, and taking my head in her hands, kissed me deeply, her tongue searching for mine. She coiled herself around me, her hands slipping down my spine, a nipping bite of her teeth to my lower lip. I pulled her to me and let my hands slide searchingly, grasping her bottom firmly, I hoped to rouse her to fuck on the scarlet bedspread, but she pulled away, placing her hands on my chest. She looked up at me admonishingly, my heart was throbbing. She winked and darted out the door, drawing it closed with a click.

I sat down heavily on the antique bed and reached into my bag for my cigarettes.

The window opened more easily than I expected, and I leant out, dragging hard, the nicotine made my head swim as I gazed out into the foreboding landscape. The line of gigantic trees and then the mountain range and the stark watchful precipice of the tallest peak of Mountweazel looming over all. I felt a very long way from home, but it occurred to me that I no longer had a home.

I heard a sound and froze. My cigarette ember glowed. My spine tensed.

It came again. I listened at the window. It sounded like the staccato half-steps of something hooved. It came again. It was below me on the decking of the porch, moving softly to and fro. Yes, it was definitely the clatter of hooves. It must be an animal, but what kind out here. A deer?

I listened closely, but nothing stirred. I leant a little further out the window, craning my neck to see the porch and the front of the house below. In response to my motion there came another clatter of the hooves. I thought of rushing onto the landing, of calling out for Pinky. I told myself to calm down. I was safe here in my room. The hooves clattered again. I started and yelped, slamming my head into the window pane above me.

I saw a figure dart from under the awning, run across the gravel and onto the grass of the meadow. It was a familiar flexing form. It was Pinky. Her blonde hair was unmistakable in the moonlight. She was wearing just a white night shirt, her lissome legs flashed silvery in the gloom. She was running as fast as she could towards the treeline, I stood aghast, my cigarette burning down around my fingers. She covered the meadow in seconds. A confused, betrayed feeling came over me, it crystallised into a sensation of horror. She really is insane. A salty taste swelled in the back of my mouth. She had reached the edge of the treeline where she turned and lingered. She was looking back at me in the window. Then she was gone, vanishing into twenty million ancient trees.

XII

I awoke with a start, the brilliant morning sunshine streaming through the casement. I squinted and Pinky leant in over me, making me start in surprise.

-Good morning, sunshine!

She beamed and leant in closer, proffering something to me. I blinked hard and sat up on my elbows, her beautiful smile broke into laughter. She was wafting a mug of steaming black coffee at me. The pungent scent of bitter alkaloid steaming spectrally in the morning sunlight. She hopped along the edge of the bed. Her grin was an ecstastic tide, like that of a zealous, experimentally minded doctor, or a newbie torturess.

-Here take this, it's so damn good.

I took the cup and placed it on the bedside table, not taking my eyes off her.

-What the fuck were you doing last night, Pinky?

Her smile cooled.

-What do you mean, Leonard? I said goodnight to you, and then I was getting my beauty sleep.

I shook my head at her barefaced lie and sat up against the headboard.

-Pinky, I saw you, I saw you from my window, you were wearing the nightshirt you are wearing now, I saw you run headlong into the trees, and I know you know that I saw you.

-Leonard, were you having one of your visions again? Is this like the real and imaginary snake?

-Pinky. I only came here for you, have the decency to tell me the truth.

-Maybe you were having one of those Charles Bonnet syndrome moments, baby?

I slammed my fist into the scarlet bedsheet bunched around me.

-Show me your feet! I screamed.

She burst into a melodious laugh.

-Jesus.

She rolled backwards on the bed, as she did so, I noticed she was wearing nothing but the white night shirt. I was fairly sure she noticed me notice. She swung both feet onto the bed in front of me, leaning back and lifting them petulantly towards my face.

-Go ahead, have a good look, inspect away, mister detective. She licked her lips, ever-so-slightly adjusting the open angle of her thighs.

Her soles were bare and clean as the driven snow. There was not a mark on them.

I pushed them away from me and looked towards the window. In the distance, I could see the range of mountains highlighted against the brilliant azure background of the limitless morning sky.

-This doesn't really prove anything. You obviously showered when you got back from whatever it was you were doing in the woods. You know that's insanely dangerous. What about all the fucking bears and god knows what else.

Pinky was just staring at me. Now it was her who was wearing a mask of total feigned bewilderment, she shook her head slowly.

-I really have no idea what you are talking about. Clearly, you didn't sleep well. Please calm down, I think you just had a nightmare or something.

-The only nightmare I am having is you, Pinky. I still know the difference between being asleep and being awake, despite your best efforts to the contrary.

-Ok, mister. Look, we can talk about this more in a minute. I just wanted to wake you up because it's breakfast soon, you get to meet everyone. We eat all our meals together here at Hecate House, and of course Tiberius is here. You can ask him all those endless fucking questions you have saved up for him.

I reached for the coffee and gulped some down. It was really, really good. About that, she wasn't lying. She was looking at me, her bewildered expression had morphed into a fairly good imitation of concern.

-There is a bathroom down the hall. Get yourself fixed up and I will see you downstairs in the dining room in ten minutes. It's right by the stairs, you will hear us. Everyone is just so excited to meet you.

She flashed me one of her sweetest apple pie–smile, which came off as mildly pornographic and then jumped off the bed and was out the door.

A few minutes later, under the scorching jet of water coming from the most antique shower I had ever seen actually functioning, my head was clearing as I took in great lungfuls of steamy air. I resolved that I would not let her brush off last night. I had to start this thing on some kind of equal footing, establish an even psychological keel.

I looked at my face in the fog of the mirror. I didn't entirely recognise myself. The sun and everything else that had happened recently had caused a slight change to my appearance. It was something around the eyes. I spat toothpaste into the basin and then hastily changed into a clean pair of black trousers and a fresh white shirt.

Descending the second flight of stairs, I heard the sounds of the breakfast in full swing. The unmistakable auditory fingerprint of Tiberius's laughter echoing from the dining room that ran the full length of the left-hand side of the house. Hearing his familiar ribald guffaw was a tonic. I felt my spirits lift, and I was excited to be here, despite last night. A smile came to my face, I hopped down the last few steps and turned the corner into the dining room. I froze, stunned by the scene that met me.

There was a long wide dining table of exquisitely carved French oak. On either side was a row of striking young women, four on one side, three on the other, all dressed in white flowing Hellenistic dresses. At the far left hand side was Pinky, she was seated directly next to Tiberius who was at the head of the table.

Tiberius Red's eyes had locked with mine the moment I entered. He was dressed entirely in red. A long red yogi master's robe. His cyan blue eyes were glinting in the bright morning light and clashing with his incarnadine garments. To his right was an empty place laid for breakfast, next to that there was a large well-built man with dark hair wearing a simple black tunic. He, like all the other dining guests, was staring at me in silence. Next to him were two more young women, one looked like she was French or Spanish, the other was Japanese. Then finally, next to her, to my utter amazement, was the brunette popstar with the flashing green eyes. The brunette who liked Vonnegut, the one I had played a deranged game of hide-and-seek with at the Chevaliers's wedding. The brunette who had leaned in and whispered her name in my ear that evening. She whispered the name, 'Lucia.'

The smile on my face soured to a sallow rictus grin. Time passed in the way that it does when you are listening to a lecture in a language you do not understand. A grandfather clock was ticking. Tiberius rose and broke the silence.

-Mr. Leonard. You made it. We are so very happy to have you here. You are, once again, my humble guest.

He strode around the table, his robes billowing and his long bearish arms outstretched. He embraced me firmly, patchouli oil and his sickly spiced smell filled my nostrils. He led me briskly towards the empty place set for breakfast beside him at the head of the table. I felt all the eyes of the other guests follow me as we orbited awkwardly around the room. He pretty much placed me down on the long bench. The large man in black moved up with a grunt. My eyes met Pinky's, she was smiling widely, a little too widely. There was something in her look that felt like the memory of a terrible teenage prank. Tiberius returned to his throne-like seat, he directed a broad inquiring smile at me. It was as if he was trying to read some text that was inked on my face without me knowing it.

-So, what do you make of our beloved MountWeazel? Isn't Hecate House a total babe?

-I mean, yes, it's wonderful, it's one of the most gorgeous spots I've ever seen. This house, this house is like something out of a...

-A dream isn't it? – Pinky cut in.

Tiberius was still gazing at me.

-It's perfect for the work we do up here, Leonard. It's really the only place for it.

I smiled back, meekly.

-For what?

-You shall see. He snapped, narrowing his eyes.

-Now eat, you must be starving after your long journey here. Pinky tells me it was rather eventful.

I looked at Pinky, but she was gazing at Lucia. Tiberius leant forward and poured more of the delicious coffee from a Victorian coffee pot. Replacing it on the table and shooting me one final probing look of assessment, he rose to his feet, placing both his ornately bejewelled hands on the table before him.

-My dear guests, enjoy your nourishing breakfasts.

He dropped a perfectly toasted slice of spelt bread onto the plate before me.

-It is so exciting to have you all here for another of our little gatherings. This is the one we have all been waiting for, I suspect. Now, we shall reconvene in one hour, down at the stone circle. That is where we shall begin our great work.

His eyes roamed the table meeting each pair of eyes individually. A parental look played over his face. Then he turned with a flourish and exited the dining room doing one of his odd dances.

XIII

-Can you actually believe this place is real? It makes the whole world feel enchanted again. The willowing trees, the holy mountain, the sacred silence. The sky, the meadow, the grass, the tinkling of the river. It's all here beneath the nurturing eye of Apollo. Come kiss me under the Californian sun, baby Honey Bunny!

Pinky was kissing me and squeezing my hand quite firmly as we and the other guests wound our way over the meadow. We walked across the gentle descent towards the tree-lined perimeter of the complex that I was now beginning to understand as Mountweazel.

-Yes, Pinky, it is so beautiful here, the place would probably make François Boucher picturesquely wet himself.

Pinky squealed with laughter and kissed me some more. We were walking the exact same route I'd seen her take last night at four in the morning. I chose not to mention that, there was no point, not just yet.

I glanced around at our companions. Four of the young ladies were blonde and deeply tanned. Their hair tousled and greasy but in a pleasing unkempt way. One of them was much fairer skinned, so pale she was almost albino. She was walking ahead of us singing a song in a language I didn't recognise, but I grasped what she was expressing. It all harmonised with Pinky's notion of paradisal enchantment.

I thought we were heading into the woods but just before the line of trees intersected the meadow, the hollow of an amphitheatre appeared. We halted abruptly, the well-built dark-haired man stood directly behind Pinky and I as we paused. She squeezed my hand even harder, he strode past us and began, long-legged, like a pink muscular crab, to descend the steep-sided hollow.

-This is the start of what I told you about in Vienna, baby.

She whispered.

-It's the start of a process. There is something special about you being here, it's a wonderful secret and I am so happy you came with me. I will tell you everything, I promise, after we have started. Oh and just one itty-bitty little thing...

She ran her hands down her white cotton dress and bit her lip.

-You are not really supposed to know about Tiberius's big plans, what we are going to be working on here, that thing I told you about.

-The writing his way around...

She scowled harshly and put her fingers to my lips.

-That's enough of that honey.

She leant in, clearly trying to disguise our hushed conversation as a stolen moment of intimacy.

-Just don't mention anything about that please, it wouldn't be...Tiberius would be very disappointed in me if he knew I had told you.

She widened her eyes at me in an imploring look, but before I had a chance to reply, she had seized my hand and begun pulling me down into the amphitheatre.

***

Tiberius was seated in the lotus position at the centre of nine standing stones, stones that did not happen to be there by accident. Stumbling down the slope, I realised that the theatricality of the environment was intended to heighten the unconscious sense of expectation, to escalate the sense of drama, and to place Tiberius in the fovea of intrigue.

The group of guests broke like a flock of sparrows and alighted upon the stone pillars. They did so with precision, as if rehearsed. They all knew their places. Pinky let go of my hand and took her own seat, two stones down from the twelve o'clock position. Everyone had a stone except me. There was just one left, at the six o'clock position, so I strode towards it, displaying more confidence than I inwardly possessed. I sat down glancing around. My eyes came to rest upon the omphalos presence of Tiberius, clad in his red robes at the very centre of it all.

-We all love music! He exclaimed.

-Music is to be Muse-ish. Muse-like? To resemble the muses when they are being icky? Mus-icky? Muse-icky— you get me?

The dark well-built man let out a low chuckle, he leant forward and slapped his rippling meaty thigh, I realised he was German. The other guests were all smiling, albeit thinly.

-I don't wish to insult the immense intelligence gathered before me. A combined collective IQ of 1985 I'd say, give or take.

He made eye contact with each one of us in turn in a slow rotation. His face resembled a sly humanoid camera.

-By virtue of the fact that you are sitting in this circle, you are already innately aware of the secret relationship between music and magic. Isn't that right?

He paused, visibly pleased with his opening oration.

-The origin of magic is about a state of mind. It is about space and time. Let's talk a little bit about the origins of magic:

All eyes were fixed upon him, he was in his bleeding element.

-It's hard to say for sure but I'd place the origin of magic at around 7000 years ago, during what is known as the cognitive revolution. That is the time when we started to get a real handle on language as a species. To really grasp hold of words. But the weird thing is language actually precedes consciousness.

He said this in a low stage whisper.

-That is very important.

-To be precise, language precedes consciousness of the *modern* kind, the one we all enjoy today. Before that we had a basic animal awareness, but it wasn't until we had language that our modern consciousness emerged.

With this statement he produced an orange, seemingly out of nowhere and holding it up wistfully added,

-Funny thing about an orange, is it's *orange*, and it's called an *orange*.

He laughed a hysterical laugh and started to peel it methodically. I wasn't sure if I should laugh too. He continued through a mouthful of fruit.

-Now that astonishing jump between simple primordial awareness, and the lights coming on in the entire *Haunted*

Palace of the mind is the experience of suddenly having a consciousness. The unexpected arrival of a modern mind inside our skulls. What must that have felt like?

I glanced at Pinky, she was riveted by Tiberius.

-What must have that felt like to those human beings who were alive during that transition? It would have been absolutely terrifying. Imagine all the voices in your head before you had a word for 'thoughts'? Imagine all the pictures in your head before you had a word for 'images'? Or all those 'dreams' before you had a concept of consciousness? Where could they have come from? Our ancestors would have assumed that if not from gods, then from spirits and other supernatural forces. It would have felt like you were possessed by demons that chattered away and showed you hallucinatory, disturbing internal visions. What a crazy time that must have been.

He popped another segment of the orange in his mouth and chewed down hard.

-Magic was originally our way of understanding our new consciousness. A kind of folk psychology. It was also the birth of representational art, and abstraction. Magic is almost one and the same as art, and still is, despite the best efforts of materialism, and scientism. Magick remains, unchanged as it was at the birth of mankind, and the birth of the mind.

He inhaled sharply:

-And at the core of magic was ecstasy. It was ecstasy that was being evoked by the very first shamans with their dancing and singing at magical rituals. Drums, fires, masks, and sacrifice. They were creating almost the entirety of our modern culture in doing so. Dance, storytelling, theatre, painting, songs, music. All genres and disciplines of art emerged from those early shamanic rituals intended to invoke a pure form of ecstasy.

Pinky was nodding enthusiastically.

-They realised that art was a way of altering the collective consciousness of their community. It was a way of evoking the sacred power of ecstasy. It was their first god or goddess and so Dionysus was born.

He was staring directly at Lucia. She was dressed differently from the rest of the guests. She was wearing a black chiffon dress and the well-made Parisian high heels I had spotted in the shoe rack last night. The same ones she had been wearing the first night we met in the Henry Miller library.

She was staring right back at Tiberius but did not seem at all as supplicant and enthralled as the rest of us. She actually looked mildly annoyed. For some reason this made me smile. I internalised this smile in a way that must have made me look like a young and ambitious serial killer.

Tiberius reached for another segment of the orange which he held between his forefinger and thumb. His eyes flickered to Lucia's for a hesitant second before he continued to speak.

-Now, a great deal of time passes. We humans start to evolve and we somehow get the idea of living in settlements and then the agricultural revolution happens. This makes bigger urban dwelling possible. Towns and citadels emerge, and once you have civilization with a food chain supplied by organised farms, you start to have a population freed from constant toil and labour. Meaning, instead of people spending their whole time working the land, they can start to do lots of other things. Alternative activities. Entertainment. Parties start to happen. Psycho-spiritual explorations occur. So inevitably, what you get next in this new society just finding its existential feet is a priest caste. The priest caste is going to set up formal religions, or at least the beginnings of formal religions. This is in essence a power grab that is going to take away traditional folk magic's spiritual component. Seizing control of ecstasy. Renting out the numinous is big business. Then, of course, with the loss of innate spirituality you are going to get those bastards artists, poets, writers, and musicians, suddenly coming into existence, they are going to usurp and monetise magic's visionary role.

Tiberius inhaled deeply, he threw his head back to the sky. The wind rustled around the trees as if in response to his very utterance. He returned his gaze to his mesmerised audience.

-But, that's all ok. That is what they call 'progress.' So magic lost its place in this new civilization, but magic had still got 'science' and 'medicine' and 'the inner world' and this all ticks along very nicely until...

The wind rustled about his robes.

-The Renaissance. The fucking Renaissance man, at which point science is totally cleaved from magic. It is torn from its twin.

-Up until that point, magic and science were one and the same thing. They weren't even running in parallel, they were totally entwined, indistinguishable. Take, for example,

Doctor John Dee. He was one of the first scientists, one of the giants that Isaac Newton was standing on the shoulders of. wrote the book on navigation that made Great Britain a famously naval nation. His visionary insights provided its monstrous British Sea Power, and its Empire. Dee wrote books on mathematics that are the foundations of today's computers. He was the great 'scientist' of his day, and even invented the first secret service. But he spent most of his life talking to spirit beings, which for diplomacy's sake he had to describe as 'angels'. He was staring into crystal balls and studying the tarot. You see he really thought of himself as a magician, as an occultist.

He took a dramatic caesural pause, revelling in a moment of high oratory drama. I was now absolutely certain he was a raving lunatic, but I was thoroughly enjoying myself.

-So, science and medicine, these are more or less taken away from magic to become subsumed into parts of the new modern culture. Hence the origin of the word 'culture' comes from the word 'cult.' See what I am saying, my beautiful babies?

He tossed away the remains of the orange, chortling to himself.

-Magic, at this point in the story, is left limping along with the 'inner world,' and it is just hanging on to 'ecstasy' because that is the one thing that culture cannot actually assimilate. An urban settled culture has absolutely no place for ecstasy. Ecstasy is the last thing you want if you are the one in charge. You outlaw people becoming ecstatic left, right, and centre, because they won't do that according to a timetable. They won't do it according to a shift-pattern, according to a hard day's taxable work. It is spontaneous and socially disruptive. It is also emancipating. So if you are the government, you definitely don't want any ecstasy spontaneously occurring in your populace.

Tiberius took a cheroot from a tin. He brought his white zippo to bear upon its tip, for an instant the flame engulfed his entire visage.

-The last thing any civilization wants is its hard-won people becoming ecstatic. The formal religions, they now had their well-paid priesthoods to maintain. Anointed ones who acted as intermediaries between you and the gods. They were a profitable prophylactic. A harsh and holy condom. An institutionalised, bureaucratic, and beleaguered Rubber Johnnie, intended to prevent you from coming into direct contact with any of that pure ecstasy stuff. Preventing any spiritual impregnation. Ladies and gentlemen, during your stay in Hecate House, as your humble host, I want nothing more than for you to touch upon the bare flesh of the very gods themselves as often as you can. Fucking is life. Fucking is god.

He dragged upon the cheroot, his eyes locked with mine for only an instant. I nodded back at him eagerly.

-So, yes, we still had ecstasy left, we had hung on to it, at least those of us who knew how to conjure it had.

He held his hands behind his back and for a moment I thought he was actually going to produce a rabbit from a hat.

-Other than conjuring, my friends, we just have 'the interior world.' A world that brings us crashing down into 1910 Vienna with Sigmund Freud and Carl Jung. These two goddamn motherfuckers come along, and they are using ideas that had been commonplace in occult circles for centuries. They start doing 'psychoanalysis.'

He chuckled, his arms by his sides, in a Charlie Chaplin–like gesture, hapless but insanely powerful.

-Psychoanalysis is just occultism dressed up in a lab coat. Psychoanalysis can never be a real science, it is talking about the interior world. A world in which things cannot be reproduced in a laboratory. Where the things of study are not really available for empirical proof. But nonetheless, the inner world was taken from magic as well.

He cracked his knuckles glaring at the ground.

As the 20th century began to have its first contractions, when the womb of life began to want to expel humanity from within, all magic had left was theatre. So it found itself with pretty frocks, fancy words, and nicely painted wands and the playful simulations of rituals. The dramatic air, the eerie, the weird, the aura of spookiness. Shakespeare, Marlowe, Lovecraft, The Beatles and Black Sabbath. It is this 'spookiness' that has attracted people. It is what gave birth to the entertainment industry.

He ran his fingers through his long main of thick black hair and finished his cheroot.

-So, what I want to suggest to you all is that over the coming months, you all collaborate to compose new songs. Create new ideas. Let us combine your talents into something that cannot be multiplied, quantified, measured or eventually manufactured and mindlessly consumed. Something new and eternal but not for everyone. Not for the masses. Not music for mass consumption.

-By throwing some rune stones, I will select a partner for you to write with over the next few days. When the time is right, we will all reconvene to hear these new songs.

Tiberius rummaged in his robe and produced a small leather pouch. He emptied the contents into his hand. I cast my eye to Pinky, who was clutching her legs in schoolgirl excitement. My eye flitted to Lucia, directly opposite her, she had her head in her hands, her dark trestles obscuring her face. Her shapely legs were outstretched but visibly tense and pretty.

Tiberius was talking to himself. I couldn't hear what he was saying over the wind willowing about the branches. Then he thrust forward in a balletic lunge, his hand extended releasing the contents of his palm. Two small stones fell on the ground before him. Rune stones. He gazed at them and I saw his beard bristle.

-One goes to seven. He declared.

The Japanese lady stood up and walked into the centre of the stone circle. She was joined by the dark Germanic man, who had been sitting at the seven o'clock position. I realised it was a kind of lottery...or possibly some sort of variation on car keys in a bowl.

Tiberius reset, and the action was repeated, as the runes fell, another couple from the circle peeled off, ascending the hill, deep in conversation, it was the French lady and the albino-looking girl. Tiberius threw the rune stones once more.

-And will six go to three.

I looked up, Tiberius's eyes met mine, squinting a sharp 'I dare you' look at me.

I walked towards the centre of the circle. Lucia was moving in a straight line to transect mine. I had hitherto always thought I was just dabbling with magic. That I could somehow knowingly rise above the occult. I could wear a mask with my music and get away with daft dramatic things like moving to a haunted church or singing diabolical blues songs in slaughterhouses at midnight. But as Lucia and I convened at the nexus point of that circle, I began to realise my mistake.

I hadn't been playing at magic, magic had been playing at me.

Lucia took my hand, but instead of turning to climb up the steep sides of the amphitheatre, she gestured and I followed her, like the night we first met, into the darkening forest.

XIV

We stumbled into a clearing, she turned to me, her thin dress fluttering about her nubile form. It was hard to put an age on her, she was both 22 and 32 at the same time. She looked at me with the wide eyes of a pythoness and I could see before she spoke what she had on her mind.

-It's you! She said, glancing back to ensure we were out of earshot.

-Well, what the fuck was all that about? She laughed and unleashed a brilliant daddy-bought-and-paid-for smile. Flashing her orthodontically perfect oxide-white teeth like a beautiful brunette high fashion rabbit.

-I think he explained all of magic from its origin right up to the modern day. I toured with him a few months ago and there was a lot of this sort of chat. *A lot.*

-You toured with him? What do you do? Are you a musician too? You didn't really tell me anything about yourself the other night.

I tried to smile mysteriously, but I just sort of revealed my eye teeth to her, making me look like a confused wolf.

-Well, who are you Lucia? And what do you do? Why are you here? You played the part of a femme fatale wonderfully when we met at the library two nights ago.

We started walking up the steep wooded slope, stepping over tree roots and thickets. In the archetypal fairy tale tradition, we were getting ourselves lost in the deep dark woods. She was a shade more muscular than you might have imagined, and when shod of her high heels she clambered lithely over the bracken and thistle like a saucy mountain goat.

We paused by a giant redwood trunk. She leant against it catching her breath. I noticed a fine sheen of perspiration had formed on her blemishless tanned skin.

-So seriously, what are you doing here?

-Ok look blondie, I am a popstar with great expectations. Tiberius came to a concert of mine a few months back. We ended up partying pretty hard. Manhattan Loft apartments of the rich and shameless... cocaine, DMT and witchcraft stuff.

-Oh and let me guess, Tiberius was interested in talking to you about songs, a certain song in particular?

-Yes! Yes exactly that.

She narrowed her green eyes, suspicious.

-Well he did a similar routine with me, kept insinuating secret meanings or relevance behind the songs, or the process of songwriting. As if there was some great secret that I had unwittingly stumbled into, a secret that he was at some point going to reveal to me.

She ran her hands slowly down both sides of the tree. Her eyes didn't leave mine for an instant, but I sensed an easing of tension around her jaw, she clearly believed me, perhaps indicating the first intimations of trust forming between us. A tenuous, delicate confidence.

-Two nights ago, in the library, before we played our little game, you mentioned you were only there because of Pinky Capote?

I looked away, staring up the narrow path. I wondered when was the last time that two humans had stood in this place and conversed, or if that had ever happened before. Were we the first two people since the beginning of time to be here in this exact spot using language to communicate?

-Well, which is it? Which was it that brought you here? The intrigue of Tiberius Red or Pinky Capote? I mean I've heard a lot of things about her.

I kicked the soil with my boot, it was a teenage gesture, but something about Lucia seemed to bring that out in me. I kicked the soil again and looked up, her verdant eyes, with the quality of freshly washed grapes, bore into me.

-I suppose it was a little of both. I am in love, or lust, or something with Pinky, and I am fascinated by whatever Tiberius is always going on about. How could I not be?

She was thoughtfully sucking in her cheeks ever so photogenically.

-Uh huh, she nodded.

I gazed into her deep green eyes, and quietly told myself that I must not, under any circumstances, tell her what Pinky had told me about what Tiberius was really working on up here.

-Well, I think we both need to just chill out, my blonde British friend.

-Let's just relax a little. It's obvious Tiberius is trying to spin us out. We should try to resist, play it cool, not overreact to anything he does or says. I mean, all he's asked us to do is to write a few songs together. Maybe this is all just an extraordinarily over-the-top songwriting workshop. The hits don't write themselves after all.

I laughed. She knew what she was doing, she was a keen-eyed operator. A narcissist of the most attractive kind, and it takes one to know one.

-I have some really good sativa in my room, and a great little record player, and some killer records.

-All I got was a bed and a writing table.

-What else do you need?

I laughed, catching a bat-squeak of flirtation and started to follow her as she descended the slope. She was several paces ahead of me, when something flickered in the corner of my eye. Peering out from behind a redwood trunk, about ten feet to my left, was the perfect face of an angel.

I blinked and gulped simultaneously. The angel didn't move. I blinked again. It was a statue. It was a huge statue of an angel. I reached out a hand to touch its arcing wings, the cool touch of carved marble met my fingertips.

-Hey blondie? Are you coming? What're you doing? Are you Pissing?

I popped my head around the tree. Lucia's eyes met mine from twenty yards below.

-I'm coming, I just thought I saw a...cat...a mountain cat.

She cocked her head in incredulity, but before she could ask any more questions I strode down the track towards her. We emerged at the very far left hand corner of the meadow, the afternoon sun had started cresting the trees, silhouetting Hecate House on the horizon.

I looked over to the stone circle, it was now deserted. I wondered where Pinky had gone. I wondered where everyone else had gone. I suppose they all might be wondering where Lucia and I had gone. I looked at Lucia and realised that once again I was forging an intimacy with a total stranger. I didn't know this enigmatic popstar at all, but I had the overwhelming desire to take her hand as we gently meandered across the meadow.

XV

-Come on in, and please, please excuse the mess.

She laughed and then shot me a pleading and playful look as the door of her chamber swung open, which was situated directly below my own room. Little did I know last night, as I tossed and turned, that it was just these thin floorboards between us.

The red eye–sun was framed by the wide window, casting deep shadows and picking out details of a huge suitcase that appeared to have undergone a controlled explosion. Clothes were festooned on every surface, garments hanging from everywhere. A litter of expensive shoes were laying all over in unusual places, one stiletto hooked on the edge of the lamp, a cowboy boot on a bedside table. As I walked in, I slipped on a selection of silk nightgowns like a surrealist oil slick beneath my feet.

-Sorry. She reached down and pointlessly picked up an Italian fedora and tossed it on the bed where it came to rest among a ball gown and a dozen pairs of jeans.

I trod carefully to avoid priceless pieces of haute couture that I was about to render extinct under my boots like unclassified florian treasures of a newly discovered colony.

She closed the door and promptly tossed her high heels onto the chaise longue in a habitual way that immediately explained the mess. She sat down on the bed, I chose to loiter at the foot of it, eyeing the chaos and weighing up my options.

I was becoming accustomed to being in intimate spaces with total strangers. After a subtle moment that was scored in the air as a silent symphony of carnal yearning, she said huskily.

-Ok, let's have a smoke Mr. Leonard. By the way does anyone ever actually call you Saint?

She rolled over the bed to a side table, reaching for a small glass pipe and a huge baggie of marijuana. It was genuinely the biggest baggie of grass I'd ever seen. She expertly stuffed the bowl and, applying a lighter to it, inhaled a deep meditative drag. She exhaled a plume that billowed dragon-like in the scarlet afternoon sunlight. She took another hit and handed me the pipe.

-What would you like to listen to Leonard?

-What have you got?

-Well mister blonde, mister strange, mister unexpected *Saint Leonard*.

She giggled and sort of flopped sideways and started throwing random items of clothing, underwear, scarves, fur coats and expensive handbags, over her shoulder revealing a stack of records next to a mint condition Crosley Sterling record player that was connected to two huge handmade speakers. She picked out an album sleeve and deftly slid the vinyl onto her palm. I knew what she had chosen without even needing to look, she dropped the needle.

I'm an alligator, I'm a mama-papa coming for you
I'm the space invader, I'll be a rock 'n' rollin' bitch for you
Keep your mouth shut, you're squawking like a pink monkey bird
And I'm busting up my brains for the words

XVI

For several days we wrote, spoke, sang, and smoked. We slipped down for strange meals at odd hours in the communal dining room. Tiberius was often conducting rites, rites like 'the rites of spring,' upon our fellow initiates. Pinky was here and there, but was most notable in her absence. She found shadows that fitted her form perfectly whenever Lucia or I entered a room. She was always observing like an adjudicator, keeping score of the movements of our bodies over invisible boundaries. She eyed our every communication and sensual transgression. Once I even thought I saw her watching Lucia and I while we were fucking like feral dogs on the chaise longue, but when I looked round it was just a shadow in the hall. The house itself became a flexing mirror of fancy. It seemed that whatever we sang about in Lucia's room almost instantly came to pass, as if the spirit of the house itself was listening at the door. A wanton voyeur eager to facilitate our increasingly lascivious appetites. Hecate House was heady and chthonic and seemed to operate entirely by its own demented logic. Rise and write, and then drink and dance and make love and write. Then we'd take tabs of acid that Tiberius was handing out with the alacrity of communion wafers.

What is this you are giving me– it doesn't matter what it is, it didn't matter what it was, and then get thee back to bed and perchance to sleep to dream: dream the things you think of are just the outlines of your fettered desires: all things are about to come to pass, to be. And you can laugh and laugh and laugh until you cry, there are only a few of us here: do what you like – no one minds, and even if they did mind or got upset or you just took a little too much, yes yes yes, you took too much my friend, just a little out of your mind: Don't freak out baby honey I could very quickly with a shake of the incense burner, with a little draught of this, with the touch of a tongue-tied toad, with a sniff of willow of wisp and the crushed eye of newt, remove the hot sensation of dysphoria from you, take it all away from you, everything gone, return you back to the red-eyed room of miss nymphet Lucia where you will write and write and write and write and write some more because those ancient singing stones are waiting out in the meadow and they want to hear the best tune you have for them. They are waiting for their song, they won't wait much longer and neither will I. So don't ask if you should do it, just run off into the night and do it again and listen to 'Scary Monsters' on so loud it makes the whole house shake, listen to 'Heroes' and 'Low' and 'Modern Love' so loud so loud so loud so loud until you render the house a shroud of sound that settles eventually down, because that is what you are here to do, and when you've written your song come back to the singing stones, come back to your friends, come back to the golden ones of Mountweazel, so we can all hear it too. I will get on my knees for you, do anything you want to do.

XVII

One bright idyllic dawn a few days later, Pinky's jealousy painted itself upon the malachite canvas of the Mountweazel paradise like a violent streak of an indelible colour. She threw my precious black notebook down on the dew-covered ground and stamped upon it with her kaloftiagménos feet. The erotically charged appendages she used normally to dance and seduce she was now deploying as nubile poediristiac wrecking balls. She was clearly determined to destroy my notebook. I stood staring, thinking of her as Kali. I badly needed to drink some water.

She was raging. She was a woman scorned. God knows what she had been up to the night before, doubtless her favorite heady mix of mescal, cocaine, and quaaludes had been taken. As she spat and hissed in my face, I sensed that the events of the last seven days had worked upon her like the sanding plane of a diabolical luthier. Shaping and hollowing out her fine body until she could resonate only these dissonant chords of rage. Wailing wolfnotes of fierce accusation. Apologies were demanded from me that a choir of beseeching seraphims could never deliver. There were crescendos of sensual recriminations. Crotch-tightening ultimatums and fleshy threats rose from her strained vocal chords. Oh how she screamed and raged, stamping all the while on the pages of my notebook.

-What are you doing Leonard, what the fuck is your deal with Lucia?

I had sleep in my eyes and was wearing a silk nightie plucked hastily from Lucia's bedroom floor, along with my leather motorcycle jacket and my last functioning pair of trousers. Moments earlier Pinky had burst into Lucia's room, screamed something that sounded like an Arabic curse, thrown a bottle of Pernod at us, looked around frenziedly, then grabbed my notebook and ran off.

So that is why she is stamping around in the meadow. I had to admit on the face of it she may have had a point. Pinky had brought me here as her lover, as her willing accomplice. So my sudden intense and lascivious entanglement with Lucia may well be the cause of her incandescent chagrin. But then, oh god, in her rage I suddenly wanted Pinky again. In her rage I would worship her more. I would lay sacraments at her feet and make blood sacrifices in her name, but first I just had to calm her down and retrieve my notebook, then I could see about fucking her again.

I had barely the time to let that lusty notion flicker over my neurons (hazed as they were by last night's remnants of cannabinoids and champagne) before Pinky charged at me. She was clad sparingly in her La Perla petit macrame bra but she was holding a hunting knife in her hand. I danced Nureyev-like around her and the glinting blade.

-How could you do this to me, Leonard?

The blade and her body swam past me in one graceful vector. I preempted her movements and caught her arm, but she wriggled free and stalked around me, slashing the air.

-What have I done to you, Pinky?

She charged and plunged the knife directly into my shoulder. The meadow became incredibly vivid. Pinky staggered back with a horrified expression on her face. Her scream was only exceeded in intensity by the screaming note of pain that was radiating out from my shoulder. It felt like an image I had seen of two giant neutron stars colliding in deep space. Unfortunately, those neutron stars were now colliding inside my right shoulder blade.

-*Thanks*, Pinky.

My vision swam, and I prepared myself once again for the end. Pinky had her back to me. She was heaving and panting. I grasped at my shoulder and realised with relief that the leather of my jacket had acted like a second skin and deflected the knife into its thick wool lining. No mortal wound had been inflicted, just a very long scratch. The silk nightie and leather jacket were a cross-dressing accident that had somehow saved my life. I looked up triumphantly.

Pinky had turned and levelled her stance at me, the knife in her right hand glinted in the sun like a mirrorball. She had realised I was not going to die from the first wound and another would be needed.

-Pinky, what are you doing?

-How dare you, Leonard? You are here at my behest. This is so *embarrassing*.

-Do what? I was playing along with whatever it is you and Tiberius wanted. I was writing the songs as requested.

-Writing? *Writing* – you call what you've been up to the last few days writing?

I threw up my arms in a fey gesture.

-You've been fucking Lucia, you fucking British bastard! She lifted the knife again and went to charge.

-Wow woah wow! My beautiful babies, stop this now!

Tiberius roared his way off the porch, his vast gown filling like the sails of a tall ship. He positioned himself warily between Pinky and I.

-Well, what in the name of Satan is going on here?

***

30 minutes later we were down at the river. I was watching the babbling white water breaking over black mylonite rocks. Tiberius had his arm around my shoulder and the morning sun was warming everything it could lay its fiery eye upon. I had recovered my notebook, it was a little besmirched by Pinky's footprints but otherwise intact.

-I know that this experience is a little much

Tiberius said in a tone that belied the grandiosity of his understatement.

-Especially at the start, but that's the point of it. That's the way it works. It's meant to break down reality. Shatter your worldview. De-regulate your senses.

I nodded.

-To over-extend the normal range of human feeling. To let you get close to ecstasy, to get close to the goddess, you recall what I said at the stone circle?

-Yes, Tiberius, I get it. I shrugged off his arm.

Tiberius took a deep breath and then cleared his throat.

-Mr. Leonard, the time has come when we must take a walk up that mountain.

XVIII

When he stood up I noticed a red leather briefcase perched next him on the river bank. I was surprised that I hadn't noticed it before as it was the kind of item that is, under normal circumstances, quite hard to miss. He clocked me, eyeing the red case and picked it up by its intricately bejewelled handle.

-We have a very long walk and I want to get to where we are going by midday at the latest.

Tiberius turned sharply and set off directly across the meadow, casting a surreptitious glance at Hecate House. In a few minutes, we were passing the stone circle and stepping over the shaded meridian demarcating the start of the Big

Sur forest. We began to climb the same path that I had first discovered with Lucia a few days before. Christ, I thought, *that feels like a lot longer ago than a few days ago.*

The cool, pine-scented air was pleasant as we climbed, but Tiberius remained in an unbroken, edgy silence. The silence suited me just fine. I had my head down and had fallen into a rhythmic, meditative step. Occasionally glancing at the back of Tiberius's patent leather Italian slip-on shoes, which did not strike me as the most suitable choice for a two hour hike up a mountain.

I drifted into a reverie on the violent events of this morning. I was slightly appalled at my own behaviour. I wasn't really sure what I had been playing at. Who was I becoming? Some kind of total bastard. I was so deeply lost in this self-loathing that I didn't notice that Tiberius had stopped dead in the path ahead of me, and I walked straight into him.

We were at the junction in the path where from behind a huge tree trunk peeped the angelic statue. Tiberius threw up a silencing hand. My pulse quickened. The forest itself seemed to respond to his command. Not a bird chirped, nor a leaf stirred. He took a step forward onto the left-hand path that ascended steeply   past the angel. As he stepped he turned to me, his blue eyes were wide. He slowly lifted a finger to his lips and then crept softly up the path.

A few minutes later, we emerged from the gloom of the forest into the brilliance of a clearing. A grassy plateau around the size of a football pitch. I squinted into the midday sun. The plain was entirely empty aside a large wooden cabin on the far side. It looked at first sight like a scouts hut. But there was something about its elongated and warped dimensions that troubled me: *These Scouts I really did not wish to meet.* Tiberius walked on heading towards this cabin.

-Do you know much about Alexander the Great?

-Yes, he was an ancient bisexual conqueror of the world and had it off with his mum, right?

-Yes, that is correct. Have you ever heard of a hypogaeum?

I shook my head

-Napoleon Bonaparte visited a hypogaeum, following in the footsteps of his hero Alexander the Great

-What is a hypogaeum?

-Both Alexander the Great and Napoleon Bonaparte spent a night inside the Pharaoh's chamber of the great pyramid of Giza. Both did so alone and both slept actually inside the pharaoh's sarcophagi. That great pyramid is a hypogaeum, Leonard, one of the very first. There are several others dotted across the world. There is a particularly fine one in Malta, which for a long time only the Knights Templar knew about. There are several in Scotland, there are I think two in Ireland, a few in Africa, and, yes, this hut here is one too.

-This hut

He continued;.

-After his night in the great pyramid, Alexander the Great emerged pallid and terrified. When his aides asked what he had seen he said he would never speak of it.

Tiberius's eyes searched mine, vainly looking for any hint of recognition regarding what he was saying.

-1000 years later, when Napoleon emerged after spending his own fateful night in the sarcophagi, he too was white and silent. He too refused to speak of what he had seen. On his deathbed he is reported to have told a friend that if he revealed what he had experienced that night, 'You wouldn't believe me, and it might just ruin your life.' His eyes lingered heavily on mine.

-This Leonard is a hypogeaum, well a part of it. It is the first of two chambers. The other part is hidden elsewhere on the mountain.

He gestured reverently at the shabby scouts's hut. It looked to me like the sort of place where you go to sweaty discos as a teenager. He bowed his head and strode towards the entrance.

*****

The hall was shrouded in darkness and smelt of smoke and sage. As my eyes adjusted, I could see there was something covering the walls. Tiberius had vanished in the shadows. I stumbled through a small doorway and into the centre of another room.

Tiberius lit a tapered candle, and from the flickering flame, I could make out that the walls were completely bedecked from floor to ceiling with an extraordinary display of Dionysian imagery. It was phenomenal, completely otherworldly. The images had an eerie life-size proportion, jumping and leering in the candlelight. A bizarre wedding scene filled with staring black goats and shapely women descending from trees holding crops and switches to whip their fellow revellers.

Tiberius turned to me, flourishing his candle and said in a reverent tone:

-Welcome to the Temple of the Rites of Higher Initiation.

He whistled a discordant sequence of notes through his teeth.

-But this isn't really a temple though is it, Tiberius?

His eyes narrowed.

-To me this feels like a staged version of a temple. A fetishized simulacrum of such a place. This is a clubhouse. So what is it that you all do up here? Witchy swinging parties, orgies, and lines of gear in the name of the Great Goddess?

I saw a flicker of anger play across his face like the shadow of a cloud passing over a sun-dappled hillside.

-So come on Tiberius, who painted all this? Who owns this cabin, who owns Hecate House? My voice was shaking.

-I don't know. *We* don't know.

He snapped his fingers sharply, and pointed to the shadows.

-Welcome, Mr. Leonard to the mystery of the mysteries. Please step this way.

I followed him into a small black room wherein I saw terrible things.

XIX

Some time later we stepped out of the scout hut. Tiberius was carrying the red briefcase. He closed the door and locked it and set off into the woods. The redwoods grew thicker and the path darker and the climb steeper. Tiberius paused before a particularly treacherous incline.

-Tomorrow night we are going to make a potion. A very special brew of mushrooms, which we will drink while we sing a few songs, and then later on, when the mood takes us we slather a thick hallucinogenic salve over our bodies and all get really, really, really high.

-I see.

-You and Pinky are in fact going to gather those precious mushrooms tonight. You are the two who are *elected* to do so.

-Also...

He paused and looked wistfully into the ground dropping away to his left.

-I think a little time together would be good for the both of you.

He winked and then strode on up the jagged path.

The redwoods began to rarefy and were soon replaced by tall thin pines as numerous and entwined as giant bicycle spokes, whirling and whorling in every direction. Tiberius had stepped up his pace and was eliding himself between their narrow trunks as effortlessly as a willowing wisp of smoke carried on a current of warm mountain air. I trudged on. A bleak and irreligious feeling had settled upon me since leaving the hypogaeum.

Sometime later I looked ahead and saw that Tiberius had swivelled sideways to allow himself cautious side-stepping progress across the arching cat's back of another narrow ridge. His arms outstretched in a crucified trapeze to steady against the possibility of a fatal misstep. The ground dropped away to oblivion both sides of the six inch–wide path.

My head swam with vertigo as I saw Tiberius striding onto an outcrop, upon which he sat down in a lotus pose and warmly smiled as I took the last few uncertain steps towards him. A gust of wind caught his hair, and for a moment he looked like a biblical prophet on a mount.

I sat down shakily in front of him. On the far distant horizon, I could see the black brushstroke of the Pacific Ocean. To our right was the mountain which, despite our two hour–climb, still towered above us. I turned to my left and in doing so must have disturbed some loose stones that tumbled down the precipice, clattering and shattering their way down the mountainside.

XXI

-I am going to give you something special now, Leonard, and then you are going to give me something in return.

He placed the red briefcase between us. He shifted his Drishti gaze just beyond my eyeline, beyond my scrutiny. The lid of the briefcase opened lightly to his touch, and he paused looking down at the contents, an expression of fleeting wonderment and a hint of sorrow hung about his bearded countenance.

-I have had this for quite some time. It has served me very well.

He reached both hands forward tentatively, sensitive as the touch of an old jeweller. He paused again,

-I thought I would probably hang onto it for the rest of my life. But I've had a sudden change of heart in recent days. I had an epiphany of sorts, a sea change. I really don't want to explain, but it has occurred to me that I want you to have this. It is time for it to...

A gust of wind carried his words whistling over the precipice.

He looked up into my eyes. I could see that he was in two minds as to whether to go through with the transaction; his outstretched hands still hovering reverently over the contents.

He inhaled solemnly and lifted the thing from the case, the lid closing quietly as he withdrew it, and in a ceremonious arcing motion he placed it down in front of me. It was a typewriter. It was made from brilliant glinting silver metal and it was as shiny as a newly minted coin.

-I would like for you to have this and for you to use it to write the words I think you will eventually need to write. It's a special machine. It is in effect a fully operational time machine. You will, I am certain, write all the songs that you have coming to you on this, in order to uncover the truth. It will, I can assure you, carry you at the mere push of a button, right to the heart of the matter, or if needs be it can forgive you your trespasses and deliver you instantly from all evil. And, the thing is, it's entirely environmentally friendly, this baby simply runs on pure unpolluted thought energy.

In a single motion he rotated the machine around to face me. I leant forward examining the beautifully crafted keyboard. Tiberius smiled at me.

-This is now yours and do with it what thou wilt.

I nodded reverently.

-Oh, there's just one thing you should know about this particular machine, Leonard.

-Look closely at the keyboard.

My eyes scanned the familiar spread of the keys, which appeared to be made out of material that wasn't ivory but something very close to it. It had the cool surety of bone and the enamel finish of a worn tooth.

-Have you noticed anything unfamiliar that catches your eye? Look at the lettering, look at the keys.

There were extra keys, with unrecognisable symbols scattered amongst the standard QWERTY keyboard.

-There are certain symbols here, certain hieroglyphic expressions that exist, as far as I know only upon this machine. New additions to the human, higher-ape language. Leonard you will now have to go back and rectify every book in existence and reinsert into them every nuance of the world those authors have overlooked.

He looked at me solemnly.

I placed my hands onto the keys. They felt good and well used, I could sense that this machine had been laboured over for hours immeasurable. I wondered what he had written on this.

Every word which you have read of this story was typed on this very machine. It is sat before me now, in a location I shall not at this stage divulge. It was also on my lap as I wrote up the start of this all when I finally made it to the cabin in Nashville, it was with me all along the road.

-Enjoy it Mr. Leonard, it is now yours. And don't worry about the special symbols. You will, with time and application, learn how best to deploy them in the writing of a story.

The wind was gathering and the sky was becoming veined purple and bruised.

-But now, as I said, you are going to give me something in return.

-I would very much like for you to read my tarot, if you would be so good?

-What?

-I should like a tarot reading. Pinky told me about the one you gave her, and now I would like one too, after all, we are on a spiritual retreat.

He said the word 'spiritual' with a peculiarly guttural inflection that totally robbed the word of its meaning.

-I want a tarot reading right now.

-I can't Tiberius, I don't have my cards with me

He eyed me coolly, slowly massaging his jawbone through his beard.

-Au contraire, Mr Leonard, au contraire.

He produced my deck of cards from his gown and handed them to me with a smile.

He then adjusted his posture laying down in front of the red briefcase altar, supine. He stretched his legs out behind

him and shifted his head and gaze forward, his thick arms
supporting his head in a sphinx pose. I started to shuffle the
deck, and as the sky darkened above us on the mountain, I
dealt Tiberius his tarot.

XXII

As I concluded his reading, Tiberius looked drawn and
unsettled, as if all his show business chutzpah had finally
deserted him. It was the first time I had seen him look so. It
felt like seeing a heavyweight champion stumble during the
fourth round. I shuffled the deck and slipped the cards back
in my pocket. He stood up and replaced the typewriter into
its case and handed it to me.

-It is funny that one can never make a work of art, as
simply as the body understands a work of art,' he coughed
and looked up to an outcrop where the wind howled.

-Tiberius, Pinky told me the reason we were here was
that you were trying to write your way around death?

-What?

-She said, you were writing your way around death?

-Did she?

He stretched a casual cat curl and looked at me sternly.
His blue eyes glinting, shooting striations of sunlight right
back into my eyes from the moody heavens above.

-We should get back, it'll take us at least two hours to
wind our way down the mountain.

The precipice from which we descended was by a trick
of the light much narrower and more precarious then I

recalled. I noticed he had not taken the lead and instead had slipped into a closely paced stride bedside me. Each of our synchronously timed footsteps was repercussed by the tumbling of loose stones from either side of the snaking path.

-So, Pinky told you I was up here to 'write my way around death'?

-She did, and also a lot of curious things about songs. The purpose of songs and the sort of songs we were supposed to be writing here.

He pulled out his pipe packed it with tobacco and lit it. I retrieved a Camel Light and popped it in my mouth, Tiberius proffered the flame of his lighter. We stood on the narrow path and smoked.

-And what do you really know of Pinky, Leonard?

This sentence began as a question and ended as a statement.

He chewed the oaky stem of the pipe between his teeth. I inhaled slowly on the cigarette, my head swam. He stifled a laugh and his face flexed into an expression of concern, or was it a pantomime of pretend concern?

-You really have been led on a merry dance. So, may I ask you again, how much do you really know about Miss Pinky Capote?

I looked down at the razor-sharp rocks and patches of scrub 300 feet below our position. My head felt like a smoking ruin on a shattered battlefield.

-We really must get down off this mountain, and you must be back for nightfall because you have another vital function to perform before this day is through. And if we don't go now we could well die up here.

He paused.

-It has unfortunately happened before.

He moved off along the path.

-The first thing you should know about Pinky is that she is not who she says she is.

-She hasn't really told me who she says she is, to be honest.

-Well yes, she rarely does and for very good reason.

-What was the point of the tour?

-Well, she described it as sort of like a harvest. She was mapping out a route that would take her to significant places that seemed to matter to her. We picked up people on the way. You, my friend, were one of them.

-What?

-She had this list.

-Hang on, the tour we just did, she knew me before we met on the road?

-Well, yes she did.

I glanced at my aching right hand. The typewriter swung like a pendulum, perfectly in time with my heartbeat.

-You know how important the songs are, you clearly figured that much out. This place is a temple to song. The tour we did together was carefully orchestrated in order to elicit a certain set of responses from you, a certain set of songs.

He relit his pipe. An owl hooted.

-It's the songs. She is using them for a ritual, but I don't have any idea what her ultimate goal is. Why she said I was writing my way around death I have no idea. I mean, you do know that songs can exist like artefacts that don't decay for millennia. Songs don't rot in the soil like other things do, they continually take new breath. They are continually resurrected in the singing. They occupy no real space or time yet somehow can overcome all our senses. And what is more, they can't age, they never ever grow old...they can never die.

We had descended so far down the path that I could see the first columns of light emanating from the meadow, and felt a faint ripple of relief run along the length of my spine. I could, if need be, just run away from him now, get in a car and leave and never look back, but of course, I knew that was never going to happen.

-Mr. Leonard, we may not get a chance to speak much further, so before we part, let me just ensure I have told you everything you need to know, for my own soul's sake. There are certain ideas that even just hearing them once can have a lasting effect upon your mind, upon your soul, that can forever change the way in which you live out your days. Ideas that were deemed so powerful they are kept beyond top secret. Totally hidden, entirely occluded from the everyday world. Protected by the workings and machinations of secretive, clandestine groups, ancient societies. The guardians of these immensely valuable ideas. It is they who choose when and where and how to transmit these ideas, at specific times, and in specific ways, so as to ensure that the ideas and thus, they themselves, remain eternally alive.

The owl hooted again, much closer.

-A song is a thing that can never decay, change nor age, once it is created it cannot be destroyed, once hummed or sung, it lives on and on. With modern methods of recording, reproduction and transmission of sound, a song can be spread around the world in literally a matter of minutes. In one broadcast seven billion people can receive a message directly into their psyche. Deep down in their minds, indelibly imprinted. The reason I've given you the typewriter is to remove myself from part of the picture. Otherwise I risk getting caught up in a *repeating pattern, a feedback loop*. I am giving the thing to you, to get out of the game, so to speak, before she...

We had come once again to where the angel stood. Tiberius rifled in his gown and produced a hip flask, he removed the cork with his teeth, threw back his head, and poured a great draught of a carmine liquid down his throat. He offered me the flask, I took it from him and drank deeply. It tasted delicious, a sweet spiced wine, and unexpectedly refreshing. I wiped my mouth and felt the spectacular hit of the alcohol shimmer in my stomach. Tiberius knelt down on one knee before the statue and outstretched his arms in a devotional posture.

-Kenosis.

He trailed off, looking beatifically into the face of the thing. He bobbed his head back and forth.

-What?

- She is after, well, I don't really know what she is after all...

-Tiberius, Tiberius please help me. I...I am beginning to think I might be a little bit fucked here.

He arose mechanically and turned to look at me.

-As I say, a song can touch a million people in a moment.

I stared into his eyes and felt a new dimension of despair opened within me.

-She has been using these songs as sigils. To call out and communicate across the chasm of time, across space...

-What?!

I screamed in his face. I felt a surge of bile blended with the sweet wine rising in my throat. Tiberius started cackling, he was wild eyed and babbling.

-You see...God's first thought was female, a female thought, and from this feminine emanation she then created all other thoughts...

I staggered away from him and pressed up against a tree and tried to stop my retching, tried to keep breathing. Then I turned and ran away.

XXIV

I don't know how long I slept for but I was awoken by a sharp knock at my door. The sun was already setting low over the distant mountain. I looked from my bed onto the meadow, a haze of reddish greys, purple, and burnt oranges gathered around the exact spot where I'd read Tiberius's tarot earlier this morning, many miles away. I still had my head on the pillow, still thinking about the tarot, his tarot; when the knocking came again, louder and more insistent.

It was Yuki, the beautiful and brilliant Japanese artist. It was a surprise to see her standing at the door, as she had not really had much to do with me at all apart from the odd late night sing-song. I felt she had hitherto avoided me. She smiled and held up a crisp white envelope.

-For you. She smiled brightly, thrusted it into my hand, turned, and was spirited away by the deepening afternoon shadow of the corridor.

I sighed, closing the door gently behind me as I stepped towards the window.

'Leonard' was written on the envelope in a delicate cursive scriptI tore it open, there was a single loose sheet of handmade French writing paper.

Dear Darling Leonard,

We have been charged with the very special task of harvesting the Psilocybe azurescens mushrooms by full moonlight tonight. It is very important we are successful in this undertaking as the entire ritual depends upon them.

Meet me on the porch at 11 PM. As ever, yours insufferably, Pinky,

I sat down on the end of the bed and read the letter back over again. I showered for a long time, trying to put what I'd seen in the scout hut out of my mind. I tried not to think about what Tiberius had told me. I tried not to think about his tarot.

I changed into my tatterdemalion black suit trousers and a black shirt. As I was rummaging through my suitcase, a picture of my ex-fiancé and I, taken at a music festival a year before, fell out the lining of the case. I held it up to the pale yellow lightbulb on the writing desk. It was hard to process how inconceivably distant my previous life felt right then. A lifetime, six months, and six thousand miles ago.

I lay on my bed reading Blake and letting my mind wander, occasionally allowing my eyes to drift shut. I folded the photograph of my ex fiancé and I, and saw that scribbled on the back in my handwriting were the words 'we are lived by powers we pretend to understand.' I stuffed the photo down amongst the coiled bed sheets.

I looked at the bedside clock, it was 9.30. I returned my eyes to the lines of verse. A moment later I glanced back and the clock read 11.07 PM. I leapt up, pulling my boots on and stumbling out the door, bounding down the stairs three at a time. I stumbled over the rack of shoes and grasped the brass door handle which swung open to my touch.

XXV

Low light, gaslight, Pinky standing there in an amber half halo. She was dressed to my surprise like Little Red Riding Hood. Her cheekbones clipped the light like the sharpest notes in some sacred, ancient symphony. Her little black dress covered by an enveloping scarlet cloak, ankle-high riding boots on her feet, with a tobacco-chewing expression on her face. I smiled. She frowned.

-You're late.

Before I could respond she threw her arms over her head and in a loud incantatory voice exclaimed:

-SANDHYAS! SANDHYAS! SANDHYAS!
SANCTUS! SANCTUS! SANCTUS!

She dropped her arms and scowled at me.

-I'm really sorry, I overslept.

She cocked her head and flickered her eyelids.

-This is very important darling. How are you?

-I'm ok.

-Good. Now pick up that lamp, Leonard, take the map and the basket too.

I followed her eyes over to the low wooden bench with a wicker picnic basket, a powerful looking torch, and a large piece of paper with looping black script. I paused, not entirely sure if I should take my eyes off her and reach for the objects. She placed her hands on her hips and adjusted the inclination of her chin. I picked up the basket, the map, and the lamp, and as I turned around, she glided silently into the night.

She was a little ahead of me and moving with a quick unsteady gait, I assumed she was drunk.

I cleared my throat and looked up at the approaching treeline.

-What is 'Sandhya'? What does that mean?

She glanced back over her shoulder, flashing me the faintest of smiles without breaking her stride.

-It's Sanskrit. Sandhya means the magic moment between two world aeons. The yawning abyss between two swathes of time. Two psychological states. It also means twilight, the moment between dark and light, sunset and sunrise.

We had cut across the lower southeastern aspect of the meadow and were approaching the spot where I had sat with Tiberius earlier this morning, recovering from Pinky's attempted stabbing. I whistled a calm descending melody as we strode over the moonlit meadow. Pinky slowed as we approached the steep-sided bank leading down to the river.

-We need to cross here and get over to that low ridge on the other side. There are stepping stones, but they're slippery and hard to see, follow me closely.

She removed her boots and dipped her toes into the fast-flowing water. Clasping the basket, map and torch to my body, I followed her, but misstepped and plunged hip deep into the current. I heard her giggle ring out over the roaring water. She stepped daintily from stone to stone, as I slipped and stumbled along, soaking myself in the process. A few minutes later I staggered cold and breathless onto the riverbank.

-You made it!

What do you really know about Pinky Capote?

Without warning she turned and kissed me deeply, racing her hands down my back. I felt the rapid pulse on her lips as she pulled away, looking at me fiendishly. She thrust forward and kissed me again, more forcefully and more urgently. My blood began to rise, but she pulled away again, stepped back and coquettishly straightened her riding cape.

-There's no time for any of that. The moon is full and high, and we must harvest, there's not a moment to lose. It's a very narrow window when the moonbeams charge the lady fungus. Hand me that map.

She snatched the map from my hand and started wheeling left and right, getting her bearings against it. She sucked her cheeks and then shot a look up at the sky, adjusting her stance to orientate herself to some distant constellation. I peered over her shoulder at the map. It wasn't really a map. It was a scrawl of text in an unrecognisable language overlaid with complex geometric shapes. There was a discernible outline that may well have been the shape of the river we had just crossed, and a row of hatching that could possibly demarcate the boundary of trees. I could make out a strange obelisk shape that might vaguely represent the position of Hecate House. But overall the thing appeared as indecipherable as the scrawling on the wall of a sanatorium. There was something terrifyingly childlike about it too. She stuffed the map into her cape and grabbed the torch from me, swinging it in the direction of a towering escarpment of rocks.

-You see that ridge over there and the small hill behind it? The valley is just on the other side. Careful where you tread though, there are pools of quicksand dotted around, and keep an eye out for lions and bears of course.

She set off swinging the torch and singing 'Lucy in the Sky with Diamonds' under her breath in a low, croaking, monotone drawl.

We had crested the ridge that was covered in dry husky gorse as if a wildfire had run through it recently. It was crowned with three petrified trees that had the eerie redolence of the three crosses of Golgotha. Pinky turned to me as we passed the trees and pulled a ghoulish face.

After a short climb up a hill that was densely grassed, we paused at its rolling summit. I could just about make out a precipice several feet ahead of us. I turned to Pinky who had stopped and was eyeing the edge warily. She turned to me and smiled.

-You know Timothy Leary came out here once?

- I didn't even know this place existed five minutes ago.

-Well, he did. He came out with some of his friends, his loyal psychonauts, aetheric travellers, deep-sea mind divers. He really fucking loved it. You see there is a very special kind of fly-agaric mushroom that grows in that valley below us. It only flowers on certain full moons and only on certain years. And guess what, Honey Bunny? This is one of those full moons, and one of those years!

- How convenient.

-We need to get down there and gather from the great mother as many mushrooms as we can carry. We're going to need a lot if tomorrow night is to be a success.

-About that *ritual* tomorrow...what qualifies as a success exactly?

-These are very *very* magic mushrooms – she continued

-We must wander gently, thoughtfully, even, dare I say it, *erotically* through the Goddess's vegetable queendom.

She took a few small steps to the edge of the precipice and gazed down. I followed, stepping cautiously next to her. It was a truly staggering sight below; the valley was a narrow trench that dropped sharply down 30 feet to a wildly flowered and tree'd canyon. The whole valley glistened with crystals and glowed with bioluminescence.

-What the fuck is this?

-It's a vein of extremely rare quartz rock that literally glows with vibration when the full moonlight hits it. This, in turn, creates a chemical reaction in the soil here that not only allows the most magic of mushrooms to grow, but encourages the growth of mosses that possesssimilar qualities to bioluminescent algaes. This is the only place on Earth like it. That's why I wanted to bring my Honey Bunny out here to help me harvest the food of the gods.

-It is staggeringly beautiful.

-Darling, there is something else you should know, it's very important. If we're to pick the wrong mushrooms, accidentally gather the wrong kind. We could all die, horribly. Really fucking horribly.

She held me in the obsidian pool of her eyes, the lights of the luminescent valley dancing within them.

-It happened here not long ago. A vacationing family went out mushroom picking to make a wholesome soup, and well, they mistakenly picked the wrong ones and they ended up having a very bad trip...a very very bad trip. When they were eventually discovered holed up in their cabin, they'd ripped each other to pieces with their bare hands and then partially *eaten* each other...the children too.

-They *ate* each other?

-Yes, Honey Bunny. Now come on in, the moonbeams are lovely!

And with this...she jumped directly off the edge of the precipice.

XXVI

-Pinky!

I screamed into the empty air hanging in front of where she had just been standing. I screamed again and staggered to the edge, fully expecting to look down upon her shattered body 30 feet below on the valley floor. What I looked down upon instead was the pretty oval of her face beaming up at me from a small recessed step a metre or so below where I was.

-Did I scare you Leonard? Did I? She giggled.

-Why must you be such a perpetual cunt?

-Get down here, baby, there are roots like a ladder we can use to climb down, it's easy, just follow me.

With surprising ease we descended the valley wall and in moments were standing in a thoroughly phantasmagoric landscape. Pinky took the basket from me and in combination with her red riding cape and the luminescent setting, the feeling of being transported into a hysterical fairytale was complete. She let out a joyous yippee.

-Jackpot, baby, come look at what the Goddess has given us.

She was crouched holding back a giant Jurassic heather to one side, peering down into a recess of glowing crystalline rocks. Leaning in, her blonde hair brushing my cheek, I saw a clump of mushrooms with bright watery orange caps, narrower and pointier than the varieties I had seen before, protruding delicately upwards on thin long stems.

-Look at these beautiful babies.

She leant closer in; I breathed in her unique scent, more starkly aromatic in the damp fresh air of the valley. She plucked one of the larger specimens from the group. Holding it up to the moonlight, it responded to the silver beams with a shiver that ran over its burning orange skin.

-Psilocybe azurescens, the rarest, most potent, and most magical mushroom of them all.

She purred in the breathy tones of a religious zealot gazing at the holiest of holy relics.

-These mushrooms are a chemical skeleton key to let the Goddess slip right into the sprawling mansion of your mind. They let her in, turning on all the disco lights, cranking the hifi and really getting the existential party started. They will have you galloping down the fast track to the Know Thyself Fun Palace in no time darling.

-Can I see? I reached for it, half expecting her to snatch it away like the craven, grasping buccaneer she appeared to be. Instead she slipped it into my fingers.

-Examine it closely and come to know its consummate beauty.

I held it closer to my eye, again detecting the faint rippling of light over its glistening skin.

-You see how the stem is white but the ring around the gills and lower side are black? Well, mark that closely, and you see at the very centre of its crown is a white five-sided star? That's what you are looking for. No star, no deal. The ones without the star will kill you dead.

She promptly took the mushroom back from my hand and bit it in two, swallowing a hunk of its brown gleaming fleshiness and then proffered the remaining morsel to me.

-What are you doing?

-Microdosing, it will help us hear her brothers and sisters singing to us, come on Leonard.

I dispatched the mushroom into my mouth.

-Happy hunting, my little psychonaut.

She pranced, nymph like, deeper into the enchanted valley.

XXVII

Where am I...The magic mushroom canyon...I wonder what this place is called?

I realised I hadn't moved for awhile, in fact I had just been staring intently at one of the glowing moonlit rocks next to me. I looked around, all the colours were tracing and leaving marvellous swirling firework trails and stuttering after-visions as I moved my eyes. In the distance I could just about see Pinky, dancing and pirouetting on the horizon at the very far end of the canyon, how could she be almost a mile away? I stood up with a sensation like the flickering footage of an Apollo rocket leaving the launch pad.

-Hey Pinkyyyyyyyyyyyy.

An infinite cascade of reverberation from the several billion acoustically reflective surfaces of the canyon amplified and dissipated my question into the rapidly expanding entropy of the unanswering and ultimately uncaring universe.

-Hey Pinky, what is this place called? Called? Called? Called? My voice seemed to come from a distant position at a far remove from my mind. I was the audience to my words rather than their progenitor. A not unpleasant dissociative euphoric wave washed over me, well I say 'me,' I was unsure who I was referring to, I mean I knew who I was, but really who was I? My words were flowing in a neon stream out over the canyon. Everything was alive. I turned my head slowly and it was as if all the flowers leant and bent their heads in to meet my gaze. Pinky was still a very long way away, and doing the wildest dance I'd ever seen, her arms and legs moving in anatomically improbable angles. I gently steered the prow of my fizzing psyche towards a comfortable looking arrangement of rocks and moss. As I gently lowered myself down I was certain I heard several disembodied, gentle voices, below my descending backside say 'aaaaaahhhhhhh.' I was alive in a pan-psychic wonderland.

I looked up and Pinky was suddenly towering over me, she had traversed a mile in a moment.

-Oh hi therrrre.

She was looking down at me, clutching the picnic basket that was overflowing with mushrooms.

-What were you asking darling?

-What ---- is this ------ place called?

-Well, lots of people call it lots of different things, it has many names, depending on what people come here to find. I mean, I call it Circe's Garden, others call it Hades's playground.

I stared at her, a smile like a wicked crescent moon had cut into her face. Several versions of her knelt down in front of me.

-What's in a name anyway? The human brain is the only thing in the universe that actually named itself.

She tapped the side of my head.

-Okkkkk.

-Come along , Leonard, we just need a few more.

She hauled me up.

-These things are stronnnggg, really strong. I mean stronger than anything I've had beforrre.

-There is an even stronger strain that grows in a certain spot down here.

She caterpillared deeper into the glowing canyon. I followed in her eddying psychedelic wake. The moon was moving too fast, rapidly transecting the slither of night sky visible in the aperture formed by the steep sides of the ravine. It had moved significantly since when we climbed down, and now as we walked a   third of the canyon was in near complete darkness. Pinky paused, there was a deeper ravine, a cracked fissure forming a gaping abyss before us. She put her hands on her hips and stared into it.

-I believe that magic mushrooms are an alien intelligence that is exploring the cosmos by interacting with the various nervous systems it meets along the way. The mushrooms are connected by vast mycelium networks beneath the soil stretching for miles at a time, the colourful bits we pick and consume are like an apple from a tree, the rest of the tree grows deep beneath the ground.

She gestured at the gaping abyss before her. I swayed slightly.

-This alien goddess breeds these mushrooms because she wants us to eat her, Leonard.

-So, she can get inside of us and have the experience of being a human. Of having arms, legs, eyes, and ears, to touch, feel, taste, and experience the emotional spectrum; dancing, music, quiddity, the thisness of this, the wineness of wine, to exhale the smoke of cigarettes, kissing, caressing and the filthy pleasures of sex. I mean having sex on mushrooms is essentially like having a threesome with an alien goddess, if you think about it, Honey Bunny. It's a consciousness that knows what it is and knows what it wants. The more you pay attention to her, offer to her, adore her, the more she endlessly wants to play.

-Right

-And, she can help us to get in touch with the great Goddess herself.

-Ok...but what if this Goddess doesn't actually exist Pinky?

-What do you mean?

-What if the Goddess or whatever this is all about, what if she doesn't really, you know, actually exist? Then what are we doing here?

- Leonard, why would you say that, how dare you ask me that?

-I just spent this morning on a precipice with a tearful Tiberius who explained a thing or two to me about you.

-About me?

She straightened her back, the red riding cape coiling around her. Her face betrayed a sense of doubt.

-If the Goddess to which you've paid endless homage does not in fact exist, I wonder where that leaves you?

She leant in and tried to kiss me, but I took a step back.

-Of course she exists, and don't you ever, ever say that again.

She leant in and whispered in her most musical voice, the one reserved for heavy manipulation, the one that unconsciously betrayed her.

-But what about you and me baby?

-I don't really know who you are, Pinky! I don't know what you want or why you brought me here.

Her eyes narrowed.

-What do you mean?

The stars in the firmament above her were running like white paint daubs down a dark canvas.

-I mean being here with you, Pinky. How do you think I feel about all this?

She didn't say anything, but she seemed to think for a time, staring glassily into my eyes. I tensed, sensing she might be about to attack.

-Of course she exists. Of course she does.

She moved very slowly and without taking her eyes from mine she began to undress. Her fingers worked at the cord that held her red riding cape around her neck and she allowed it to drop to the ground, she wriggled out of the black dress and in a moment it dropped to her feet. She then unhooked her bra and slid her green silk panties down her legs. She stood before me, her skin glistening golden in the moonlight. She looked imperial and filthily erotic, as if she had been called forth out of the stygian, mythical night. She was Aphrodite, she was Athena, she was Artemis. She stepped towards me, a sephirot of some truly potent supernatural power emanating from her glowing body. She bowed before me, and with deft sleight of hand, another small piece of fleshy magic mushroom appeared upon her fingers, and she popped this into my parted lips.

-Worship me, Leonard.

***

Sometime later she was snoozing, snuggled into me, her gentle breath caressing the flesh of my arms, her blonde hair pooled over my chest. I closed my eyes and fell asleep under the smouldering canopy of those Californian stars.

Go off now on a black pilgrimage, past desolate places and cyclopean ruins and come at last to the unholy city of Chorizen, and there to a great tower of black basalt, part of an ancient ruined castle, over the gulf of stars, deeper into the avenued city within a city. There in the very centre a dozen vast Pyramids stood before me, flickering in the flames of burning torches that cast dancing shadows upon their deeply sloping sides. There I stood a while taking in the masonic majesty of these staggering symbolic structures. There was a vast pillared entrance facing my vantage point on the grand avenue. Despite the flickering torches, it was not possible to see anything of the interior, yet as I gazed I became aware of a certain swaying, shadowy movement just beyond the penumbra of this mighty and foreboding threshold.

I awoke with a scream in my throat. I was back in the ravine where I had fallen asleep. Pinky was gone, as were her clothes and the picnic basket of mushrooms. The sky was bruising in a soft rosy glow. I stood up stiffly, shaking the chill from my bones. I blinked hard as I surveyed the scene, the dream was fading with the effect of the mushrooms. I started off back along the path in the direction we had come.

Twenty minutes later I emerged clambering from the ravine and then managed to cross the river much more easily in the early morning daylight. A burnt umber hue hung over that forest scene, making Hecate House glow even more infernally, as I trudged in a soggy and clockwork motion towards it.

Your waking life is the melody and the dream world is the deep rhythmic root of your existence. The only true evidence of your existence are the songs. The words on the page, they don't decay, whatever happens to you.

I sat on the porch and lit a cigarette. Glancing back over the meadow, I saw a huge black crow rise from the river bank and swoop long, low, and looping like the markings of musical notation. A feathered four-beat crochet inking the morning sky. I tried my best not to read into it some portent of doom. I let the door of the house slam behind me as I skulked to my lonely room.

XXVIII

I awoke to the midday sun streaming through the warped glass of the window pane, refracting its rays and partially magnifying them onto the creased parchment of my face. My eyes winced like wasps stings. I had absolutely no idea where I was or who I was. Sitting up still fully dressed on top of the heavy bedspread, I gasped as all the finer details of the night before came flooding back. I groaned and staggered to the bathroom to find water. I drank down a ferric tasting draught and sat on the edge of the bath. I noticed a white gown hanging on the back of the bathroom door. Someone had been in here while I was asleep. I could well imagine who that may have been. It was a simple cotton gown with a sash to tie it together. There was a note pinned to it.

'LEONARD. 8 PM The Stone Circle. Nil By Mouth.'

I didn't recognise the handwriting. I didn't like the sound of not eating anything all day. I felt a pang of hunger roiling in the pit of my stomach already. I discovered that the house was deserted when I emerged, showered, and dressed from my room an hour later. There was not a soul anywhere, not a sound, not even the tell-tale signs of recent activity, no smoking ashtray, no still-warm seats. A piece of mental machinery clicked and whirred as I surveyed the scene.

I spent the rest of the afternoon in my room becoming hungrier and more anxious with each passing hour. Long-fingered shadows crept across my bedspread as I lay there listening to Miles Davis softly blowing his cool blue notes. I read William Blake fitfully. Occasionally I would get up and stalk around the house like a fretting cat. Panic began to show its teeth and then finally bit around the time the red eye of the sun dipped beneath the distant crown of the magic mountain. I glanced at the clock, it was seven. I was delirious and expectant, desirous and a little terrified, a compound of emotion I'd not experienced since childhood, a hazy memory of my first Halloween. I noticed the night curling around the window outside. In a mechanical motion,

I stepped to the bathroom, undressed, and wrapped the white robe about myself. The cool of the cotton brought me back to my space and time location, the silence of the house was devouring. Nothing had stirred since I'd awoken. I walked out of Hecate House for the last time. As is often the case, I didn't realise that at the time. In the same way that there is a moment in any relationship that you casually say goodbye to someone for the last time, and you don't realise you'll never see them again.

Halfway over the meadow I stopped. The silence was like the space between notes in a piece of avant-garde jazz. This is the first moment in the process, a process I only came to understand much later. Turn back now. Turn around. Calmly walk back to the house, change back into your clothes, pack your bag, take Pinky's car keys from the table in the hall, get in her car, and drive back to LA. I couldn't move, caught in a quadratic equation of the human condition. Trying to divide the desires by the compulsions, trying to calculate the square root of my soul and resolve what it was I truly wanted to do. Tiberius made my decision for me. He did so by grabbing me. I squealed as he seized me by the waist and spun me around.

-Leonard, there you are!

-Fuck off would you, Tiberius?

I glowered into his blue eyes that flashed animally in the moonlight. He was wearing a black kaftan that blended perfectly with his black beard and black matted hair. This made the flesh of his face and the azure of his glassy frenzied eyes seem all the more mask-like. He was laughing a deep belly laugh.

-We, I mean, I just searched the house high and low for you. I thought you might have left us, vanished like a thief in the night.

-What's going on Tiberius?

-What isn't going on my man, *what isn't going on?*

-I'm leaving.

-You can't. They're all waiting for you, just down there at the stone circle. Didn't you get my note?

-What is this all about?

-You already know.

He nodded eagerly

-It's what we've been working towards. I explained all this. You are about to be let in on the mystery my friend. But we can't be late, that would be bad.

He tugged at me, and we began moving down the slope. I dug my heels in and we stopped again.

-I really need to know what this is all about, where is everyone? Why the fucking robe?

He lifted his ringed forefinger to his lips, widening his eyes, and then made a flourish in the direction of the stone circle

-All will be re-re--revealed. He stuttered...he had never done that before. He continued pulling me along, in a moment we crested the rise and I looked down at the strange site below. There was a huge bonfire roaring away at the circle's centre, the flames leaping high into the air, the blaze was big enough for a wave of heat to wash over us, crackling sparks flew into the night sky. There were nine cloaked figures walking around the perimeter of the stone circle. They were all in crimson hooded robes. They were spaced several feet apart and moving in measured rotation around and around the perimeter. There was no sound save the roaring crackle of the flames.

-SANCTUS! SANCTUS! SANCTUS!

SANDHYA! SANDHYA! SANDHYA!

I pulled free of Tiberius's hand and turned to run, but before I could take a step, he'd seized me roughly and shoved me down the slope. I tumbled down the incline, the view of the blazing fire bouncing end over end in my field of vision. I came to a halt in a sprawl just beyond the outside of the circle, my robe had ridden up around my hips, my arms and legs were spread-eagle and I had tufts of grass in my mouth. I lay there gazing up at the reeling stars listening to the crackling of the fire and then a hooded figure loomed over me obscuring my view of the sky.

-Baby, what are you doing? Pinky pulled the hood away from her head, her blonde tresses cascading like a golden landslide as she did so. She reached down, took hold of my arms, and hoisted me up onto my feet. The other eight robed guests had de-hooded and were now staring at me. Tiberius arrived bounding down the last of the incline into the amphitheatre.

-You really lost your footing back there my good man, still at least you made it in the end.

-We were getting very worried about you. Pinky added.

Tiberius darted off behind the fire.

I stared at Pinky and mouthed – *What the fuck is going on?*

She saw this but chose to ignore it, she just continued rubbing my shoulders smiling grimly. Tiberius reappeared staggering under the weight of an earthenware Amphora, at least three feet deep and filled to the brim with viscous crimson liquid that was sloshing down the sides and staining his hands red. Yuki and the lithe French girl, Eloise, darted off and reappeared carrying wooden chalices.

-Now for the first of our great rites tonight, we drink a libation to the mighty, the glorious, the sensual, omnipotent, ombibulous, all-knowing Dionysus.

As he spoke Yuki knelt and allowed him to flug a great glug of the wine into a chalice. She then turned towards the fire and lifting her noble gaze to the starry firmament, declaimed:

-Oh Mighty Dionysus, the first and last drink is as ever for you and is always in your honour.

She poured the wine onto the ground before her, the other acolytes roared a chorus of cheers and whoops as she did so. Eloise and Yuki then began filling several of the chalices. The remaining guests gathered around to take up a vessel themselves. Pinky retrieved one of the brimming chalices and brought it to me.

-Drink this, Honey Bunny...this sure is going to be a fun night. This wine is going to make you feel really fucking good.

-Pinky, I want to go home right now.

-Darling, you are home.

-I don't want to do any of this anymore.

I suddenly thought of Lucia and spun around sloshing the wine over my robe. She was sitting on one of the small stones to the far right of the blazing fire, her eyes met mine, forlorn, transmitting a note of telepathic distress directly into me. I started forward but Pinky stepped in front of me.

-You don't have a home. Not anymore. Your home, your heart, stands before you, offering you the most delicious wine.

She grabbed my hand and awkwardly forced the chalice towards my lips.

-Come on, Honey Bunny, drink it down! I know how you like wine. You drink me up like wine sometimes, go on have a sip. You won't regret it.

I blinked acquiescence and lifted the chalice to my lips and drained every last drop.

She laughed

-That's the fucking spirit, kiddo.

Tiberius staggered over and heaved the amphora aloft and sloshed more of the thick wine into my chalice.

-You have had an intense few days my friend. This retreat is supposed to be about spiritual awakening, music, magic, but most of all it is about fun with a capital F for Fucking Full-On Fun. The wine unfolded like summertime. My mood lifted as it pulsed through my veins. I liked them both again. I loved them both again. Perhaps I'd just taken all of this, *everything*, just a little too seriously. My head had been in a strange place at the church. It was understandable that I may have been a little off kilter, the needle jumping a little wildly at times. Maybe it was time I just unwound and let myself go. I should really be enjoying all this.

-Cheers to you and Pinky. Tiberius lifted his chalice.

-Cheers, Tiberius, and you know, both of you, I'm sorry if I've been a bit withdrawn or even a little suspicious or whatever. I've had a lot on my mind, there's been a lot to process you know. I guess I owe you both an apology and well, thanks for having me here, this place really is pretty fucking magical.

I beamed ecstatically at them both.

-Don't be so silly, Leonard. I know how strange this place can feel at times, but that intensity, that's the fuel that fires it all. That's the engine that drives it, that emotional yo-yoing, the heartaching toing and froing is the price we gladly pay for total enlightenment. And all the fucking is great isn't it?

She said this, eyeing me slyly, as she had over martini's that night in Vienna. Tiberius and Pinky exchanged a look, I didn't know what it meant, but I didn't mind, it didn't matter. Suddenly nothing really mattered. The wine really had lifted my spirits. Tiberius banged a bronze gong that was positioned at the tweve o'clock singing stone position. The conversations hushed and all eyes turned to meet his glowing face.

-Tonight, friends, we partake in the greatest of the mysteries. Each of us has a part to play. Each of us has a deal with the deities to make. But first, we must pay homage to the gods with the offering of our songs.

He produced his ebony guitar and began to gently strum sustained elegiac chords of an unusual depth and richness. We all went to our respective sitting stones, the same positions as we had taken when I was first partnered to write songs with Lucia some months ago as decreed by the runes. I looked over to Lucia, she was gazing intently into the fire. She hadn't gotten into the swing of the evening at all: her face was pale and withdrawn. The night drew in, the fire died down and Tiberius began to sing his song.

But he didn't sing his song. He sang my song. The song from the Yorkshire game house. My heart started pounding and I felt a retch of wine rising in my stomach. I turned to look at Pinky, she smiled directly at me and started singing too. I looked frantically left and right as the other guests joined in, all singing my song, singing it straight at me and smiling emptily as they did so.

I sent three lovers to the wilderness and one came back
She had blood in her eyes and carried in her arms a strange looking sack.

Tiberius stood up still singing and strumming his guitar, as he did so the other guests rose and started moving rhythmically in time with the music towards me. Pinky strode towards me swaying and singing.

-Come on, Honey Bunny, sing along!

Someone started beating a drum and the throng surrounded me. They were dancing and swaying and grabbing hold of me urging me to join in. I resisted, they were spinning me around and all the while their singing grew louder, the drum beat increased in tempo and then we were marching into the night. Tiberius, leading the way with his guitar screamed:

-Such beautiful music, your time at Hecate House has not been wasted, the evidence of your labour is thronging in the air around us, but now the hour has come when we must ascend. Come friends, it is time, let the great mysteries commence.

XXIX

The mob marched me across the meadow and into the woods. They were still singing and cavorting. The demented music played on. They were ecstatic, manic, and entirely out of control. Every so often I tried to make a break for it but firm, caressing hands grabbed me and returned me back onto the path.

We emerged from the woods into the bright moonlit meadow and I realised our destination was on the far side marked by two flaming torches: the Scout hut. The merry band of demented acolytes bundled me forcibly through the narrow doorway. Black candles were guttering and smoking but barely illuminated the room at all. The effect of the candles was to make the fresco paintings leap, leering from the walls. The stench of sage and something swinish was overpowering. On the threshold, Lucia pushed through those on either side of me and grabbed my hand, trying to pull me away. Pinky turned sharply on her heel and separated my hand from Lucia's, and taking it herself, led me to a curved Egyptian symbol painted on the floorboards.

-Sit here, this is your spot.

I nodded numbly and sat down glancing back just in time to see Lucia being led through one of the small doorways to the darkened room. It was the awful room that Tiberius had taken me into the other day.

Four other of our house mates, acolytes or initiates, were placed in what seemed to be random positions around the hut. Tiberius and Pinky entered in a thick plume of rank incense. They were both now clad in leathery robes and wore large golden chains around their necks. I noticed that there was a white circle painted on the floor. The other four members of the group were kneeling at the compass points inside this circle. The place where I was sitting was outside the circle. Pinky turned and whispered to Tiberius, his eyes widened, he shook his head, but she leant in, whispering again, insistent, her hand reaching for his. His face was stern and his jaw set, but after a moment he moved forward and with an air of resignation stepped into the circle.

The candles were extinguished. Tiberius rose from his kneeling position and approached the silver cauldron that was the source of the foul vapour filling the room. He picked a satchel and started to throw handfuls of herbs into the coals.

-The purifying rites.

His voice was solemn, shorn of its Manhattan musicality. He threw more handfuls into the smouldering crucible. The four people within the circle began intoning a *basso profundo* incantation, their moaning was reminiscent of Gregorian chant, but the intervals were uneven, harmonies not in thirds and fourths, and too closely aligned. The rising dischords were atonally poisonous to the ear.

-AAAA
EEEEE
IIIIIIII
OOOO
UUUU
The chanting rose and fell.

-Ilex, fennel, ichor, nectar, aconite, hemlock, hellebore.

Tiberius held up a flask of wine and poured that into the smoking thurible with a hiss.

- The apple of Aphrodite herself, the sacred sacrament, Psilocybe azurescens.

He emptied the picnic basket of mushrooms into the smouldering cauldron. I went to stand up but before I could even get up to my knees, Pinky and Yuki beside me fell about my shoulders. Their hands locked in place across my back. I was firmly pinned. The room plunged into darkness. I heard a noise, something was moving near me. The noise came again. An animal noise. A heavy animal panting snort. It was moving around the outside of the circle. Then it stopped somewhere close in the shadows.

Straining my eyes I could just make out Pinky moving to the thurine and taking up a pointed surgical-looking instrument. The pulse in my neck started to throb hard enough that my vision began to warp in time with it. She submerged this implement into the thurine filling it up and then removed it and turned in the direction of the panting animal. Whatever the animal was, I could now see it was holding a shotgun in front of itself, the barrels pointing upwards. Pinky moved forward and began to pour liquid delicately into the barrel; it must have been almost a pint in capacity. Once the first barrel was filled to the brim, she turned and repeated the process methodically. She set the instrument down on the floor and curtseyed to the animal. She took a black bandage from her pocket.

-What we need you to do, Honey Bunny, is something that has been happening in secret for millennia, for time going back beyond time. We need you to see something

special for us, to go somewhere special for us, and commune
with someone very, very, important to us.

-Pinky

I thought I was screaming but it came out as a whisper.

-Baby, you really don't have any choice, so you don't
have to say that again. Let me explain. You are going to take
a dose of this special potion we've made here. And what we
need you to do now, we need you to do it *willingly*.

I sobbed. She moved back to the animal and whispered
something into a hairy ear. It moved forward heavily on its
hind legs, proffering the shotgun at me. Pinky started to
wrap the black bandage around my head.

-Pinky, stop it please.

-Shush.

-Now, you're going to put that gun in your mouth and
you are going to drink every last drop, and you are going to
enjoy it, you are going to really *want* to do this.

-Please, Pinky.

-Because, Honey Bunny, if you don't, our lord and
master will squeeze the trigger and blow your blonde head
clean off your shoulders. So I think you will drink every last
drop for us, won't you?

There was a clattering of hooves and Pinky's fingers
clamped around my jaw. She slipped her fingers over my
lips easing my mouth open further as I screamed, and I felt
the metallic apertures of the shotgun meet my lips.

-There we go baby, softly softly, here comes the
aeroplane, open up nice and wide.

I shook my head pathetically trying to bite her fingers,
but Pinky had clamped her left hand around my forehead

holding me still. The barrels continued their progress, forcing their way between my teeth and I felt the first of the bitter fluid enter my mouth. I retched as it surged over my tongue. The angle of the shotgun adjusted upwards horizontally and my mouth was entirely filled with foul liquid. I felt Pinky's fingers pinch my nostrils, finally cutting off my ability to breathe. The shotgun was jerked encouragingly. My lungs started to ache and burn. I was choking. I gulped. The concoction seared as it went down my throat, and the instant it touched my stomach I heaved, but I suppressed a vomiting retch and just kept gulping. I knew the animal would take great pleasure in seeing my head explode like a watermelon. I felt the last of the fluid drain from the barrels.

I heard a distant whistling sound, a whistling that seemed to be emanating from within my skull. It sounded like a distant howling gale. It sounded like the wind I had heard in my dream of the black pyramids. The shotgun was still in my mouth. I heard shuffling, and the hands around my shoulder blades released, a moment later the blindfold fell from my eyes. The hypogaeum was empty. Pinky alone stood in front of me, she was now holding the shotgun. The animal was gone.

-Well done, baby. I am so proud of you.

She pulled the trigger. Both hammers fell with a dull metallic click. She lifted the gun out my mouth laughing so hard that she almost dropped it.

-Baby, you didn't really think we'd blow your brains out, did you?

I slumped forward on my knees crying.

-You evil fucking cunt.

I tried to lunge at her but just sprawled helplessly at her feet.

-Don't do anything silly now, just you sit down for a second.

Fluorescent strip lighting hanging from the ceiling flickered on, bathing the room in harsh white light. There was a noise by the door and two large men in suits entered. I recognised them, they were the men from the flight to Vienna. Pinky knelt down and spoke to me in a hushed, urgent tone.

-In a moment these nice gentlemen are going to escort you to somewhere else on the mountain. You are going to go with them, *willingly*. I really need to be sure you do this willingly as otherwise the next bit doesn't work properly and that will be a problem. Do you understand me, Leonard?

Pinky took my head in her hands and gazed at me intently as if divining something in my reeling eyes.

-If you try to run away, they will simply leave you. And given how many grams of Psilocybin you have surging through your veins right now, you don't want to be left helpless and intoxicated on a mountain side in Northern California overnight. You will be discovered smashed to pieces at the bottom of a ravine in the morning, or possibly months from now your mauled carcass will be found by a luckless hiker.

She smiled at me and licked her lips, stood up and smoothed down her robe, running her fingers through her hair.

-You really have done so very well with all this darling, really no one has ever responded to this process quite so calmly. You really were quite cool. I think you may actually enjoy the next part of the process, well at least, I do hope you try to enjoy it.

She looked at me with an earnest encouraging smile and moved over to the far side of the room, popping a small Dior bag over her shoulder.

-I will see you soon, Honey Bunny, have a wonderful trip!

She strode out the door with imperial authority. I sat motionless with my legs sprawled out in front of me, the lights flickered. The large men look down at me solemnly and without pity.

XXX

Time started passing in a way it had never done so before. The striplights slowed their flickering. The slices of darkness between the light elongated, strobing to a slow blink. The room began unfolding like origami, becoming divergent and dislocated. Things were flowering, telescoping, fracturing apart, and blossoming into a tesseract of golden lotuses. *All things begin and end in eternity.*

I looked at my hands, they were pink long-legged aliens. In the stroboscopic lighting, they began to take a myriad of forms, flexing and shapeshifting, transforming into newborn entities attached to the end of my arms. My head swung with the momentum of a mediaeval anvil in the direction of the door. The two men were both wearing mirrored aviator sunglasses...no, they were not wearing mirrored aviator sunglasses, there was something terribly wrong with their faces. They were wearing flesh masks. The floor flexed and a liquefying ripple radiated around me. I inhaled a hot desert wind that howled over my canyoning mind. I blinked and the universe glitched, reversed, stopped and began again. I leant forward and a trillion megatons of nuclear material stored in the heart of a distant white dwarf erupted, cooled, and then reignited.

I was off my feet being dragged and then hurled out of the scout hut. It took a really long time for me to hit the ground. I landed in the tall grass that was growing before my eyes. The four legs of the Russians moved mechanically towards me. I laughed uncontrollably, a laugh that soon devolved into awful sobbing. They shoved me forward. A troop of nymphs and naiads emerged from the glowing ravine. The two Russian men now seemed to be stately equines squiring me along. I stumbled and fell every so often. They hoofed me up and carried me until the knife pangs of nausea subsided. The grass was now at head height and the ground was sloping upwards at 86 degrees. The man to my left had the head of a pale grey horse. He turned and neighed at me, his white horse teeth glinting in the moonlight. The one to my right still had his human head but his lower body was now that of a stallion, he was a centaur. I had the thought that they should somehow combine to form one complete horse which I could then ride to our destination. I tried to vocalise this but discovered I was unable to speak at all.

A small hissing sound passed from my lips. I must have a slow puncture. The heavens above were imploding.

We burst from the jungle of grass onto a barren-cresting plain hellscape. Day was night, night was day, and all was disordered. The sky was one flat shock of brilliant white, the horizon a fine black obsidian line. There was tundra extending away from me following the undulations of trees and earth into an inverted counter-Californian nightmare. We turned onto a set of worn stone steps carved into the side of the mountain, and I looked around this blasted shadowland, this negative photographic plate of a landscape previously idyllic. The horse-headed man and the centaur would turn and look but always continued dragging me along. We descended further into a ravine that lay hidden in the lea of the great mountain.

She'll be coming round the mountain when she comes.

My steads slowed. The one to my left, the centaur, produced a flashlight, and as he clicked it on, the sound echoed like a sonar along the length of the narrow valley. The beam shimmered brilliantly, and I was able to see white light refracting and splitting into the seven constituent colours of the rainbow. I kept my eyes closed for a time. When I eventually opened them, we were standing in front of a stone entrance cut into the side of the mountain, two pillars, and a plinth in classical Grecian style. Carved on the lintel piece was the phrase:

VOCATUS ATQUE NON VOCATUS DEUS ADERIT.

The Russian to my right grabbed my head in his hands. I was so startled that I didn't notice that he had transformed back into human form. He looked into my eyes and examined my face. He let go of my head and turned to the other man.

-On v poryadke...kak dolgo, poka my yego ne otpravim?

The other man nodded slowly and glanced at his wrist watch.

-Fifteen minut ponimayesh'?

He peered into the doorway and then back at the other man,

-Da, da.

My examiner took out a packet of Parliament cigarettes, offered one to his partner, took one for himself, and then just before popping it in his mouth looked back at me, our eyes locked. Lurid watercolours were running from everything. He offered the pack to me, I extended my alien appendage, and took a cigarette.

-Spasibo. I murmured.

I inhaled the tarry tobacco and realised that I was acclimatising to the huge dose of hallucinogens in my system. The cigarette tasted really good. Both men finished their cigarettes at exactly the same time and stamped them out. The one on the right with the flashlight clicked it on and cautiously peered inside the entrance. He grunted and then turned to me and gestured in the direction of the entrance. We had taken just a few steps inside when he stopped abruptly and shone the torch beam onto the floor in front of him. There was a round stone trap door. It had a rusted iron handle in the middle. The first man handed the torch to the man beside me, and kneeling took the iron ring and heaved with leg trembling exertion trying to lift the stone. He readjusted his stance and barked.

-Nebol'shaya pomoshch', pozhaluysta.

The other man stepped forward and clasped hold of the ring and together they heaved. The stone trap door lifted and rolled away, exposing a small black hole in the floor.

The first man stood back panting and picked up the flashlight.

He swung the beam into the hole. I was able to make out the smooth stone sides descending directly down and on one side iron rungs of a ladder sunk into the tunnel.

He turned to me and gestured.

-You go down.

I shook my head. He gestured at the narrow aperture again with the torch beam, and the other man took a step towards me.

-No.

The second man grabbed me by my arm and held me up to the edge of the hole. I looked down, a sheer drop into unbroken blackness. The beam of the torch only penetrated for a few hundred feet before dissipating into the void.

-Down you go. You climb.

-No, no please.

-Or we drop you down. It makes no difference.

He shoved me again, the other one grabbed me, spun me around, knelt down and placed my shaking foot on the first rung of the metal ladder. I looked up at him, my eyes pleading, my hands shaking, I clasped them together in a prayer gesture.

-Please, *please*.

He put his head to one side, disgust played on his taut lips. Little flecks of spittle clung to the corners of his mouth. He put both hands on my shoulders and pushed down hard. My foot on the rung slipped, but I managed to place the right foot next to it. He pushed again harder.

-Down you go.

-Please.

I felt myself slipping backwards, if I slipped, I would fall to my death in the pit below. I relinquished and slunk down, my left foot extending for the next rung, which flailing in the air below it, blindly found. I began to descend. I looked up and the flashlight flared in my eyes, both men were leaning in and grinning at me. The one on the left reached for the stone trap door, their faces began to shift and morph once again, but this time they were not pretty horses.

-Wait wait.... no. I protested and started to scrabble out of the mouth of the hole.

-Noch' Noch,' said the other Russian.

The stone slid over the hole dropping perfectly into place with a terminal thud, just above my head.

XXXI

I couldn't tell you how long I screamed for, but it was long enough for me to no longer be able to really make a screaming sound anymore, something in my throat just gave out and I had a hot metallic taste in my mouth. The tunnel pressed in around me. I could feel its granite constriction on all sides. It was black. Pitch dark. The demons and other things appeared one by one. They are never far from my waking mind, even now, years later and many thousands of miles down the line. I can be back there, in that hell state, in an instant.

These visions came in awful swathes. I could feel my breath condensing on the cold stone directly in front of my face, droplets running down my hands that were gripping the iron rung. I squeezed my eyes shut in an attempt to clear my vision of the swirling hallucinations. I counted slowly to four on my inhale, held my breath, and then exhaled counting to four. I repeated this for quite a while. Gradually I felt my racing heart begin to slow, my head cleared ever so slightly.

Eyes open or eyes shut made no difference. The hallucinations came and went of their own accord. All I knew of my surroundings was the brief glimpse of the tunnel I had seen from the torch beam. There was only one possible axis of travel, straight down.

I let one exploratory foot dangle from the rung I was standing on, at the expected distance below, it touched upon another iron rung. I stepped onto it, then the other foot followed, my hands gripped onto the next rung, I tentatively repeated the process, my feet found the next rung, and the next rung, and so began my long descent into the blackness.

Time passed, perhaps a lot of time. It was impossible to have any notion of how long I had been climbing down the ladder. A dull throb was becoming torturous in my thighs and my palms were starting to burn from the abrasion of the rungs. And then, something actually quite lucky happened to me. I stopped. I stopped dead. I have no idea why I did this. My foot dangled down, cautiously seeking for the next rung. I crouched on one leg, extending my other leg as far as I could – nothing, just the smooth stone wall of the tunnel. There was nowhere to go up or down. I felt strangely calm. Taking my hand from the ladder I fumbled at the hem of my robe, my fingers sought out one of the brass buttons. Getting hold of one, I ripped it from the fabric. I extended it out into the darkness and let it drop. It clattered less then a second below, clattered and rolled to a stop. It had clattered onto stone. There was ground very close below. I ripped another button from my robe and repeated the process, paying even more attention to the echo. A metre maybe, a metre and a half at best, I reckoned, perhaps a little wishfully. It did not take me long to weigh up my options. I thought of things I regretted and people I would miss, one person in particular, I thought of a few memories.

Close to heaven, close to heaven, close as a kiss, close to you.

Then I leant back and let go.

XXXII

I fell for less than a second. My back hit the floor only about two metres from where I had been standing on the bottom rung, hard enough to knock all the air from my lungs, but I had never been happier to be so badly winded. I moaned with strange delight as I rolled around, gasping, trying to get my breath back. Then I lay still in the true and total darkness, the visions swirling and returning with renewed potency. Elves and dwarves were rustling around me in the bituminous black. A deep fatigue from my hours of climbing set in. I resisted the urge to succumb and forced myself to my feet, deciding I must find something out about the place I was in. I staggered to and fro, until eventually I connected with a jagged rock wall on the far side, away from where I'd fallen. I traced my hand around this, marking a circumference of some several metres. A large solid rock chamber. There were no other openings, I was summarily trapped. I had climbed into an oubliette.

I crumpled to the floor, total despair coming upon me with the finality of a wrecked transatlantic liner slipping into the seabed. I moaned. The elves were rustling to and fro. I felt another wave of the hallucinogen surging within, probably combining with adrenalin to create a terrible new chemical compound. Madness, or some form of awful self-slaughter was now a very real possibility. Dashing my own brains out might be my only way out. I sobbed onto the stone and the dwarves and elves and grey wraith things gathered around and looked down at me.

I must have lost consciousness, because when I opened my eyes, stars and distant nebulous galaxies were passing by. I was still imprisoned in my black, featureless sarcophagus. I lay back and watched the universe unfold for what felt like an aeonic passage of space and time. And then I was once again awake, back in the cave, but there were no elves or dwarves, and the swirling galaxies were gone, and something else had taken their place. A glimmering light coming from behind me, illuminating the damp glistening walls. I sat up and turned around. Pinky was standing in a red robe, holding a hurricane lamp, looking at me coolly and luxuriating in the moment of her perfectly stage managed discovery.

I saw her folding and unfolding as if there were an endless sequence of reflecting mirrors behind her, or a television feedback loop. She lifted her hand in beckoning gesture and I saw in slow motion an endless succession of Pinkies, one after the other, after the other.

She looked sensual and electric. A dopamine wave or something wonderful crashed over me, warm as a Calima breeze. I wondered how she had come to be standing there, but I didn't really care. Watching the light play amongst her auricomous hair, I considered, once and for all, crawling on my hands and knees and begging her to marry me. Then she winked and vanished between two atoms. The light went with her, but I could still hear her singing:

I sent three lovers to the wilderness
And one came back
She had blood in her eyes and carried in her arms
A strange-looking sack
As I laid her down, she never made a sound, save for
these words of misery...
So I looked inside the sack
Then said my prayers,
Changed my name
And never looked back...

I stumbled forward as the lamplight faded and saw that there was indeed a door. A narrow slit, no more than a foot in width, where two palisades of stone lay almost overlapping. I shoved myself through the aperture, which led to the delta of a narrow passage. At the far end she was waiting, smiling coquettishly. Catching my eye, she turned the corner, singing as she went:

I wandered to the water's edge to find a ship
Found a one eyed sailor and offered him all I could give
I climbed aboard and turned to shore to say goodbye to
my land
And looking back there was a statue of me and howling
sand.

I hurled myself after her, but as soon as she had rounded the cornerstone the lamplight was once again gone and I was running in pitch dark down the uneven passage. A few footsteps later and I caught sight of her. She turned and stepped down another passage. It was a labyrinth, not one made of words or illusions but of solid stone. I realised that if I lost her, I would never find my way out. I would be condemned to wander blindly down these alleys of eternal night until my heart gave out. I saw her lamp glowing again up ahead, and a streak of her rufescent robe as she turned. She lingered, waiting for me. I ran on and took another turn pivoting where last I had glimpsed her, and was confronted by emptiness. I had lost her. I was lost forever too. I screamed her name. I was now the loneliest minotaur that ever lived. I sobbed again and rocked my head into the stone of the maze floor.

That's when I heard it: a distant reverberation, her unmistakable mezzo-soprano. She was still singing to me. She was still singing my song. I started to scramble on my hands and knees along the passage, straining to follow the familiar melody down the maze of passageways. I was seeking her by her vibrations; she was leading me out of the labyrinth with her siren song. I made a sudden sharp left and tumbled clear out into a bright golden chamber, and there was my lover, my enemy, my goddess, my muse, my destroyer, my creator, my queen, my executioner, standing patiently, smiling and singing.

She looked at me for a long time. I was still on my knees, arms outstretched, ready to receive divine instruction.

-Oh, Leonard.

In my kingdom you have to run as fast as you can just to stay in the same place.

XXXIII

-Kalisti!

As she stressed the three consonants, she released from her palm a golden orb which arced through the air toward me. The cold heft of the gold slapped into my palm as I caught it. If I hadn't, it would have knocked my front teeth out. I held it up. It was a golden apple, perfectly sculpted. An utterly bewitching object. Engraved on one side of the apple was a K, and rolling it over, I recognised Pinky's own fine cursive script:

For the most beautiful

- Bestow the apple upon one that you wish to. In fact that is the very next thing you shall do.

An ethereal ascension of piercing bright notes aspirated within the golden chamber, and lo and bloody behold, there was Tiberius Red. Perched on a stool that looked like it was made from the polished tusks of a giant narwhal. His rosy lips embouchure'd delicately to a long bone-white flute. I stepped closer, his eyes were glassy, he was in a trance, and his vacant expression reminded me of a carnival medium. His ensemble was offset by a huge red pointed wizard's hat. A wooden door on the far left of the chamber opened, and there came a row of naked women. Tiberius increased the intensity of his flute music. The nine naked women formed a line and turned to face me,   their backs to the wall   . Pinky strode towards them.

-Now you must choose the most beautiful one, the *Kalisti*, and you must bestow upon your favourite the Apple of Discord.

She stepped towards a marble pedestal atop which was a large sand clock.

-You have 23 seconds.

She turned over the hourglass. The inverted reservoir of sand began to flow. I looked from the glass to the row of naked women. As I looked something dreadful began to happen. The nine women in front of me, none of whom I had immediately recognised, began to morph and melt, like waxwork mannequins in a factory fire. Their faces were changing, re-arranging, and then new faces began to emerge and ooze, new bodies too, but these were ones that I recognised. They became girls that I had known, girls I had briefly possessed, and girls I had chased. They were glaring, demanding askance, with medusan accusatory expressions flashing over their faces.

One night stands, ones that got away, ones I could only dimly recall making eye contact with over a bar, ones from when I first even became aware of girls, old flames, new flames, wives of my friends, every women I had ever felt a pang of passing interest or lust for, women I had sung to and tried to woo, women I'd pretended to be someone else in order to ensnare. A horrifying fleshy firing line of indiscretion and duplicity, all loaded and aimed directly at me. At my shallow, manipulating, wanton, desirous, self-serving self, all targeted at the very heart of my psyche. I felt my knees buckle under the weight of unendurable shame. I heard her laughter. She was laughing at me. She stamped her foot and clutched her sides, steadying herself on the pedestal,

-Well I must say, this is amusing. Ten seconds to choose, honey bunny!

Their unrelenting gaze, rods of scorn, like the archers of Agincourt, piercing and penetrating. I saw a familiar face laughing ghoulishly.It was that of my former fiancée. I screamed. Time slowed. One of the changelings coalesced into the shape of Lucia, my betrayer. She had sold me out. Lucia, who had clearly been part of their game and had obviously manipulated me since the moment we met, probably since that night at the wedding when we had played hide and seek. Smiling and murdering while she smiled. I stood up, my vision narrowing. The flute music was unbearable. If there was a Hell, I was there. I staggered towards Lucia. If anyone deserved the Apple of Discord to be placed upon their palm, it was her. I took one final step towards her. I thought I saw a flicker of a familiar, gentle, caring, pleading expression flash in her dark green eyes. I narrowed mine in reply. I extended my right hand, clutching the heavy golden apple. She flinched, her eyes beseeching me, my right hand came forward, the apple glinting. I saw its orb move across her wide black watery pupils, her mouth shaped slowly into dreadful swollen horror. Her left hand lifted mechanically, her palm open and trembling. I looked deep into her eyes and dropped the apple into her hand.

-*The most beautiful.*

The flute music instantly ceased. The room brightened.

-The KALISTI!

The other eight female phantoms peeled away. Lucia snapped from her trance and the terror of realisation broke across the delicate lines of her face.

-What have you done?!She screamed in my face and doubled over. Before she could fall, the two Russian men appeared from either side of the chamber and seized Lucia's crumpled form and dragged her, screaming and writhing, towards the door. I ran forward, her head lifted as she was dragged backwards, dark matted hair obscuring her distraught twisting features. Her green streaming eyes met mine, and they flashed a dreadful message back at me.

I turned to Pinky

-Stop all this!

She ignored me and walked across the black and white tiled floor to the centre of the room. I reeled around, enraged, and was about to grab one of the heavy brass oil lamps when a large hairy hand seized my arm, twisting it sharply behind my back. I could tell by the sickly stench of the aftershave it was another fucking Russian. He glided me over the floor towards Pinky. Tiberius stood and started to walk in a swaying sashay, in wide circles, blowing a sickening adagio on his bony flute. Pinky's eyes met mine warmly,

-You are doing so well tonight, my love. I really wasn't sure if you would make it this far – you seem so...so *fragile* sometimes.

Two more Russians came forward from the gloom, carrying stately golden thrones, with royal purple satin. Pinky reclined serenely on the throne to the left, the Russian still clenching my throbbing arm, shoved me onto the other one. I went to stand and a heavy hand fell on my shoulder holding me in place. Pinky extended her own delicate hand onto mine.

-Settle down, it's time for a play. I remember you telling me all about your favourite plays. You love plays.

-What?

-A play, baby, a very special play, put on especially for you...Well, it's all about *you*.

Two more Russians had joined the attendants, and in a pantomime of regal ceremony carried Pinky and I aloft, the thrones resting on their shoulders. The interior of the next cavern was a perfect recreation of a seventeenth century proscenium theatre with a shimmering arch and raked stage. There were two tiered half circular balconies above us, both entirely empty. The stage was lit by limelight. Two attendants hurried forward, one of them placed a crystal glass into Pinky's outstretched hand into which he decanted the effervescing contents of an open bottle of Krug Clos d'Ambonnay. The other attendant stood over me and with a flourish extended a length of grey gaffer tape. He leant forward and started taping my wrist against one of the ornate armrests. He fastened my other wrist to the other arm rest, then wrapped a length around both legs until I was firmly affixed. Finally, two lavish crowns were ceremonially lowered, one on my head, the other onto Pinky's. Reclining back into the velvet and sipping from her glass, she beamed at me.

-This is something really special. Very few people ever get to experience anything like this. Catharsis...You get to purge all your pity and all your fear.

A bell rang out across the empty theatre. The house lights were dimmed and Tiberius leapt onto the stage.

-O for a Muse of fire, that would ascend
The brightest heaven of invention,
A kingdom for a stage, princes to act
And monarchs to behold the swelling scene!

My Lady and Gentleman, I present to you – The Golden Chain of Homer!

Pinky clapped, stamping her feet against the floor.

-Our play is taken from an ancient Greek legend about the chain that connects heaven to the Earth. Each scene is a theatrical expression depicting a series of alchemical rules that are part of that great hermetic philosophy.

He produced a glistening chain, brandishing its twelve entwined links in the air.

-Each symbol encountered in the story is a transitional step from one state of being to the next.

He adjusted his grip on the chain and as he spoke he moved through the links like a set of rosary beads.

-The apotheosis of this golden chain in alchemy was known as the Materia Prima or the Azoth. it could remove impurity from the living to make them immune from death.

This extremely experimental process is the *matter* of the play we now humbly present to you.

He took a deep bow. I heard the shuffling of stagehands and when the limelight lifted it revealed an incredibly detailed set. The black backdrop had been replaced with a series of stained glass windows, looking out onto a painted scene of a graveyard and distant rolling moors. There was a rug, a spiral staircase, a large bookshelf, a Chesterfield sofa, a table that had once been an altar, a seventies hi-fi replete with German-made speakers and a stuffed black and white cat perched on the windowsill. A perfect recreation of the Church of the Horses, set as it was on the night that I had received Tiberius' invitation. I turned to Pinky, she had a feigned expression of surprise on her face.

An actress entered from stage left. She was dressed and made up to look exactly like me, a staggeringly accurate likeness of myself. Her medium length blonde hair was brushed back and tucked behind her ears; she had stage makeup around her eyes and cheekbones and fine dappling that gave the appearance of a few days of stubble. She worea white shirt and black suit jacket, slim fitting black suit trousers and a pair of cherry red Doc Martens. Pinky giggled.

The actress playing me crossed to one side of the stage, knelt down and selected a record, placed it on the turntable and danced across the stage quite badly to the music. She lit a cigarette and knocked back a glass of red wine while twirling around the church interior. I looked on, half disgusted.

A clunky prop phone buzzed as the actress danced over to it. She was over-acting, reading a message and then throwing her hands up in a gesture of startled excitement. A thumping orchestral show tune kicked up, and from either side of the stage poured a chorus line made up of the other guests of Hecate house, dressed in boiler suits but with angelic tinfoil wings on their backs. They started dancing a choreographed routine around the actress playing me. The raucous show tune built to a crescendo with the actress darting over to a writing desk and scribbling a note down, before one of the angels, with the vague demeanour of Higgs, handed her a suitcase and guitar. Then the actress swanned out of the church followed by this chorus line of angelic showgirls.

The music faded in cue with the lights dimming, just a prop candle left burning near the writing desk on stage. There was a sound effect of a snowstorm blowing and the creak of a rusty gate. The front door of the church, at the far left of the stage, swung open and through it entered another female actress, made up to perfectly resemble my ex-fiancée. Her peroxide blonde hair tied in a bun, a pencil tucked behind her ear, a smouldering rollie cigarette on the go, her simple dress paint-splattered from a day at work. The actress playing her stumbled out of the storm and dropped her bag by the door and looked around, an expression of confusion playing over her hard northern countenance. She walked across the stage, her alarm at my absence visibly growing with each step. She grabbed the note that I'd left on the desk. She read it over and over, she clutched her head, and looked around searchingly again. She read, frantic and panicked, and then slumped down onto the rug, clutching the note to her chest. Her sobbing echoed across the auditorium. My tongue was a dry husk. Pinky whooped and cheered in delight, stamping her feet and sloshing back more champagne.

-Bravo! Bravo!

She laid a gentle and patronising hand onto my white straining knuckles.

-Don't get too excited, that was just the first scene. We don't want you wearing yourself out prematurely. There's so much more to come.

She ran her tongue around the outside of my ear. I squirmed, the crown slipping down my forehead and partially obscuring my vision.

I could not say for certain how long I endured the play. The performance style and theatrical techniques possessed a molten quality. Sometimes it was blank verse and mime, at other moments were perfectly rendered farce, then in the next scene it slipped into some restrained 19th century domestic drama, then suddenly became a Broadway musical, then Kabuki; a mad whirring merry-go-round of moments, a collage cut from the fabric of my life. All the episodes were retold from differing points of view. I was re-experiencing them at a remove. No longer the I of experience, but as voyeur and judge. I had to admit as I sat strapped to my throne gasping, sobbing and wincing, that the play had a devastatingly upsetting but also, hugely *valuable* effect.

***

Lucia, or an actress who looked just like Lucia, swayed languidly across the stage. The projected pattern of trees moving like radar lines across her body. She had a paperback novel in her hand; she occasionally glanced down at the open page, scanning a phrase or two and then looking up and out into the audience with an elevated thoughtful expression. She twirled in a graceful daydream motion to the centre of the stage; she let her arms fall languidly to her sides and then started to sing in her inimitable dulcet tones that I recognised from the nights I'd spent writing with her, but this was not her song, it was someone else's, it was old and familiar:

Some enchanted evening,
You may see a stranger,
You may see a stranger,
Across a crowded room,
And somehow you know,
You know even then,
That somewhere you'll see her
Again and again...

A big band instrumentation swelled in accompaniment to her singing.

Who can explain it?
Who can tell you why?
Fools give you reasons;
Wise men never try.

And then the actress playing me entered stage left. She had changed into the exact costume I had been wearing the night of the Chevalier's wedding. The actress playing me spied Lucia and started to approach her from downstage, there was a touch of *What's the Time, Mr Wolf?* about the wide stepping gait the actress deployed in the recreation of my approach. As she was drawing close, at the very last moment, Lucia whirled around.

-Oh hello there stranger. I thought I caught you looking at me back there in the library.

Lucia said, exactly as she had said to me that night. The actress playing me froze midstep, floundering to find words, a wideeyed expression of surprise lighting up on her face. I stood frozen, as the words which I had not too long before uttered, and those which came in reply, were regurgitated back to me now through the miasma of gaudy theatre, now somehow become ridiculous.

-Say, would you like to play hide and seek with me?

They darted to and fro about the stage to the notes of Berlioz's *Symphonie fantastique*, struck at a rending volume. They danced a dance of hide and seek and I watched, strapped to my throne, and wept.

The choreography grew in complexity and ambition and before long I realised I was watching an entirely new form, each fluxing mood expressed in coordinated gestures perfectly poised to Appoline movement concordant with the symphony. Sickeningly brilliant dancing. As the first movement attained its serrating finale, the deafening timpani drums resonated in my diaphragm. My tears blinded me. I realised that I was a traitor. I deserved to have my throat cut, my tongue torn out, and to be buried in the sand at low tide. Dark shadows emerged from the stage periphery as the lights flared. Lucia convulsed and twisted, seized by stagehands. She screamed and broke free staggering towards the front of the stage, her green cat's eyes flashing. She was terrified.

-You have to help me! You have to, Leonard!

She let out a piercing scream, and two men grabbed her. Tiberius strode to the centre of the stage. He stood staring directly at me. As the last of the shuffling kicks and muffled screams of Lucia being dragged away died down, he announced in an officious tone:

-The Theatre of Memory is now closed.

XXXIV

And with that the curtain fell...a rough Hessian sack was pulled over my head. The tape around my arms and legs was ripped away and I was dragged from my throne and spun around in several rotations before being briskly marched out. I was hauled down onto a steeply descending slope. The air was foetid, with a sepulchral chill. The men escorting me stopped abruptly, pulled me up and had a terse exchange in Russian. There was a sound of metal grating against stone, a door was heaved open. I was shoved forward and I stumbled into an even steeper descent. There was a pungent odour, an unctuous blend of storax, frankincense and galbanum, but there was something else too, that burnt swinish smell that always lingered around Hecate House. From our echoing steps I inferred that we had entered a much larger space and I felt an intense blast of heat. I knew there were others present. The sack was whipped off my head.

I was in a huge cave. Its ceiling must have been several hundred feet above my head. In front of me was a roaring fire pit. Next to that stood Pinky in her scarlet gown. And next to her was a crude stone altar and, beyond, a horrific mural, a dreadful thing. It was rendered in the charcoal-black and blood-red colouring of cave paintings. An utterly revolting image.

-Bring him here.

Pinky's voice echoed across the cave. The two men seized hold of me and I shrugged them off. They glanced at Pinky, who nodded her assent. I walked along the flagstone path surrounding the roaring fire pit and joined her in front of the altar.

-I hope you enjoyed your play. We all worked very hard on it. It will help you slough off the dead skin of your old self, your old soul.

She fluttered her eyelids at me.

- I want to go right now.

-Oh don't be like that,

She rubbed my arm.

-This is such a special night for you.

She broke off and moved to the right of the altar where a large red leatherbound book was open on a reading stand. She started turning the huge parchment pages.

-Can I fix you a drink, my love?

She produced a bottle and a crystal tumbler. She poured generously and handed it to me. It glistened in the roaring firelight. I took it from her, weak, acquiescent and vacant. She smiled and bit her lip. A look of uncertainty passed over her features like a line of fine ink dropping through water.

She returned to leafing through the huge red book. I sipped the whisky; it tasted good. I glanced around the cave. There were all the guests of Hecate House in a silent congregation around the edge of the fire pit. I could make out more robed figures in the darkness beyond. *Just be cool.* Pinky found what she was looking for in the big red book and lifted it from the stand.

-The power of Abraxas is twofold but you see it not, because in your eyes the warring opposites of this power are extinguished. What the god-sun speaketh is life. What the devil speaketh is death. But Abraxas speaketh that hallowed and accursed word which is life and death at the same time. Abraxas begetteth truth and lying, good and evil, light and darkness, in the same word and in the same act. Wherefore is Abraxas terrible? It is the love of man. It is the speech of man. It is the appearance and the shadow of man. It is illusory reality.

She sighed and I felt the first throbbing of a minacious energy. I looked up at the obscene mural flickering in the flames and in that instant I understood all the ancient mysteries of cave painting.

-This song is nearly sung,

She replaced the red book onto the stand and walked towards me, her irises predatorily dilated. She stepped close enough for me to smell her familiar odour of Chanel and Marlboro Red.

-Do you know, Leonard, that the process by which I *acquired* you, and the process by which I fell in love with you were very similar?

I stared at her eyes and tried to remember loving her.

-It was all illusion and trickery, sleight of hand.

She made a profane wanking gesture and ran her finger along my nose and then down the length of my torso.

-I love your songs. I adore your grand allusions and that hyperbolic way in which you speak about even the most trivial of things. Yes, I really do love the way you talk. Fuck, how you talked and fucking *talked*.

She pulled me close to her.

-Do you see that you were only ever here to amuse me, Leonard?

My back bumped into the edge of the altar.

-What?

-Oh, don't look so upset. Everything is ok, I promise.

She took another step and did a nuzzling thing with her cheek.

-Now you're going to stay here with me on Mountweazel forever. I need you to stay here, writing away, writing about me, singing about me, and your goddess will do anything in return for you.

She extended her hand, vibrating like a piano wire. She placed her index finger gently between my lips. It tasted of ash...with a mousing hint of fish.

-You are my chosen one and I will give you everything your heart desires. I will shower you in golden wishes.

She massaged her finger against the tip of my tongue.

-Just one last sacrifice.

-What do you want?

-I want Babalon and adrenochrome.

-Babalon? I mouthed the word over her index finger. Adrenochrome?

-Yes, honey bunny, Babalon. The first feminine. The
Red Goddess. The heart wants what the heart wants. And
we want the adrenochrome for ecstatic kicks. It's a *party*
thing.

She gestured towards the mural and the robed audience.

-I need you to finish your song, the one that you started
that lonesome night on the moor.

A scream reverberated around the cavern. Lucia was
being dragged by the Russians from an opening just below
the mural. I surged forward but Pinky grabbed my hand.
They manhandled Lucia onto the altar and proceeded to
bind her ankles and wrists. She fought wildly but they easily
overpowered her, pulling a piece of tape over her mouth,
silencing her squeals. They nodded at Pinky. Lucia's eyes
fixed mine in silent pleading, I stared back at her.

*Beauty shames the ugly, strength shames the weak,
innocence shames the guilty.*

Pinky turned to me. In her left hand she held a glinting
silver athame with a ten inch razor blade. In her right hand
she held a silver stemmed chalice. She pressed the items into
my hands. She moved to the head of the altar, looking down
on Lucia as she writhed.

-Now I need you to kill Lucia for me. I need you to fill
that chalice with her blood so we can all drink her.

I moaned. Pinky lifted a finger to her lips. She cocked her
head playfully to one side and produced my black notebook.
She started to leaf through the pages.

-Oh, look at all your lovely songs, Leonard. You have
been busy here. Writing down every last detail. If you do as
I ask, we can make sure the entire world hears your songs.

Don't you like the sound of that? Your songs will grant you the power of the Gods. You and I will be able to do whatever we want for the rest of our endless lives.

- You think all this is real?

-You refuse to play along? Leonard, do you really think I'm just playing now?

-Yes...of course I fucking refuse.

Her face hardened.

-Well, that is a really bad decision, honey bunny.

-It's a bad decision to refuse to murder someone?

She laughed and rolled her eyes. I really, really hated her.

-You would leave me with no other choice but to kill all the members of our little club at Hecate House, everyone. I'd have to do it in a really awful way, of course, to cause as much scandal as possible, to distract from what has really been going on up here. And I would kill Lucia anyway, just *because*, and of course I would kill you too, but I would have some fun with you first, I would find very pleasurable ways of torturing you. Oh, and then we would make certain to frame you for all this. It would all play out perfectly, like *Helter Skelter*. How do you like the sound of that legacy, Saint Leonard?

The razor blade and the chalice felt hot in my hands. The room swam and I rocked and swayed.

-Pinky, don't be so fucking stupid,

-Oh, honey bunny, I have more than enough footage of what you've been up to these last few weeks at Hecate House. All those acid-fuelled orgiastic fuckfests. Hours and hours of the most extraordinarily shameful filth, I must say.

-What?

- And of course you're well known for your interest in the dark arts. The tarot readings at your shows. The occult references in your lyrics. It won't be a stretch of anyone's imagination that you came to California and went off the deep end and ended up murdering a bunch of gullible hippies.

I groaned and the cavern ebbed.

-Now, let's get on with it shall we?

The acolytes took a step forward, tightening the circle surrounding the altar. They picked up torches from the floor and lit them in the flames. Only their glowing eyes were visible beneath their cowls. They began to incant the same discordant hymn they had sung earlier when calling to the animal.

-This is complete perfection. We wear all black. Black cut from the breast of the red star. Renew her blood. Lay it out on a white sheet. Place her heart upon it with blood of birth, since she is born of thy flesh and by thy mortal power give us our wishes on Earth.

The athame and chalice felt as hot as curling tongs in my hands. I found myself standing at the head of the altar, my eyes bleary and unfocussed gazing down at Lucia. She was writhing in terror, eyes reeling, bloodshot and streaming with tears. I felt nothing, nothing but a throbbing ache in the base of my spine. A pleasurable pain that wanted to ascend and stretch its wings. The pain felt good, all of it felt good. Pinky looked up from the red book, smiled, and moved to directly face me from the far end of the altar.

All was red. My vision glowed infrared. Red as love, red as hate, red as shame. I blinked and it all remained, redder than any rose madder. Everything was incarnadine. Pinky was an animate flame. I looked down and Lucia was a thing of liquid gold. She looked delicious, a mouth-watering divinely entwined ouroboros. I wanted to sink my fists deep into her, dive into her golden maw, penetrate her golden soul and embrace her there, holding her heart forevermore. I looked up from the altar, the glowing red goddess was smiling lustily, encouragingly.

-Don't you want a little drink, darling?

I nodded slowly and she stroked my cheek.

-Go on, just do it. She tastes wonderful.

I lifted the knife. All I needed to do was dip the tip of the blade into the lustre of Lucia's skin and fill the cup and drink and perhaps Pinky's prophecy would come true and we would all live happily ever after. My right hand moved in accordance with a deviant scripture, it arced through the air towards Lucia. I felt the shudder of resistance as it encountered a meniscus. I pushed on, applied more pressure, the blade slipped further, the glistening fluid swelled and quelled, the feeling was one of letting a fever break. I leant in harder, my heart throbbing in my chest, I felt my hand touching hot wet flesh. With that the glamour broke. I dropped the blade. A scream. A scream and hysterical laughter.

When are you gonna come down?
When are you going to land?
I should have stayed on the farm
I should have listened to my old man
You know you can't hold me forever
I didn't sign up with you

I'm not a present for your friends to open
This boy's too young to be singing the blues
So goodbye yellow brick road
Where the dogs of society howl
You can't plant me in your penthouse
I'm going back to my plough
Back to the howling old owl in the woods
Hunting the horny back toad
Oh I've finally decided my future lies
Beyond the yellow brick road

THE MARRIAGE OF HEAVEN AND HELL

I

I have no interest in persuading you of anything. As far as I am concerned the events that I am about to relate exist beyond the realm of the regular empirical parameters of scrutability and credulous assessment. This is not a shaggy dog and there's no weighing it up. This is a rabid Irish wolfhound of a tale, baying at the moon, and I advise extreme caution. These are my caveats.

It's something that I wish had never happened to me, and to be directly, inflexibly honest, as I sit here now, I have reservations about setting it down. Prior to this I had only ever recounted these events to two of my closest friends and it had upset them. It perplexed them. It led to difficult questions being raised, and then questions, gently, graciously, and silently dropped. Questions of lifestyle and sanity. Questions of morality. It remains as it is, and was, and always shall be an unsettling red thread running through the spectral fabric of my last album, *Good Luck Everybody* - and it begins exactly where most good stories do.

We had been in a bar on Sunset Boulevard, aptly named
Little Joy, for five hours. Lucia was beginning to get fruity.
She snapped an answer at the journalist sitting in front of
us and then gazed at her phone. She was ready to leave. We
were there for Lucia to do some press meetings about her
forthcoming record release. I was there to drink tequila
and orange juice and to lend some kind of moral support
and perhaps a little pith to proceedings. Detecting a subtle
shift in her psyche, I drained my glass. We signalled cursory
goodbyes and in silent acquiescence stepped out into the
vermillion dusk of an October LA evening.

We barely spoke as the town car edged its way through
the early evening tide of traffic. We had an arrangement
that we would both do the necessary thing to allow the
other to exist in a state of near-perpetual emotional non-
engagement, a sort of hedonic calculus that felt like free fall.
I think of it now as a sort of symbiotic trance.

The car inclined upwards as we started the long climb
up Mulholland on our way to her house, a gaudy seventies
megastructure nestled in a blind alley not accidentally
situated about three hundred feet from the Hollywood sign.
On this occasion, and unlike on the mountain that fateful
night, the set designers had left little evidence of their art.
It was a palace of stately isolation, open plan, equipped
with a spectacularly ostentatious view of Los Angeles.
Floor to ceiling windows, discrete mid-century furniture,
exposed concrete, rugs, and Californian ephemera. She had
chosen it to frame her existence precisely, the ancestral seat
of a goddess of the silver screen. It had an atmosphere of
unease and oozed paranoia like wet ink. In the air, and on

every surface, vibrating resonances of newfound fame and fear. It was as if the place had become a tuning fork for our relationship; it was where we had signed our treaty of chaos and dysfunction, that ever-widening gyre that I, in my naivety and self-imposed amnesia, had found profoundly exhilarating. I loved that house. I had been living there with her since the night we left Mountweazel.

The car took a sharp left. Lucia slipped forward and I reached for her hand. She looked at me unblinkingly, she had a disquieting habit of levelling a gaze at me that felt like it was the first time she had ever laid eyes upon me. A bat squeak of something illicit passed between us. She smiled, leant forward and turned up the radio. *The Mercy Seat* reverberated through the black interior of the car. I turned to look out the window at the vertiginous hills rising either side, the curiously clichéd lights of LA now glistening below and the red eye of the sun going down over the Pacific. I had a resurgent pang of a feeling that had persisted for the last few weeks, of not knowing who I was, or who I was becoming, and how I had ended up in this situation. It manifested as a sort of dissociative rush, a wave that would crest over my mind, time would stand still, I felt weightless for a moment, and then it would submerge back into my unconscious murmurings.

In my mind I was able to compose the sequence of events, order them, see the causality, and yet still not make any sense of my circumstance. I had decided to make another album, and to get over the end of a terrible relationship. I had been recording in a studio on Melrose for six months. I had made new friends and constructed a purposeful life in this city. But everything had been very wrong since that night on the mountain.

There is a rather archaic word, *widderschynnes*, for which there is no definite translation. It roughly means counter, against, unlucky and backwards – somehow all out of whack. Well, everything had been *widderschynnes* since that fateful night. Lucia and I had fallen in love over a debilitating distaste for our own sense of self-awareness. We also shared a fascination for magick, music and the applied imaginative use of the will. We had become a double act as practitioners of the esoteric arts. Some of these we would intuit and just make up the process for ourselves, other aspects we studied and investigated like unattended children. Either way we had been getting results, of a sort. The fact that we stayed in the house pretty much all the time had advanced us rapidly down this arcane path. I would go to the studio between 3pm and midnight. God knows what she got up to during the day but once I returned we would immediately set about on some line of investigation, usually until the sun came up.

The car pulled to a halt at the gates of the house, the driver switched off the radio (...And *The Mercy Seat*...).

- Will you be needing me later, Miss?

- No thank you – we're staying in tonight.

The car door clicked.

We walked across the secluded drive. Graceful palms and high cicada branches curled around a nine foot fence, meaning that the house was completely concealed from the road. Not that anyone ever came down here. It was a blind dead end. That's why she liked it. It was a house designed with privacy as paramount. I had never adjusted to how quiet and remote a feeling it was, despite being in the centre of one of the most frenetic cities in the world.

The gravel of the path glowed a reddish tinge, pebbles like embers in the last light of the sun. I gazed too at the diffuse glow emanating from the skin of her exposed shoulders as she rifled through her purse for the keys. I noticed two small scars just beneath her right shoulder blade and wondered how and where she had acquired these wounds. She glanced back at me but before I could speak she had found the keys and in a moment we were over the threshold into the gloom of the large open plan lounge.

The blue light was dispelled by her immediate lighting of the legion of candles arranged in the centre of the low circular table. She lit her cigarette off one of these and reclined on the voluminous red satin couch. I walked over to the glass double doors that looked out over the most singularly arresting feature of the house: a 40 foot square balcony, built into the hillside itself, a stroke of tasteless grandiose architectural genius. Standing out there you felt as if you were levitating over the city itself. We sardonically referred to it as the Mount Olympus of comedown locations. From its far right hand corner you could look across to the Hollywood sign and down into the steep ravine below. The balcony was flanked on all three sides by sheer drops, all of which terminated in the trees and jagged rocks below. Staring down into the shifting lights I said,

-I think it might be time for a latch-lifter, darling.

I walked to the round corner tiki bar, transplanted from perhaps the seediest cocktail lounge on the strip some 30 years previously. It was maintained by her housekeeper and was a pentagon of intoxicants. At that time our drink *du jour* was a couple of inches of Johnny Walker Blue with soda water, no ice and a glacé cherry for Lucia. We could usually rely upon it to get right to the heart of the matter, or near enough.

Laying back on the couch, we silently observed the gloaming, a meditative mood settling upon us. The room shuddered and jumped in the quivering candle light. Handing me the last gasp of her cigarette she moved to the record player that was positioned on the floor in the very middle of the room, surrounded by an archipelago of records. Records which she purchased obsessively and treated in much the same way as she treated most things in her life, with a degree of carelessness that was both infuriating yet enviable.

I drew on the cigarette, tasting her lipstick and watched as she methodically flipped through the discs. She paused momentarily, selecting an LP; her hair had fallen forward and I couldn't see what selection had caught her eye. Moments later Berlioz's *Symphonie Fantastique* flooded the room. She turned and walked back to the sofa, flamingoing to remove her stilettos. I noticed that her wide green eyes now betrayed a shift in mood and emotion.

-What's it going to be tonight, Leonard?

Ever since fleeing the retreat we had been studying the work of Dr John Dee, Enochian magic, Abramelin the mage and several other Goetic high magic practices. Devising and scrying invisible geometric pathways in time and space. Communing with the angels every other day, working from tarot correspondences and the Kabbalah – all the usual. I reached for the deck and began to search for a particular card. We were looking for a new kind of overpowering folk magic to protect us from whatever it was we had encountered up on Mountweazel. We were both disturbed, self-medicating nightly with magic and blood thinning whisky.

***

At some point in the evening I must have lost consciousness. I awoke on my back beside the table. I sat up; the room was suspended in a profound, upside-down darkness. The candles had all burnt out, save one, flickering on the sideboard near the spiral staircase. I was alone. I stood and groped along the edge of the couch, reaching into my pockets for my lighter. It was then that I noticed my trousers appeared to be covered in honey. My mind flashed to a memory of our magical undertakings that night, and as I relit the candles on the table before me there was indeed the empty jar of Californian honey, along with the razor blade athame, a chalice and the blurred charcoal markings of the pathway we had been working. Jesus Christ. I lit a cigarette and stared at the xenon sky in the windows above. A few moments later I walked over to the tiki to fix myself a drink. It was then that I discovered I was not alone. Nestled in the space between the bar and bookshelf was Lucia, naked, save for her jewellery. She was asleep.

I went to the record player and put on Jacques Brel. I didn't feel like waking her up, her moods being unpredictable if she was roused at this hour. Jacques was singing about Amsterdam. I found my mind wandering to the streets there, to the Paradiso Venue and to a show I had played a year earlier, and the events that had followed. It was then that I heard a sound.

The candles were guttering and I stumbled to the record player to turn it off. As I lifted the stylus, the sound came again. It wasn't a sound I had ever heard before. Here I will do my best against the inadequacy of language; it is too blunt a tool for accurately rendering the real experience. What I heard clearly for the second time in the silence that had settled on the room was a kind of mechanical laughter. A rushing, ticking and whirring sound, mingled with a cackle. A human sounding cackle, fleshy, reverberant and fiercely corporeal, but not in any way something you might mistake for an animal sound. I felt a sensation of terror descend upon me. A keen and almost intelligent terror, a terror impelled by the knowledge that something truly evil is very nearby. I froze. The room pitched briefly. Silence, nothing at all. I cocked my head. Nothing. The double doors were still wide open, leading to the balcony beyond. A gentle breeze was nuzzling the remaining candles. Still nothing more. I stood up very softly, not taking my eyes from the balcony doors. I was certain that was where the sound had originated from and I felt myself attuning to an awareness of a presence just beyond the reflective planes of glass, out on the balcony. I stood staring back at my silhouetted reflection in those glass doors. I felt the breeze from the canyon beyond cooling the broken sweat on my brow. I am not sure how long I stood there unmoving, staring at the darkness beyond the doors. I had almost begun to recover my composure when it came again, longer, more malign and more assured this time. There could be no mistake; it came from something that stood just beyond those doors. Someone was on the balcony laughing mechanically and dreadfully at me.

The kind of fear I felt I can't get down on these pages, it was in no way a common fear. It was nothing like the fear I had felt at the scene of terrible accidents, or when being threatened by lethal force. It ran, in some perverse way, backwards and forwards through time. I knew, innately, that whatever was on the other side of those doors, whatever was in the inky depths of the concrete balcony, was of a calibre of maleficence I had never encountered before... Never thought even possible before.

Looking back now it seems curious that I didn't entertain for a second that the intruder might be a human being, a villain or an opportune thief lurking on the balcony of a big house. I knew that whatever was there, making that sound, was something that I was not going to encounter in a strictly terrestrial way.

I flicked my eyes to the sleeping form of Lucia. The laughter came again. I felt like screaming, screaming to wake her up and screaming to warn her, and screaming at whoever was making that awful fucking sound. It sounded just a shade closer too. A footstep closer, perhaps.

I reached for my cigarettes and lit one, slowly. Inhaling deeply to let the nicotine sink its teeth into my nervous system. My head cleared. Still my eyes fixed on the black void beyond the doors. I decided very quickly to step towards the doors. Before I knew it I was at the threshold, my reflection looming large in the thick glass. It was slightly ajar, a narrow opening before me leading out into the black of night. No sound came. I exhaled smoke that rushed out through the aperture. There was a small sound. A grunt.

I stepped out into the night. I could see nothing at all. I could however now feel something, a presence. I speculated it was about eight feet away from where I was standing. Beyond the gloom I could see the shimmering, infinitely distant city lights. There were shadows cast on all sides. I heard nothing. I took a step forward (I actually cannot tell you why I did this). I heard a movement and the rushing mechanical sound swam around me. It was significantly louder and now nauseating. It was then I knew that whatever was out there with me was truly demonic. It definitely wasn't human. It moved in the blackness, it moved like a sea within a sea. A voice came, a voice of similar tone to the laughter, shrill and ticking. It spoke to me. I found myself speaking back, in a language I did not entirely understand. It moved. A staggering of hard heeled feet on the concrete, I too stepped forward again, and now there was a close communion. I cannot relate what was contained in those moments. I distinctly recall a sudden awareness that I either had to flee or fight, and to flee from what was before me would mean to flee in one of the three remaining directions I could move in, and that meant down to the rocks several hundred feet below the balcony. The thing standing before me had started to make broken, wild sounds.

At this point, I spoke a few words (which cannot be replicated here). From where they came, I know not. After I spoke, I knew that I had a few moments, a few footsteps to get back into the house. I can still feel the sensation of the door slamming closed. I can also recall the thirty seconds of shrieking as I stood staring back at it through the glass, past my own reflection, into its grotesque writhing and seething. Lucia didn't stir. I poured a drink and curled myself around her. I would tell her everything in the morning. I left the remaining candles burning, and before closing my eyes tossed a handful of Palo Santo into the flame.

***

Four months later. I am recording *Good Luck Everybody* again, and this time at Stanley Kubrick's estate just outside of London. We have finished the last take of the last song of that day's session., It is 3:38AM when the band and I retire to the control room. We want to hear the mixes of the songs we have worked on that day. As the tapes spool, I step outside into the freezing February evening to catch my breath. I return to a scene of disarray. The producer and engineer are fraught. The red book, the A5 red book in which we have been noting every stroke and moment of the recording, composed of every 'to do' list, the schematic masterplan of the album, has gone missing, inexplicably. A frantic search commences. We roam every aspect of the estate, no stone unturned and no maggot left lonely. We split up and searched the entire grounds, retracing our steps from the dining room, across the lawn to the studio to no avail. A raging wind blowing, but no rain. It's bitterly cold. I find myself alone in front of the house. I am standing between the arching pillars of the entrance and the overgrown garden halfway down the crazed paving, the gale is howling off the porticos of the building behind me. I know the red book is hopelessly lost – if it was dropped it would have been carried aloft into the eternal. I pause on the path, arrested for a moment by a sound I hear soaring over the tempest. I hear it, unmistakable and recurrent and exactly as it was that long strange night in California. A demonic rising laughter, mechanical and clipped. However, on this occasion I found myself laughing back.

II

Lucia woke up in my arms, shaking. She pawed at my face and I came to with a searing hangover.

-What happened last night?

I rolled onto all fours and crawled to the corner bar. Hoisting myself up to its counter I selected two tumblers and decanted a restorative dose of Kahlúa into each. I swung my gaze to meet hers as I tossed two half melted bits of ice into the glasses.

-Something has been going on, hasn't it? I knew before last night that there was something wrong. All yesterday during the press I felt it. I felt it from them, and I felt it from you. It is like something bearing down on us, something projected and faraway. Something is lurking behind, and beneath and within everything.

- Yes, there is something. I've felt it too. I've seen it.

I paused, trying to decide whether I should tell her what really happened last night. I decided against it.

-I saw something following me on the way back from the recording studio the other night. I think we're being stalked, again.

-Stalked or talked about?

-Stalked, darling, stalked. An agenda behind every smile, an eager eye at every bar, a distant acquaintance pretending to be a familiar friend. You know.

-It's her, isn't it?

She stood up unsteadily from the couch and went towards a pile of her clothes. She slipped pedicured and rubicund painted toes into a hemline that had been hand-sewn in the backroom of Yves Saint Laurent in the mid 1960s. A priceless piece of high couture reduced to a dressing gown in the haze of another mid-morning existential crisis.

-What do we do?

She necked the Kahlúa and her eyes met mine. She was eclipsing the rising West Coast sun and looked half demented and half divine.

-I have no idea, darling, I have absolutely no idea. We've been away from that place for six months. Living like hitmen in the shadow of your public gaze. If only you weren't so fucking famous it might be a lot easier. Perhaps she's coming for us.

-I think I saw her .

-When?

-Two nights ago I pulled over at that stupid place you love, the hot dog place on Melrose. I thought I saw her when I was picking us up a couple of chilli dogs for dinner.

-You saw Pinky?

-I saw her. I saw her in the passenger seat of a Mustang, a newish one.

-What did she do?

-She didn't do anything. She just sat staring at me for ages. I was going to go up to her, but as I paid and turned around the car had gone.

I fumbled around the counter for her white Zippo and shoved a Gauloises into my mouth.

-Why didn't you tell me?

I lit it and looked at her, already feeling the Kahlúa lift like birdsong.

-I knew you'd freak out.

-So what the fuck do we do?

-I think we need to go to the desert. It's harder for them to get us there.

-The desert.

She looked at me and adjusted the dress.

-There is a thing that I found in my room at Hecate House that I think will help us.

-Lucia, I can't take any more of this.

-I found this box of stuff. Notebooks, polaroids and other things.

-Other things?

-It was a box of stuff marked *Jack Parsons: Care of the JPL Laboratory 1966.*

III

It felt good to see the city melting away in the haze behind us. Lucia had got us in the Range Rover armed with a bottle of white wine, a pack of valium and some Reese's Pieces. Just before departing she darted back into the house and returned with a battered office file under one arm and her favourite Spanish guitar. We were spiritual pioneers, we were two knights gallant, but best of all, we were anonymous. No one knew what we were doing for once. To be honest I didn't really know what we were doing either. Lucia had said she would explain on the way. I didn't mind. I'd become accustomed to allowing lassitude and disaffection to dominate my moods in the last few months. A kind of spiritual resignation, a longing for an innocence lost somewhere up on Mountweazel. I sighed, turned up the radio and watched the endless parade of billboards flow by the tinted window. I must have dozed off for a time – what with Interstate 40 being one dead straight line, and two Valium washed back with white wine, this is easily done. The car pulled up sharp.

-Where are we?

Outside the sun was setting on barren scrubland.

-I don't know exactly where we are, Leonard. I just pulled over to talk to you.

She turned down the radio that was playing a Johnny Cash ballad. She had the knack of framing every moment in a celluloid sheen that seemed to generate charismatically around her.

-I think I know what's going on and what really happened to us at Mountweazel. And I think I know what to do about it.

-Oh good.

I stretched out and looked around for my cigarettes. I felt like I had been here before.

-I read through all the papers I found in that box. I read them back in Hecate House and I asked Tiberius a few questions – when I could sneak them in undetected.

-Yes, I recall those kinds of conversations. Awkward prying silences over the long dinner table, narrowed eyes and evasive non-answers. I swear the place was bugged.

I dragged on my cigarette and felt sick.

- So what did you find out?

-I am certain that Pinky was Jack Parsons' daughter. She was sired in the love cult that he was the founder of. I also figured out what that cult was really all about. It was a re-enactment of an ancient rite. Something Aleister Crowley had uncovered by accident years ago and tried to keep a lid on. Jack simply picked up where he left off.

-Let me guess...I exhaled the smoke into the car. He too failed in his bid for immortality?

-He failed. He failed spectacularly. He blew himself to pieces. Heavy. And so Pinky has gotten it into her head that she is destined to complete his great magical working.

-The Babalon thing she was going on about at the end?

- Yes, the Babalon working.

-So, my love, where does that leave us?

-We broke the spell. We walked out on her, we laughed at her, we banished her with laughter, we stopped her manifestation, but we left the ritual incomplete. The door was left half-open. Now the thing that she summoned is trying to come back and complete its task.

-What task?

-Yeah, I don't really know what that is. But from what I gleaned from his papers...

She cast her eyes to the office file, set on the back seat like a third party in the conversation.

-It's very, very bad.

I dragged on my cigarette and nodded, stifling a retch.

-So we have unfortunately caught the attention of demonic entities from a realm of existence incomprehensible to our understanding of reality.

She looked at me, her eyes narrowing incrementally with every passing syllable. It was really sexy.

-Well, imagine it like this, Leonard. We walk around our neighbourhood in Melrose and we see cats all the time, right?

-Cats?

-We see cats sat on porches, we see cats on the sidewalks, we see cats looking back at us as if they can see through time. But we don't really pay attention to them. We may occasionally stroke one that crosses our path, but imagine if a cat, or say a couple of cats, got together and started studying the occult, and they began to piece together our human language, and started to gather and practise saying things in English; things that we might just understand. And one day, when passing by a cat, we looked at it, and it looked back, and in a catty voice said: 'ERLLLOO! EOW DU EUWWW DUW? miaow miaow.'

I rolled down the window and flicked my cigarette away. I looked back at Lucia, she still had a feline expression across her sharp dark features.

-What would I do if a cat spoke to me in the voice of Dick Van Dyke? I'm not sure, Lucia. I am really not sure.

-You would pay attention, Leonard. You'd pay a lot of fucking attention.

- Well I suppose I would – if a cat actually spoke to me...

-You'd be amazed, you'd never ever forget it, and if it ran away, vanished into the night never to be seen again, you'd think about that cat endlessly. You'd wonder about that cat, look for it, wonder where it had gone. You'd want to talk to that cat some more.

-So you are saying that these inter-dimensional demonic entities that Pinky Capote conjured to complete the unfinished masterwork of her deranged father are now obsessed with us? They want to know why we were speaking their sacred language and they are coming for us? Demons are now actually hunting us, that's what you are saying?

-Yes. That's what I am saying.

A gust of a rising wind kicked up sand and shattered deadwood particulates that tintinnabulated about the metallic skin of the vehicle. The idling motor was the throbbing backbeat of the silence. I think we both felt equally embarrassed and uneasy when facing the insane facts of our own lives. She put the car into gear and we continued down the desert highway.

It's 125 miles from LA to Pioneertown. I couldn't tell you how long the drive took –my mind was elsewhere. I was lost in the swirling cloud of a threatening thought storm.

I was beginning to get a really, really bad feeling about coming out here.

I hear a train a-comin, it's rolling round the bend.

Joshua Tree is the last stop before the Mojave Desert swallows you alive. Perched near the Coachella valley, it's not so much a town as a single street that looks like something straight out of a Western. It was purple dusk when we arrived, our car creeping down the desolate main street. I looked at Lucia. Her eyes were searching the shuttered roadside.

-What are you looking for?

-A motel.

We had almost reached the end of the strip and the last streetlights of civilization before the oblivion beyond. Then, at the last minute, a shabby sign flashed: The Safari Motor Inn: Vacancies. It really was the last joint in town. The last stop between us and the black sands. We pulled onto the forecourt.

A pool of glowing yellow light spilled onto the tarmac from the open office door. Shutting off the engine Lucia darted from the car and vanished inside. A few minutes later she emerged, followed by what I assumed to be the proprietor. A stout, weathered, fortysomething, callow faced man followed taciturnly behind, checking out her arse as he did so. I got out of the car and grabbed the box, the guitar, the wine and walked towards room number six on the far end of the single level complex. The proprietor fumbled with a key and then swung open the door. He paused, casting a weary eye of assessment back and forth between Lucia and I. Apparently satisfying his own mysterious criteria, he turned and walked back towards the office from where I could hear the faint sound of a ball game in the final innings.

A fourteen square foot room where a single bedside lamp glowed. I walked in, dropping the box and guitar on the bed, and paused to look at the only decorative feature in the room. It was a picture of the space shuttle Discovery landing in Houston in the early 90s. It didn't make a great deal of aesthetic sense. Lucia turned from the bedside table, where she had been making a note of something on the small Safari Inn embossed notepad.

-Do you ever get hungry?

-Yes, I could eat something. Do you think there's an Off Licence around here?

-A what licence?

-Yeah, let's get something to eat. Pizza?

-Darling...unless you are actually pizza, I can live without you.

She cracked her greatwhite smile and leant in to kiss me, much more deeply and tenderly than I had expected.

***

A few sweaty and breathless minutes later we were walking arm in arm along the lonely strip. We appeared to be the only inhabitants of Pioneertown that evening. All was shuttered and not a single car had passed by as we walked.

-Where will we get a slice of pizza?

-There will be somewhere, baby, this is America.

-Yes, but...where is everyone?

-It's out of season, I guess.

The stillness out there, God almighty. Surrounded as we all are, all the time, by infinite space. But we just don't notice it, that we are all eternally wandering in the eternal. A neon pizza sign glowed up ahead. Lucia pointed, squeezing my arm.

-It's a sign, Leonard.

We quickened our pace, neither of us mentioning how the deserted street was making us feel.

-You know, I read somewhere that our experience of life is actually a trick that we play on ourselves. We think we're awake when really we're asleep.

Lucia looked at me like she either completely understood or completely disagreed, but in the half-light of the streetlamp it was hard to tell.

-You know how overpowering dreams are? You know that they seem to live inside and outside of us, and how we can't control them? Well where are you when you are in a dream? Where are you observing from and who is creating it, if it's not you? And it can't be you, as you never know what's going to happen in them. Dreams are naturally occurring stories, now isn't that a disturbing thought?

Lucia squeezed my arm even more firmly.

- Our experience of reality is really a dream state and the intensity of our waking world just drowns out the experience. What I mean to say is the overpowering quiddity, the very intensity of the neon pizza sign up there for example, well that illusory reality inoculates us from seeing what we are truly experiencing: the real *dream* world in which we live. The veil of Maya.

-Ok baby. We are going to have a slice of pizza, a big old glug of wine and then get ourselves rid of Pinky Capote. Then we're free to listen to Lou Reed in my lounge on repeat forever. And you can explain all that to me again.

She pushed open the door of Two Guys Pizza Pies. The place was unsurprisingly empty. I was beginning to feel like we'd driven to the actual end of the world, but then a smiling waitress appeared.I barely registered her as Lucia had already seated herself in a red vinyl booth.

-Two Large Johnnie Walker Blacks, no ice please.

Lucia ordered our drinks without looking up from the menu.

-Are you going to tell me now what we are doing out here?

She looked up, biting her lip.

-I am not sure I can or even should. I think I should just do it and you come along for the ride.

-What?

She cocked her head to one side, her brunette fringe covering one eye. She raised her eyebrow and stuck out her tongue, for a moment in her leather jacket she was transformed into a beautiful, dangerously exotic she-bat.

-Come on. Don't you trust me, baby?

-No, I absolutely don't.

The waitress slammed the drinks onto the light blue Formica.

-What can I get you two? she drawled.

I didn't look up, knowing that Lucia would order for me.

-Oh can we get one Four Horsemen of the Apocalypse with extra cheese, and a side of the Light My Fire   Meatballs'

-Anything else?

Lucia picked up the scotch and knocked it back,

-Another two of these, please.

-Sure. Coming right up.

My eyes settled on Lucia. I felt a stirring of lust for her.

-Well?

-Well what?

I belted my scotch and blinked, watery eyed, Lucia looked at me wonderfully.

-I have to go out to this place. A spot on the edge of the reserve. Actually we both have to go. I've got to sing a song and you've got to sing it too. It's the only thing left for us to do.

-What the fuck are you talking about, Lucia?

I set the glass down, feeling ethanol erupting in the pit of my empty stomach.

-You've driven us out to the actual middle of nowhere to sing some songs around the pissing campfire?

-This is the last song I am going to sing for a while, and it's not like any song we've sung before.

-Oh – *one night only*, I see. This just gets better and better.

I felt my temper uncoiling in the amniotic of whisky.

-I found it in the notebooks.

I nodded, but I was also thinking about what I was going to do to her in the motel room later.

-It took me a few weeks to actually figure out what it was. It was in fact a melody. It was a song, a set of encrypted lyrics and chords.

-What do you mean? I said, my attention snapping back.

-Well on the page it sort of just looked like a really complex mathematical formula, all quadratics and algebraic symbols and whatnot.

-This was a box belonging to Jack Parsons. He was a rocket scientist – did it occur to you maybe that it was actually rocket science and not your next smouldering pop song?

She froze, fixing me with her gaze.

-Don't patronise me. Anyway, one night I got Tiberius to talk – well...dance and talk – and he told me how to decode it. He told me what the mathematical language was and what it really meant.

-What?

-That was about two days before the final ritual so I didn't get a chance to ask him any more about it. I played him the very start of the song that night, but he stopped me before I got to the chorus.

-Tiberius is a raving nutjob like she is. I don't think he actually knew what he was saying half the time.

I said this dismissively but I didn't really believe it. No matter what Tiberius' involvement had been, he was no fool, he was in fact the opposite, and whatever he had been getting out of the arrangement at Hecate House and his weird collaboration with Pinky, there was something of profound importance underlying it all.

-What have we got to lose?

I was about to reply when the pizza arrived. I was feeling the scotch. The waitress placed the food down with a bang. I swigged more scotch. Lucia reached for a slice, my eyes settled on the pizza pie before me. A perfect disc. The Four Horsemen of the apocalypse as advertised, four cheeses on a thin crust. My eyes focussed on it, watching Lucia lift a sizzling slice, tendrils of membranous melting cheese thinning as she lifted it like a stretched spider web. That is when I saw it. Inscribed on the pizza in a rank black oily substance. It was the enneagrammatic symbol that had followed me relentlessly. The one that looks a bit like a pentagram but isn't. The symbol carved onto the cat's head Pinky had given me in Vienna, the shape that was sketched out connecting the points of the tour map together, the one that had glowed on the head of the mushrooms we had gathered in the valley. I reached out to grab Lucia's hand, arresting the slice in mid-flight from the plate to her mouth. She yelped at me and looked down at what she was about to put in her mouth.

We both froze as the recognition tore into us. I stood up in the booth and whirled around, simultaneously knocking the poisoned pizza slice from Lucia's hand. There at the end of the empty restaurant, standing by the counter, was the doe-eyed waitress that I'd not paid any attention to. She let out a cackling laugh...It was Pinky.

-Enjoy, hunny bunny! I'll be seeing you.

With that she tore from behind the counter and ran out the door. The bell rang as it closed. Lucia was already on her feet, tears refracting the animal glare in her eyes.

III

We were pelting down the empty street. Lucia was a little ahead of me, I could hear her sobbing as she ran. There was another sound, too, the sound of another pair of nubile feet, but they were distant, echoing as they scampered down a side street. Lucia rounded the corner into the car park of the motel several yards ahead of me. I had breathlessly reached the open door of our room as she emerged, carrying her guitar aloft, a wild eyed whaler armed with her harpoon. She strode across the lot, crossing the black meridian that demarcated the end of civilization in North America. In a few paces the tarmac turned to sand.

-Lucia, where are you going?

-We're looking for the two big power lines just outside of town. The point at which they cross, beneath that X, lies the spot.

I followed her out into the Mojave night. Minutes later she stopped, hearing the hum of the cables carrying electricity over the desert. It was not as dark as you might imagine. The light that had existed since before our primordial ancestors, before the single cells, the dinosaurs, before the glaciers and the waterfalls, fell brightly across her face as she sat on a curiously shaped rock. She took up the guitar and began to play.

We heard the lightfooted steps of Pinky Capote approach us as we began to sing those bright twisting vespers into the night. I took out my notebook, and retrieved the nine pages of this book that appeared that night in Nashville with the crow, and I lit a fire with them. The three of us started to sing.

Later the townsfolk would talk of having seen queer shadows dancing around a fire that night. Of atonal moaning and profane hymns being sung. A family that lived on a nearby ranch claimed they'd been woken by a horrible pleading animal scream but had decided it was just a coyote being devoured by its own offspring. Suffice to say, I never saw Pinky Capote ever again.

When the sun rose that morning over those desecrated sands, Lucia and I walked hand in hand back to room six. I stayed up for days and days writing songs that would contain those moments, hovering between the aethers, like angelic feathers, gliding on the breath of euphony. On the third morning in the Safari Motor Inn I awoke, and Lucia was gone. I stumbled to the door. Her car was gone too. She had left me. I staggered to the end of the bed, and tucked into the frame of the mirror was a note.

Look after those songs of ours, they're our firstborn. Please take care of yourself– and yes, I will love you forever. LCF

***

A few more days were spent in Room Six. It took me a while to get my head together. I'm not sure if I ever really did. I made some ranting phone calls, played guitar and stared at the wall, watching the shadows ascend, lengthen, cascade and then decline. For a while it was always night.

***

I awoke one bright fine morning. It was the start of June. I walked down to the diner in town. Higgs was waiting at the table he had guessed was mine. He had rung the phone in the motel two nights before saying he was coming to pick me up. I sat down at the table. There was an iced coffee and a Jameson waiting.

-Well?

-Well, I'm here, aren't I? I said, as if that would just about cover it.

I pressed the tumbler to my forehead.

-I've been looking everywhere for you.

-I know. I just had to get something figured out.

A waitress delivered him a six egg omelette. I looked up, double-taking at her just to be sure. Higgs didn't eat, he just looked at me over the steam rising from the plate.

-I've missed you, Higgs.

-I've missed you too, Leonard.

We laughed to banish the pain of re-acquaintance.

-You know Leonard...I've realised something over these last few months. Something has become crystal clear to me.

I sank the iced coffee in one, holding the Jamesons to my temples.

- What's that?

-Everything you wrote about on your first album has now come to pass. The church, the first class flights, the fleeing your lovers in the dead of night. All of it, every bloody word down to the very last detail has come to pass. You wrote about it before it had happened. What the fuck is that about?

-Say that again, Higgs.

-I've noticed that all the events and details in the songs –
all of it has now actually happened.

-Well yes, I suppose it has...When you put it like that.

-So what does that really mean?

He drove us back to Los Angeles, down that dead straight
road, listening to The White Album on repeat. He didn't
say another word about the matter.

SONG OF SONGS

I am sitting at my old writing desk. It's dusk. I'm by the window, looking out into our wild and semi-secret garden. It's early spring and the night air is sweet with sap and punctuated with the traffic noise of the distant city below. I am writing about writing. I have a glass of Castillo Del Montino Rioja wine next to my typewriter. The typewriter that Tiberius gifted me, on the side of that magic mountain, some two years ago now. To my surprise it arrived one morning in a misshapen parcel sent from a Mexican address. ago now.

Thought you would be wanting this. I retrieved it from your room at Hecate House after you quite rightfully fled that dreadful night. I hope you get some good use out of her. She's a great machine – she's a time machine, a telepathy machine, and all that other stuff we talked about. Hope to see you again at some point down the road, no hard feelings, and just remember: Life can be so original.

Ciao, Tiberius Red

I have written all of this book on that typewriter. A cosmic document, a magical papyri. A nomological screed, an epic of ecstatic awareness, a deep draught of gnostic intoxication, a blissful buddha sartori, an endlessly interpretable ink blot, a sprawling fugue. Or perhaps it's just a misguided self-help exercise that got well and truly out of hand. *The hands of time grind slowly, but boy do they grind fine.* I take a drag on my cigarette and place it in the aphrodite seashell ashtray next to the typewriter. I walk over to my record player and peruse the stack of records, but, changing my mind, I return to my desk and place my fingers on the keys:

Music represents patterns of being, all the melodic details of being alive. We are all moving to a time signature. Being is simply a structure of layers of pattern constantly interacting in a relatively harmonious way. Music mimics the layering of all life patterns. People adapt to patterns of being in their lives, so does the dancer adapt their body to the patterns in the music. Music is an embodied display of the place of the person within the great Cosmos itself. This is the reason that evolution always selects for singers.

In writing this book certain truths have revealed themselves. Certain mysteries have become unveiled. Yet still the sphinx at the heart of this story remains inscrutable. Steadfastly guarding her secret. 'Some mysteries,' she whispers 'can only ever deepen, baby honey hunny'.

The Ebbinghaus curve, that curious phenomena whereby memory drifts towards error over time. When we remember, all we are doing is remembering the last time we remembered that memory. A xerox, of a carbon copy, of an impression. Hence why so much of our past appears to us dream-like and mythic. It has so many other narratives and moments woven into its weft from the unsound process of recollection. Ghosts in the fleshy time machine. Our lives are houses that

we haunt with our darkly-mirrored, pirouetting poltergeists,
garmented in rags of regret and animated by our own restless
wills.

One night recently, I took my dear friend Josh T Pearson,
who happened to be in town, to my beloved Boogaloo Bar
that sits on the crossroads just around the corner from
where I live. I wanted him to meet my friends Gerry and
Munroe, enjoy a Guinness and set this unrighteous world
to rights. Josh is taken with the place. He sips his pint. His
eyes wander to the bar and then flick back to mine.

-My friend, with your writing, you have to step with all
your weight.

-Well, Josh, the book is getting very long, and it's already
taken me over two years, and I don't know if I am losing my
mind but I am beginning to think that the book is more real
than real life itself.

He places his glass gently onto the table.

-I mean why else would anyone read it, buddy?

He winks.

-Isn't abstraction more real than reality, Josh?

-How so?

-Well, for example, in the way that pure mathematical
representations are the most real of all possible phenomena
in the universe.

-If you say so, but I know a hundred-dollar piece of ass
when I see one.

-Being a powerful mathematician certainly grants you a
tremendous amount of control over the world. Trade, travel,
astronomy, time keeping, technological advancement,
finance, war, love, and sex. All these things are executed and

depend upon a mastery of extremely abstract conceptual phenomena. You could argue that all human existence is contingent on abstraction.

He lifted his glass with a lone-star smile.

-I think this may be getting a little bit above my pay grade, buddy.

He pauses.

-But just remember: When the book is done, it's done forever.

***

I settle at my desk. My cat, Atlas, is on the windowsill keeping a watchful eye on his nocturnal empire. I pour more Rioja from the newly uncorked bottle and set it beside the silver typewriter. Its keys, with the extra layer of mysterious glinting glyphs, are now familiar as I rest my fingers once more upon them, finding their instinctive grooves. Slipping a new sheet of paper into the machine, a certain song springs to mind. A melody, a memory.

This is a diary of desire, this is a love letter.

I hear tripping footsteps coming down the garden path. She is winding her way to my door. Those womanly steps, those of a goddess, the sweetest of sirens. For she is singing something, a delicate melody barely audible above her breath. I lean in, willing my being to hear her sweet song.

Written on location in:
Nashville, Hollywood, Los Angeles, New York, Big Sur, Humboldt, Grinton, Yorkshire, London, Paris, Sussex, San Sebastián, Athens, Hydra, Spetses, Delphi, Ithaca, Highgate, Ramsgate and Berlin.

www.ingramcontent.com/pod-product-compliance
Ingram Content Group UK Ltd.
Pitfield, Milton Keynes, MK11 3LW, UK
UKHW040900040525
458182UK00001B/21